Praise for Ventoux

'Where the novel succeeds most is in its wonderful blend of humor, suspense and poignancy, which will appeal to non-cyclists as well as those of us who understand what it takes to scale a mountain as evocative, daunting and symbolic as Mont Ventoux'
FELIX LOWE, author of *Climbs & Punishment*

'Wagendorp's book manages to be funny, shrewd and moving, with a complex structure that never feels cumbersome, and a finale so intense that you want to read it very slowly, almost one word at a time'
The Guardian

'Bert Wagendorp keeps his readers firmly in this glorious tragicomedy about friendship'
De Morgen

'Hilarious, stirring, feel-good'
NRC Handelsblad

'Takes in the nature of friendship, musings on the nature of time, and the small choices we make that can change our lives; very funny, and often very touching'
Cyclo

'Twists, unforeseen developments, and heart-breaking truths; the plot is peppered with moments that urge you to read on'
Life in the Saddle

'A touching and well-crafted novel about friendship and life, that's also got some bikes in it'
Road.cc

'Within the main story, there are plenty more relatable sub-plots woven in: of personal journeys, triumphs, of tragedies, humor, success and of disaster—and of course, of cycling. It's a novel which grips you, it's a novel which makes you think, and it's a novel which makes you reflect on your own choices. And it is a novel well worth reading'
Road Cycling UK

'*Ventoux* is a stunningly accurate depiction of male friendship told in a subtle and sensitive style. This feel-good novel about old friends who find their way back to each other is a delightful and easy read. Especially recommended for cycling aficionados who will recognize Mont Ventoux as the scene of many classic races through the years'
Battle Books

'Instantly likeable, the heady mix of angst in Wagendorp's characters, and their love of cycling and music coupled with a desire to leave lasting, revered legacies instantly resonated'
Seven Day Cyclist

'A fictional cycling story with camaraderie, romance, love, intrigue and treachery. Quite brilliant!'
The Bike Lane

'*Ventoux* is so convincingly written that contrivance is a factor that never once rears its potentially ugly head. The characters are thoroughly and naturally believable, as are their various interactions, while the book's 285 pages provide compulsive reading from page one'
The Washing Machine Post

BERT WAGENDORP (1956) is a writer and columnist for the Dutch national newspaper *De Volkskrant*. His novel *Ventoux* was proclaimed Book of the Month by the leading Dutch television talk show *DDWD* and received unanimous rave reviews from the press, selling 100,000 copies within the first six months. The book has been adapted into a Dutch-language film of the same name.

PAUL VINCENT (UK) studied at Cambridge and Amsterdam, and after teaching Dutch at the University of London for over twenty years became a full-time translator in 1989. Since then he has published a wide variety of translated poetry, non-fiction, and fiction, including work by Achterberg, Claus, Couperus, Elsschot, Jellema, Mulisch, De Moor, and Van den Brink. He is a member of the Society of Dutch Literature in Leiden, and has won the Reid Prize for poetry translation, the Vondel Prize for Dutch-English translation, and (jointly) the Oxford-Weidenfeld Prize.

Bert Wagendorp

VENTOUX

Translated from the Dutch
by Paul Vincent

WORLD EDITIONS
New York, London, Amsterdam

Published in the USA in 2019 by World Editions LLC, New York
Published in the UK in 2015 by World Editions Ltd., London

World Editions
New York/London/Amsterdam

Printed by Sheridan, Chelsea, MI, USA

This book is a work of fiction. Any resemblance to actual persons, living or dead, or actual events is purely coincidental.

Library of Congress Cataloging in Publication Data is available

ISBN 978-1-64286-017-7

First published as *Ventoux* in the Netherlands in 2013 by Atlas Contact, Amsterdam

The publisher gratefully acknowledges the support of the Dutch Foundation for Literature

N ederlands
letterenfonds
dutch foundation
for literature

Twitter: @WorldEdBooks
Facebook: WorldEditionsInternationalPublishing
www.worldeditions.org

Book Club Discussion Guides are available on our website.

For Hannah

'I finally sat down in a valley and transferred my winged thoughts from things corporeal to the immaterial, addressing myself as follows:—"What hast thou repeatedly experienced to-day in the ascent of this mountain, happens to thee, as to many, in the journey toward the blessed life. But this is not so readily perceived by men, since the motions of the body are obvious and external while those of the soul are invisible and hidden. Yes, the life which we call blessed is to be sought for on a high eminence, and strait is the way that leads to it."'

PETRARCH, *The Ascent of Mount Ventoux*

Prologue

For years the photo had been in an envelope, at the bottom of a white storage box. On the brown tape with which I had sealed the box sometime in the mid-1980s, I had written 'Miscellaneous'. At least eight times I took it out of a dark cupboard, down from an attic, or out of a shed, and put it back without unpacking it. Now that she had suddenly turned up again, I knew immediately where to find the envelope.

Photos of other holidays are neatly arranged in albums with titles such as 'Italy 1984' or 'Route 66, 1986'. This one was hidden away, deep in my memory and in a cardboard vault, until the moment came to retrieve it. Time had added a hint of orange to it.

I placed it in front of me on the dining table and absorbed the image. For minutes on end I gazed absently into the eyes of the people in the portrait. Then, slowly, the memories came. The sounds, the smells, the words. I remembered that I stared into the lens and thought: one day, later, much later, I'll look at this photo, and I'll remember that this was happiness. Time seemed to disappear, until I had almost become the young lad standing there. I felt the excitement, the joy, the expectation again. I felt her body against mine again.

It's more than thirty years since it was taken, on the campsite of a little place in Provence, one day before Joost, Peter, and I cycled up Mont Ventoux. On the back it says: 'Camping in Bédoin, June 1982. From l. to r. David, Peter, Laura, Bart, Joost, André.' In the background you can see a blue bungalow tent and a small orange trekker tent. There is a racing bike leaning against a gate. The girl is wearing a red bikini and white flip-flops. An embarrassed smile is playing around her lips, as if she is not completely at ease about this, of all moments, being immortalized.

André has a roll-up in his mouth and is facing the camera with indifference through a cloud of smoke. Joost is posing ostentatiously with his hands on his back and his chest thrust out; David has raised his right hand in a warning gesture—the photo was taken with his camera and he had set the self-timer.

Peter is wearing a little hat and sunglasses. As a result, you can't see his eyes. There is a vague grin hovering around his mouth. With his hands in the pockets of a pair of cut-off jeans he is leaning against Laura with his bare torso. You can see she is perfect, see how beautiful her breasts are and how endlessly long her legs. Her eyes take you prisoner, even on a Kodak print. I have put my right arm around her and am looking triumphantly into the lens, like a footballer allowed to hold the championship trophy for a moment.

I

My name is Bart Hoffman. Actually it's Johannes Albertus Hoffman—Hoffman as in Dustin, with a double *f* and one *n*. I was born almost fifty years ago in Zutphen, a town on a river in the easternmost part of Holland. My father was the head of a Christian primary school.

I'm a crime correspondent with a national newspaper—I belong to the generation of student dropouts who found their way into journalism. A guy I knew from studying Dutch wrote the occasional piece for the arts page of a big daily. He heard that they were looking for someone in the sports section to type in the results on Sunday morning. When they were short-handed, I was occasionally allowed to go to an unimportant football match. Writing came quite easily to me, and when they were looking for a reporter, I applied for it and got the job.

It was painless, packing in my studies. I didn't like the other students. I didn't like all the hot air they talked about Dutch writers like Reve and Lucebert, or Chomsky's generative grammar. I was the only person in my year who read *Football International*. The fact that I could effort-lessly recite the first five minutes of the TV commentary of the 1974 World Cup Final, a fantastic ready-made art-work, made no impression on my fellow students. Long before it came into vogue, I had a very good imitation of Johan Cruyff in my repertoire, but they didn't even recognize it.

After two years, the paper's cycling reporter retired and I was able to take over from him. In the spring I followed the peloton and reported first on the Paris-Nice or the Tirreno-Adriatico and then on the classics, and in the summer I went to the Tour de France.

During the day I would drive slightly behind the peloton and afterward talk to the racers. Then I would type up a piece, and in the evening go out with colleagues to a good restaurant to talk over the race and life in general. I couldn't imagine a better existence, and I was always sorry in the autumn when, after the world championship, Paris-Tours, and the Giro di Lombardia, it was over for another five months.

When I was 24, the week after Holland became European football champions, I moved in with Hinke. She was beautiful, and had the Nordic white skin and clear, challenging eyes. She could easily put her long legs behind her neck, since she had done gymnastics from an early age. I was in love and thought she was a very nice person, but that was before I had awakened a less nice side in her.

On the fourth birthday of our daughter Anna, in 1995, she gave me a choice. I could choose between fatherhood and the nomadic existence of a cycling correspondent. In the case of the former, she would continue to be a part of my life, and in the latter, she would disappear from it and take my daughter with her. I chose to become a real father.

I went to the editor-in-chief and explained my situation. A month earlier, our crime correspondent had died of a heart attack. The editor-in-chief asked if I knew anything about crime and justice.

'I've been a cycling correspondent and I've read *Crime and Punishment*,' I replied, more or less as a joke.

'Okay, then you're the man we need. Congratulations.'

When I turned 40, I stopped smoking, got my old Batavus out of the shed, and began cleaning it up. It was, may I say, one of my better decisions. On the bike I began slowly but surely to realize that you can go right, but also left. That you can always take the same route, but can also choose a different one. That things sometimes happen to you, but that you can do something for yourself. Anyway, it was another five years before we got divorced. Anna was 18 by then, and there was no longer any reason for Hinke and me to stay together.

Ever since I've been alone again, I've lived in a spacious flat in the centre of Alkmaar. I once moved to the town because I found Amsterdam too big and the people too noisy and far too full of themselves, and now I don't want to leave. The flat is sparsely furnished, but that doesn't bother me. Everything I need is there, and I like space around me.

I know every metre of cyclable road between Den Helder and Purmerend. On the bike you think time is standing still, or at least that it is no threat at all. The bike protects you from despair.

Anna has bought a Bianchi—she was well brought up. Not a German racing bike via the Internet, not some new American racer, but an Italian classic make. She knows who Coppi and Bartali were, and likes the Giro better than the Tour.

'Brilliant colour,' I said, when she brought it to show me. 'Nice sea-green.'

'Celeste, it's called.'

Never knew that; you have to be a cycling woman for that.

'La Dama Bianca,' I said.

'Giulia Occhini.'

'The doctor?'

'Locatelli. Enrico.'

'In?'

'Varano Borghi.'

'On ...'

'Lago Comabbio.'

'Never heard of it.'

'Never existed, it's the tears of *dottore* Locatelli, mixed with the sweat of Fausto Coppi.'

'And the love juices of Giulia Occhini.'

She started roaring with laughter. 'Bart! The child is here!'

The latter was a quote from her mother. I immediately saw the tent before me, on the Italian campsite, the rickety table with the breakfast on it and Anna's conspiratorial smile.

'Passion or betrayal?'

'Passion. If she hadn't gone with Fausto it would have been betrayal.'

'Very good.'

'Bart! You're making the child completely amoral! Of course it was betrayal.'

It was one of our set dialogues. We had about ten of them, and both of us knew our lines perfectly. This one was extra special. On a holiday trip when she was 10 we rode to Varano Borghi, not so far from Lago Maggiore, to see where Giulia came from. I had just seen a play called *Fausto and Giulia* and wanted to know whether there was anything to be found in the village that evoked the most famous love story in sport.

There was nothing. I asked a passer-by if he knew where *dottore* Locatelli's old house had been, but he shrugged his shoulders.

It was the end of February; people were still talking about the Eleven Cities Skating Race, but she had already done a few circuits. She pointed to the kilometre counter: 195 kilometres. 'Four times. Not bad, is it? And alone, you know, you've got to allow for that. Average 26.1.' We made a date for two days later. I was looking forward to it— cycling together is friendship, love and togetherness, all in one.

We rode west. At Egmond we went into the dunes. Rays of sunshine were drawing the cold out of the ground. 'Take it easy, Dad,' shouted Anna. 'I'm still not properly in shape.'

She was talking like a pro in the early spring. I held back, rode alongside her, and gave her a push in the back. 'You're pedalling too hard! All women pedal too hard. It's because they're always toiling along on those crazy Granny bikes. You must keep it supple. Change gears more lightly.' She did as I said. I put my hands on the handlebars and just for a moment touched happiness.

In a café in Bakkum, a handsome lad served us coffee. Anna had taken her jacket off and he looked at her jersey.

'Suits you,' he said.

'Thank you,' she said, and gave him a heavenly smile.

'Bottoms suit you too.' She waved him away with a casual gesture.

I drank a mouthful of coffee and looked at her. 'Strange things are happening, Anna,' I said.

'*Very* strange things are happening. In America, a panther walked into a house on a new estate and fell asleep on the sofa. I read it this morning on ...'

'With me. With my life.'

'Oh. What kind of strange things?'

'Well, first I see my old friend André in court.'

'Is he a judge?'

'No.'

'A lawyer?'

'No, he's a criminal.'

'Christ. And is he your friend? Will he have to go to jail?'

'No, acquitted due to lack of evidence.'

'Lucky. For him, that is. And what else, in the way of odd things?'

'A little later I read that my friend Joost has been nominated for the Spinoza Prize.'

'What does he do?'

'He's a brilliant physicist. At least that was what the paper said.'

'Oh. Don't know the prize.'

'Kind of Dutch Nobel Prize, you could say.'

'Funny friends you've got. And the other one, what's his name ...'

'David. From the travel agency. He doesn't count for the moment, because I still see him regularly and he calls me twice a week.'

'But what kind of strange stuff is going on then?'

'Everything is coming back.'

She looked at me thoughtfully. 'I don't find it that strange, I think. These things happen. Chance.'

'There were two other friends,' I said. 'Or rather, a friend and a girlfriend, Peter and Laura.'

Now she raised her eyebrows. 'And have they turned up, too?'

'No.'

I waved to the waiter and ordered two more coffees. I

hesitated whether to tell her the story, and decided not to. The day was too beautiful.

'Or are they dead?' she asked.

I had come across André at the beginning of 2012, in the dossier of a coke case in which 'senior civil servants and other prominent people' were possibly involved. I heard myself saying, 'Hey, André'. I went to the trial and waited until the accused came in. André had shaved his head. He looked sharp, in a suit that had undoubtedly cost more than my entire wardrobe. His eyes scanned those present. I saw from a barely perceptible nod of his head that he recognized me. I think he knew I would be there before he had seen me.

A few weeks later he was acquitted. André looked at me more openly now and smiled. Undoubtedly he had also read my look and interpreted it accurately: good work, you won, well done, man.

A week later I read an article about Professor Joost M. Walvoort and his work on string theory. He was a nominee for the Spinoza Prize, worth one and a half million euros. 'A tidy sum, which you can really do something with as a researcher,' said Joost in the paper. I knew exactly how he had said that and how he had looked—a mixture of nonchalance and smugness.

I looked for Joost's name on the website of Leiden University. 'Prof. J.M. Walvoort (Joost),' it said. 'Theoretical Physics'. I could see from the accompanying photo that the years had not left any excessively deep marks. He was looking confidently into the lens, with that slightly mocking expression.

I keyed in the number and he answered immediately. 'Bart here.'

'Hey Pol, you again?' As if I had him on the line for the fourth time that day. On the bike Joost called me Pol, because the sound of it suggested Flemish cycling aces. He was Tuur.

'I thought: I should give Joost a call.'

'Great. How's things then? Prick still completely in order?'

That's the nice thing about old friendships. The fact that you call up your scholarly friend after twenty-five years and he inquires first of all about the health of your prick.

'Exceptional,' I replied.

'Good. Shall we go for a few beers again?'

'That's why I'm calling you.'

'Nice. Just say when.'

I mentioned a date.

'Fine. In Amsterdam where you are or in Leiden where I am? Or don't you live in Amsterdam anymore? Alkmaar? Then let's do it on my patch in Leiden. Huis De Bijlen, do you know it? Eight o'clock. We'll have a bite to eat first. Nice!'

With him it was no sooner said than done, and he took control, as if he had rung me or had at least been on the point of doing so.

'Right,' I said. 'It'll be nice to see you again, Joost.' I hadn't changed a bit either, immediately ready to accept Joost's leading role.

'Okay. If you like you can sleep over. Loads of room.'

He still had that slight Amsterdam accent.

I didn't say that three days before our date, I was due to go cycling with André.

II

In 1970, Eddy Merckx won his second Tour de France. I was 6, watching TV with my father, and saw Merckx, the cycling marvel. 'The cannibal,' said my father. 'So young and already so good. He's going to sweep the board. No one can compete with him.'

I reversed the handlebars on my bike and did a circuit through the neighbourhood. I imagined that I was Merckx on the Tourmalet. I looked back: no one! I'd left them all for dead. I stopped outside André's house.

He was lying on the sofa reading a *Billy's Boots* comic.

'André, let's be racing cyclists.'

'Huh?'

'Let's be racing cyclists like Eddy Merckx. You know, from the Tour. We'll reverse your handlebars, too.'

'My father's already a racing cyclist. I'm going to be a footballer.'

It was the first time that one of us didn't immediately jump aboard the other's fantasy.

'Shame.' If André didn't want to know about cycling, there was no point in my getting involved. 'Swim?'

'Right.'

But that summer the seed was sown. From that moment on, cycling catered for years to my need for heroes.

The urge to sit on a racing bike again came back later. That was after I had read *The Rider* by Tim Krabbé. I was fifteen, read it in one sitting, and knew instantly what I had to do. True, it would have been better if I had pursued the sport from the age of six, but Merckx was a late starter, too.

I took my savings out of the bank, borrowed another two hundred guilders from my mother, and bought a Batavus from Van Spankeren's cycle shop. Joost and André looked at me pityingly. Cycling was still a sport for thickos who shouted unintelligibly into the microphone. But I didn't care. I joined a training group that left from the Zaadmarkt every Sunday morning for a ride of about eighty kilometres. The guys gave me some funny looks the first time. They immediately commented on my unshaven legs and my football shorts, but they accepted it for this once.

Then they started riding me into the ground. I had kept up for about ten kilometres when I saw them pulling away from me. They didn't look back; of course they knew it would happen, it was an initiation ritual. During the following week I rode out a couple of times by myself, hoping that it would go better the next Sunday. I actually could keep up for a little longer in my new cycling shorts, but not that much longer.

On the fifth Sunday we went to the Montferland. On the way, Kees Nales told me that he had climbed Mont Ventoux. Mont Ventoux! I knew the mountain from the stories about Tommy Simpson, the Jesus of cycling, who suffered for all doping sinners and died on the Bare Mountain.

But Kees Nales had survived. I was deeply impressed

and resolved there and then, as our wheels whooshed towards Montferland, that I must also climb Mont Ventoux.

'How was it,' I asked, 'Mont Ventoux?'

'Tough.'

'Had you trained a lot for it?'

'Nah.' I didn't yet know that cyclists always say that they've done scarcely any training.

'Do you think I could do it?'

Kees looked at my legs, which still weren't shaven. 'You don't look like a climber. More of a sprinter, if you ask me.'

We got to Beek. Just outside the village, in the Peeskesweg, was a steep length of asphalt. The lads immediately stood out of their saddles and started sprinting up. Only Kees Nales looked around one more time to see whether I wasn't perhaps a sprinter, after all. But I knew after the first hundred metres. I felt the strength draining out of my legs.

'I'm not a climber, dammit,' I shouted, as a kind of indictment of the Creator. No one heard.

At the top, the lads stood waiting until I arrived. They looked at me pityingly. Couldn't climb, poor fucker.

'I thought so,' said Kees Nales. 'Too heavy and no climbing muscles.'

A little further on they went up the Eltenberg. It was a bit steeper and longer than the Peeske. They didn't even wait for me at the top. I decided to cycle alone from then on. I tried to get André onto his father's old bike, but failed.

Cycling is a sport of the imagination. On my own, I was the talented one, and my unshaven legs didn't matter. Others rode me and my fantasy to pieces.

I celebrated my 45th birthday alone, since I was divorced a few months earlier. One day, after everything was settled,

I bought a Pinarello Angliru, blue with red and grey high-lights. As a consolation, I told myself, but actually it was more of a reward.

Then Ventoux came back into my head.

III

The first time we heard Joost say anything, immediately after he had entered our classroom, he made us laugh. It was because of his accent. It was 1969, October or November, I suspect, as we were making dolls of chestnuts and matches.

Miss Hospes introduced him. 'This is Joost,' she said, with those nice Eastern os.

'What a small class', said Joost. 'In Amsterdam the class is much bigger. And we have an aquarium, too. Our teacher is called Miss Prins.'

'Joost's father is a doctor,' said Miss Hospes. Joost nodded. 'First Joost's father was a doctor in Amsterdam, now he's a doctor here. Perhaps you will be able to go to Joost's father sometime, if you're ill.'

'Or if you die.' Joost laughed out loud, but we were shocked and Cora Berg started crying.

'Don't say those funny things, Joost,' said Miss Hospes.

'And my mother plays the saxophone.' No one knew what a saxophone was.

'Really, that's nice. So tell the class what nice songs she plays.'

'No songs. Mummy plays jazz.'

'Oh,' said Miss Hospes, who knew more about psalms.

'She puts on records by Charlie Parker and she plays along. It drives Daddy crazy. "Can't you stop that tooting," he shouts. "It's just like a cow." Then she shouts, "Prick."' Joost must have found that very funny, because he almost got the giggles.

'Do you have any brothers and sisters?' asked Miss Hospes, with a blush on her cheeks.

'I have sisters. One is called Louise and the other Sandra. Louise is seven and Sandra is seven, too. They're twins. I can't tell them apart, they're so alike. But I like Sandra better than Louise.'

'Right, Joost,' said Miss Hospes, 'go and sit next to Bart. Bart is that boy with the red sweater. Can you see him?'

'Yes, he looks like a leprechaun.'

He came over to me and said we were going to the clay tray. He paid scarcely any attention to the other children. I beckoned André, who was sitting opposite me at our table. 'We're going to the clay tray, come on.'

'This is clay,' said Joost at the clay tray, as if he were giving a commentary. 'When I pick up a piece of clay, I can make something out of it. For example, a little man. But when I throw the man back in the clay tray and I give him a thump, he becomes clay again.' He sounded really surprised, as if he himself were listening to something new. André looked at him open-mouthed.

Within a day we were inseparable. AndréJoostandBart.

IV

André lived in an apartment complex in South Rotterdam. I parked my car by the water, crossed the road, and walked toward a large glass door. I looked for number 85 and rang the bell. I had traced his address through a lawyer with whom I was friendly and sent him a postcard. On it I had written that I would be at his place on 16 March at 11 o'clock, and he should let me know if that didn't suit him. I got an email in reply. 'Bring your bike with you,' it said. 'You looked as if you were in training.'

'Bart!' cried a familiar voice. 'Good to see you, man! Same as ever! Didn't shave this morning, I see,' There was a buzzing tone. 'Door's open. Come right up. Fourth floor. Got your bike with you?'

I didn't reply, but pushed the door open and went to the elevator.

Of all my old friends, André is the most precious to me. Or perhaps I should say: the memories of André are dearest to me. Our friendship is older than we are. Our mothers were friends because our grannies were already friends. We went about together when our mothers sat opposite each other at table with their big tummies. Once we were born, a week apart, we were immediately an inseparable duo.

I have a photo in which the two of us are sitting in a playpen, two boys of eighteen months, in the same pink knickerbockers and the same white jumpers. 'November 1965, Bart and André', my mother has written on the back. We are playing with blocks, me with my left hand, André with his right. We have put our free arms around each other. 'The two of you sat like that for hours,' says my mother.

I think friendship is based more on shared experiences than on compatibility or attraction. I share more with André than anyone else.

He gave me a Russian bear hug, long and powerful, kissed me on both cheeks, and beamed at me. He was moved, and I was probably the only person in the world who could spot that.

'Bart, man, I'm so pleased to see you again.'

'Me too, André.'

'Coffee? Cappuccino?'

'I'd love one.'

The huge room was white. White walls, a floor of white tiles, and a white ceiling. In the middle there was a black Gispen table with six Jacobsen chairs around it. In front of the window with a view of the River Maas stood a large sofa; hanging on the wall was a TV screen of cinema proportions. In two corners were two tall speakers. Apart from that, the room was empty.

André's father was caretaker at the Baudartius, our secondary school. He had been a renowned amateur cyclist with a powerful finishing sprint. In André's parental home, the living room was full of lamps, vases, and other knick-knacks that old Gerrit had won in the criteriums of the eastern Netherlands. Perhaps that explained André's sparse interior.

The emptiness spoke for itself and did not beg to be filled. In that emptiness stood a bike, a splendid racing bike. I walked around it once, I touched the stem and stroked the saddle. It was soft brown, like the tape on the handlebars and a strip on the tubes. The bike itself was white. Gold leaf seemed to have been applied on the down and seat tubes of the triangle of the frame.

'Wow,' I said. I saw André smiling contentedly as he came into the room with two cups on a tray.

'Listen a minute.' He took a remote off the table and pressed the button. I heard a guitar, and a little later a couple of violins, and then Nick Drake: 'When the day is done, down to earth then sinks the sun ...'

André sang along, in a rather hoarse voice. 'When the night is cold, some get by but some get old ...'

He turned the sound down and shot me a questioning look.

'Fives Leaves Left.' He nodded with pleasure. 'Sjaak's first LP, 1970, I think.' Sjaak was his elder brother.

'When he was out I always played this track, do you remember? I actually wasn't allowed to touch his turntable. There were all kinds of scratches where I put the needle on, just before "Day is Done". We were very young, weren't we? Right away, I thought it was the greatest song I'd ever heard. And I still do. That guitar at the beginning, or those violins. I had no idea what the words were about. I do now.'

I didn't understand why he was playing the track. 'What a fabulous bike, André. A bit different from that old Raleigh of your father's.'

He laughed mysteriously. 'Pegoretti, hand-built. Dario Pegoretti is his name. I went to Caldonazzo, where he lives. Plays only jazz in his workshop. Love, man, love. I've never seen so much love. I just stood and watched and I never wanted to leave.' Now 'Day is Done' sounded through the room in a jazz version. 'Pegoretti is a jazz freak. I'm standing there and he puts this on, in a version by Brad Mehldau.' I still didn't understand.

He put his hand on the saddle. 'This model is the Pegoretti "Day is Done".' He stopped talking and looked out of the window.

'Do you understand anything about chance, Bart?'

'There's no such thing as chance. We call things chance for want of a better explanation. The fact that you go to an Italian cycle-maker and he's making a bike he names after a song that you played forty years ago until the record wore out only seems to be chance, because we have no idea how such a thing is possible, because we are terrified of admitting that it isn't chance at all.'

'You haven't changed a bit, Bart, you've always got an answer. So it isn't coincidence either that you're here. It wasn't coincidence that you were sitting in that court with your notepad.' He looked serious.

'It was cool calculation. I thought: I've got to see André again. Let's have a look to see where he might be. Hey, he's on trial.'

'They couldn't touch me, could they? Those guys didn't stand a chance. Suckers.'

'I'm not so sure,' I said.

'Leave it. I mustn't talk to you about it. You put it nicely. André T., unproven dealer in pleasure and oblivion. That's how it is. That's how it was, I should say. I'm going to do other things. Important things. For myself, that is.'

I looked at him and saw that he did not want to go into details about his new activities. Not now, at any rate.

'Bart, you old wanker. It's as if you were here yesterday, with that slow Puch moped of yours. Haha.'

'I was never the Kreidler type. I'm still not, as a matter of fact.'

He looked at me seriously. 'Sorry,' he said, 'for all those years of silence. I should have responded, at least to the announcement of your daughter's birth.'

'I expect you were busy.'

'Pretty.'

'No excuse, bastard.'

'No.'

'She'll be 21 soon.'

'Yes, well anyway, congratulations on your daughter's birth.'

'Thanks a lot.'

'Do you have a photo with you? I'm interested to see what you've produced.'

It happened by itself, he said a little later. 'People always want to know how it could have reached that point, how you wind up in the wrong world. The answer is simple: step by step. You scarcely realize that you're going irrevocably in a certain direction. Just like people who have the same office jobs all their lives. How did it happen to them?'

'If you ask me, you were already involved when I got married. With your Porsche and your Mandy.'

'That's right. It didn't work out with Mandy.'

'And how did it happen?'

'You say to yourself: this is easy money and I obviously have a talent for it. Let's carry on with it.'

'No pangs of conscience?'

'Pangs of conscience are like muscle ache. You massage them away.'

He made a movement with his hand. Enough of this. He took me by the arm. 'Glad you're back, Bart, really glad. Come and have a look.' He walked over to a work of art that consisted of scores of seemingly identical images of a racing cyclist on a cycle track, just before the finish line. If you looked closely, the photos were all different.

'Attack on World Hour Record by Tony Rominger, Bordeaux, 5-11-1994', it said underneath. 'Tom Koster,' said André, 'graphic designer, great bloke. He died four years ago. I bought work from him regularly. Running, cycling, skating. One day he realizes: I can't make any headway, what's wrong with me? He goes to the doctor and the doctor says: Tom, my friend, you've got lung cancer. Nothing they could do. Lived another eleven months. Sold all his paintings to pay for the funeral and that was that. He'd just bought a new bike, shame. Was always concerned with time and suddenly time was up.'

I looked at the photos and tried to see the differences.

'Stasis is movement,' said André. 'Movement is stasis. We all do our best, we all try to improve on our own world endurance record, and what's the result?' He shrugged his shoulders.

'Rominger's world endurance time was scrapped from the record books,' I said. 'Because of his bike, I think. Or because he established it in the EPO period. Whatever the case, all for nothing.'

'The most beautiful thing he left was this work,' said André, 'except that Rominger doesn't know about it. I should call him. It might be a consolation.'

Someone came into the room. I turned around and thought I was going crazy. She shook hands with me and introduced herself, but I was momentarily lost for words.

'This is Bart,' said André. He pretended not to notice my astonishment. 'I told you about him. Bart Hoffman, Dustin's second cousin.'

'Bart!' said the woman. 'André has told me a lot about you.

I'm glad to meet you at last.' She had an English accent.
'Ludmilla,' said André. 'Tolstoy. You're looking at the
genes of *War and Peace*.'

'Stop it, André,' said Ludmilla.

I was speechless. Laura. André had found her again, in
Russia, in England, Rotterdam, or God knows where. Perhaps he'd had her copied by a friendly plastic surgeon
from his coke customer book. It was Laura aged 35. She ran her hand through her hair
in exactly the same way and had the same look in her eyes,
that look halfway between embarrassment and challenge.
Ludmilla said she was popping into town. 'See you later,'
she said. 'I assume you'll be staying for dinner.'

'That's right,' said André, when she had gone. 'I thought
at first that I was having visions. But it was real. Look not
and ye shall find. Once you start looking, you lose.'

I got my Pinarello out of the car and put the front wheel
on. André was waiting on his Pegoretti, with one leg on
the ground. He was wearing a red-and-black jersey of the
Amore & Vita team. On the chest was the big *M* of McDon-
ald's.

I set the kilometre counter to zero and got on. We had to
cross the Maas; we were going to do André's training circuit, a 'River Rotte run.'

'You're sponsored by the pope,' I said.

'Yes, I spread the Holy Word. No abortion, no euthana-
sia, just love and hamburgers. Got it from Ludmilla. Little
moralist.'

After a kilometre we reached the Erasmus Bridge. 'This
is my mountain stage,' said André. 'When I feel like it I
charge up and down it ten times. On the outer section,
good for power.'

'You're taking it seriously.'

'I live like a monk. No drink, no nicotine, no drugs. I stand on my head for an hour a day. Yoga. Rest, purity, regularity, that's my motto now. And lots of cycling, to keep the head clear. Looking back, I think it's a shame I didn't ride out with you back then.'

'What do you mean?'

'When you came and asked if I would come and race, don't you remember? I was lying on the sofa with a comic. Maybe I could have built up a nice career in cycle racing. I had the genes. And I *was* mean enough.'

He stood up on the pedals and rode ahead of me. I looked out over the river. Nice escape, coke dealer at the front, crime journalist on his wheel. We rode through the city, until we reached the Rotte and turned north-east along the river.

I asked when he had started cycling.

'About a year ago. On my old man's Raleigh. Part of my inheritance, you could say. Had it done up and rode it until last month. Cycling with my dead father, that feeling. Had long conversations. Good conversations. Of course, he didn't think what I was doing would amount to anything. I'll tell you another time.' He paused for a moment. 'That bike is bewitched.'

'I know that. I sometimes think that with every cyclist you come across, there's an invisible peloton riding along with him.'

'Recently I had the feeling that we'd finished. That I had more or less told him everything. Then I thought: time for something new. That Raleigh was made in 1977, so it was about time. And I thought it was rather a weird idea, that bike. That's not that odd, is it?'

'No. I wouldn't want to ride one metre on it.'

We came to a white drawbridge. We crossed, after which we headed for town again along the other bank of the

Rotte. On the Crooswijk bend, André cycled alongside me and put his arm on my shoulder. Then he stood up and pulled away from me. A little further on he sat up and stuck his arms in the air.

I was happy, too.

I clumped into the room in my cycling shoes. André gave me a towel and showed me where the bathroom was. The floor was covered in black marble. When I looked more closely at the dark-red tiles with hieroglyphic motifs on the walls, I saw little Egyptian figures on racing bikes. Ludmilla Laura had prepared a Russian speciality, something with ground beef and cabbage. We ate in silence.

'What did you think,' asked André, 'when you saw me in court? What a bastard?'

'I've passed that stage.'

'I wouldn't have blamed you for thinking that. I *was* a bastard. And I enjoyed it.'

'You don't have to defend yourself.'

He smiled and took a second helping.

'I was a sophisticated trader, make no mistake about it.' He said 'trader', not 'dealer'. 'I saw politicians on TV pretending to be squeaky clean, though I had delivered a fresh supply to them the day before. Well-known names from TV, captains of industry, bankers. Oh, Bart, do I have to tell you that? You're a journalist, aren't you? Why do you think I got away with it?'

I said nothing.

'Exactly. Your father used to say to us that what you knew was power, and he was quite right. And who you know is even more power.'

'And now?'

'Now it's finished. My name has been in the paper, I'm tainted. All I can do is descend to regular trade, and I don't want to do that. That would make it vulgar. Anyway, I don't need to anymore. Actually I was glad I had to draw a line.'

'What are going to do, then?'

'Maybe something with vintage cars. Old Peugeots and Citroëns. I've got four of them in a shed outside of town. I tinker about a bit. Sit in them. You can smell the past in cars, did you know that? I've got a 1968 DS that I swear you can smell our nursery school in.'

'Yum yum.'

'And I read books about medieval poetry and philosophy. I go to auctions of incunabula. Do you know what they are? Do you remember, the library of the Walburgiskerk, with those books on chains? We went once a year with the class. I thought it was fascinating even then.'

'André, bullshit. You were always tugging at those chains. You drove those people nuts.'

He laughed. 'That was being a tough guy. Come with me.' In his study was a classic English desk. Along three walls stood bookshelves that were filling up nicely. On the fourth hung a photo of the six of us on the summit of Mont Ventoux. He went over to the photo and pointed at Peter. 'He has been marked out, but he doesn't yet know it. To paraphrase Death in the poem: 'That on Ventoux I saw the man / I must fetch at night in Isfahan.'

'Carpentras.'

'Doesn't rhyme.'

I touched Peter's face with my finger.

V

Joost made a valiant attempt to explain the rudiments of string theory to me. We were sitting in Huis De Bijlen. He faltered now and then and waved his hands about. Then he stopped abruptly. 'I *can't* explain string theory. For the simple reason that there are no words for it. And that, in a nutshell, is the problem with the theory.'

The fact that even Joost could see there were no words for something proved that we were in a deeply abstract world.

'It's a mathematical concept so complicated that there aren't many people in the world who really understand anything about it. I sometimes don't even know if I understand the real finer points. And I'm not talking about the reality behind the theory itself, because that is far too complex to be thoroughly understood by anyone. I am making a contribution to the mystery. There are scientists who call string theory a religion.'

'But what good is it to you, if it can't be explained?'

'Do you remember we used to sing something like "We see Thy Glory, but we cannot fathom it?" It's the same with string theory. Fathoming it is no sinecure, and sometimes

we can't even see a thing. That makes it nicely complicated.'

I gave up.

'It's another world. One in which time and space no longer exist, with nine, ten, or perhaps even eleven dimensions. We're thinking about something we can't imagine.'

'So you just sit at your desk all day, thinking?'

'That's what it comes down to. Pen in hand, though.
Beer? Yes, beer. Drink up a bit, you're being a real girlie.'

We had completed the update. Joost was still married to
the American woman he had met when he was studying
at Yale. I remembered the wedding card, with a saxophone
on the front. One of his daughters was studying chemistry, the other planned to go to art school.

I told him that I never saw my ex-wife anymore and that
my daughter was studying Dutch.

'Chip off the old block. She'll soon drop out and become
a journalist, I assume. Messy divorce?'

'No. By mutual agreement, as they say. We were through.'

'Glad to hear it. Fancy-free has its advantages. God, that
wedding of yours. What a business. At a certain moment
David had to get me off the table. If you don't come off
now, I'll knock you off, he says to me. And he lifts me just
like that, with one hand. Strong as an ox, David.'

'I remember.'

'I was so ashamed, the next day. I sent you a card with
my apologies.'

'Never arrived. Or else it was immediately thrown away
by Hinke.'

'Do you know what I was wondering the other day? What
on earth her name was.'

Joost's father had died, like mine. But his mother was
still living in the old house, with her huge collection of
jazz records.

'I still think of your father a lot,' said Joost. 'He once said to me that you mustn't let life call the tune. Strange how you remember things like that so vividly.'

'He was talking to himself.'

'We often talk to ourselves when we talk to other people.'

'Does your mother still smoke cigars?' Joost's mother was different from mine in every respect, and that was best symbolized by her cigar—not just any cigar, but a big one.

'The most expensive Havanas. The look on your face the first time you came to our place. Your eyes nearly rolled out of your head. She got them from Hajenius in Amsterdam.'

'I wasn't used to that kind of thing.'

'My mother played saxophone, smoked Havanas, and was already drinking malt whisky before you could find it in Holland. She got it from an Italian friend, or rather, from her Italian lover.' He said it casually. 'The guy was one of the owners of Caffè San Marco in Trieste. We called in every summer on our way to our Italian holiday cottage. And he came regularly to Amsterdam. Most beautiful café in the world, by the way.'

'Did she have lovers, then?' I heard myself ask. Stupid. I was nearly 50 now, a veteran crime reporter, and still Joost had managed to catch me out. The son of the bohemian mother shocked his bourgeois friend.

'Of course she did.'

'Christ, Joost, how was I supposed to know that? I thought mothers were mothers, not lovers.'

'If you ask me, she still has them. And she still smokes cigars. The woman is fed up with everything. Fine by me.' He downed his glass in one. 'Crime journalism, yes. I read a piece by you on drugs the other day. Nice article, had a good laugh. Though that may not have been your intention. Hypocritical bastards with their War on Drugs.'

'Hey, funny you should have read that.' I knew the piece he was talking about.

'Yes, I thought right away: I've got to give Pol a call. But you beat me to it.'

For convenience's sake, I believed him.

'Beer,' he said. 'First I'll go and get us two beers. Thirsty weather, tonight. Do you know how many brain cells are lost after each glass of beer? Two million. Can you imagine that. So that makes another sixteen million fewer this evening. Deadly drug, alcohol. Okay, two beers. Double trouble, haha!'

'Do you still cycle?'

'Definitely,' said Joost. 'Together with a couple of guys from the faculty, in the summer, once a week. I reckon I'm in better shape than when I was 20. We should go to Mont Ventoux again. David with that car of his. David. I wonder how David's doing?'

'I see him a few times a year. And I get ten emails a week.'

'Gotta look him up again sometime. Good old David.'

It was my turn to get beer.

'André,' he asked as I put the glasses on the table, 'have you ever heard anything from André?'

I looked at him and drank a slow mouthful.

'You were talking about that piece of mine. The one about that drugs case. Do you remember the name of the accused?'

'No, of course I can't remember all the names in a piece like that.'

'André. André T.' The glasses clinked as Joost's fist came down. I knew that his eyes would grow larger, his mouth would fall open, and that he would lick his top lip with the tip of his tongue.

'Holy fuck,' said Joost, eyes wide. 'Holy goddamned fuck. Fucking André. Into fucking drugs.'

'He was already involved when I got married. Do you remember the Porsche he turned up in?'

'I scarcely spoke to him at the time. All I remember was that he had a dreadful blond babe with him.'

'That's right. Mandy.'

Joost looked at me and, undoubtedly for the first time in ages, shut up for thirty seconds. I enjoyed the hubbub in the background immensely.

'And?'

'Nothing,' I said. 'The prosecutor didn't have a chance.'

'Oh. That's good to hear. Well done, André. Did you talk to him?'

'Two days ago.'

'You're doing a tour! Where?'

'In Rotterdam. Cycles like crazy. Has a Pegoretti with gold leaf on it and a thirty-five-year-old Anglo-Russian girlfriend.'

'Jesus,' said Joost. 'Jesus Christ Almighty ... Anything else?'

'No.'

'Beer. A very large pilsener. It just goes to show, Pol, we haven't seen each other for far too long.'

'You're right, Tuur. And one more thing. That girlfriend of André's, that Ludmilla, is the spitting image of Laura.'

VI

I gazed at the short blond hair of Marga Sap in front of me. A gold chain glittered through it. She was wearing a tight black sweater and I had to restrain myself not to stroke her neck with one finger.

It was the end of August 1978, Gerrie Knetemann had just become world champion, and Karel Giesma the maths teacher was talking about p-adic numbers. I tried to make myself invisible in order to avoid questions. The dark universe in which he moved was not mine.

Next to me, Joost was adding moustaches and glasses to the pop musicians in his diary—most of them already had moustaches anyway. He also drew in text balloons. He was bored, and Giesma couldn't tell him anything new. Joost was one of those people for whom the logic of numbers and lines held no secrets. He read *Pythagoras Magazine*.

He stopped drawing and nudged me.

'Someone winds a thread round the earth,' he whispered. 'And so does someone else, only he doesn't lay the thread on the ground but hangs it one metre high. Yes?'

I nodded with as little interest as possible.

'Right. Now the question is: how much more string does the second man need than the first?'

'No idea. It's impossible. What do they do with the oceans?'

'What matters is the principle. This is an experiment in thinking. Well?'

'Ten thousand kilometres.'

'Oh no. A little over six metres!'

'It's impossible.'

'One man needs a length of $2\pi r$ and the other one of 2π r plus 1 metre. That makes 2π metres. Say about six metres. Nice, isn't it? Now we'll do the same with the circumference of your prick.'

Marga Sap turned round. She didn't understand a thing about maths either.

'The circumference of my prick?'

'That's different from the length, dickhead. Someone winds a string round it, and someone else does the same, but at a distance of one metre. How much more string does he need?'

'Christ, Joost, shut up for a minute.'

'Also 2π metres,' he said triumphantly, and wrote something in the text balloon above the head of Freddie Mercury. Freddie already had a pipe in his mouth.

'I want to fuck Marga Sap,' said Freddie Mercury.

'Hoffman, stop that stupid laughing,' warned Giesma. He was chalking secret codes on the board.

I was wearing my black Levis and the Michigan State T-shirt my cousin had sent me. It was Thursday, and after maths I had to dash to the music school for my organ lesson, for which, as usual, I hadn't practised.

Everything happens simultaneously; time is no more than an ordering, an illusion. Joost says that time doesn't exist, André has a painting on the wall about movement that is stasis, while I'm trying to make time stand still. Our friend Peter had to knock on the door of the love cabins on his father's brothel boat when time was up. There were men who only came when he knocked. One of his poems is called 'Love is Time'.

I hummed 'You're The One That I Want' softly in Marga's ear. The nape of her neck went slightly red. I'll just run my finger along Marga's chain, play a little with her blond hair, blow on her neck for a moment—and who knows but she might fall in love with me.

Then there was a loud bang on the door of the classroom. Giesma dropped the chalk in shock. Marga turned round with a questioning look in her eyes, as if she could feel what I was planning.

'Open ze door!' yelled André from the back of the class. Joost dropped forward laughing, with his face in his arms. Giesma went to the door and, for a second, checked that his bow tie was straight. Berghout, the principal, peered into the classroom, the strands of hair falling across his balding head, and grinned with satisfaction at the effect of his sledgehammer blow.

Next to him stood a black boy.

'Come in,' said Giesma.

Berghout went over to the spot behind the teacher's desk, followed by the black boy, who was wearing a shiny light-blue shirt and trousers with wide legs that had a slight sheen and a red stripe down the side. He swung his hips loosely.

'Boney M,' whispered Joost.

The boy seemed shy, yet at the same time exuded self-confidence.

Marga turned round to me again. Her beautiful lips formed three excited words: 'He's black!'

'No, he's an Eskimo,' I whispered back.

The headmaster looked at the class and said nothing, obviously wanting to give us time to absorb this historic moment.

'Class,' said Berkhout, 'I'd like to introduce you to David Castelen. He's from Paramaribo and recently came to live here. From today David will be a member of your class. I'm counting on you to show him the ropes and make sure he soon feels at home in our school. Anyone got any questions?'

No questions.

'David, any questions?'

'No, I don't have any questions.'

'Good. Then Mr Giesma will assign you a seat and you can quickly brush up your knowledge of Dutch mathematics.'

'I hope it isn't as hard as the Surinamese kind.' There was laughter. Giesma pointed him to the empty spot next to André, at the back of the class. David walked over to it like Elvis Presley going on stage, with swinging hips.

Joost looked at me and made significant movements with his eyebrows. 'Seems okay,' he whispered.

I nodded. 'What do you think, is he gay?'

'Blacks are never gay, didn't you know that? They're far too big to be gay. The other gays can't take it.'

I saw a new red blush in the nape of Marga Sap's neck—obviously she hadn't known that before either.

David's father had a small travel agency in the Lange Hofstraat, the East-West Travel Agency. Castelen Senior himself had a deep-seated dislike of travelling, including holidays. He had come to the Netherlands because of the future of his children and, in so doing, he had used up all his wanderlust for the rest of his life.

The family home was above the travel agency, so that the

life of father Castelen, who had the whole world on offer to his customers, was confined largely to an area of ten by ten by five metres.

'I can't understand those people,' he said. 'What's the point of going to a lousy country like that? You catch diseases, the food is terrible, your daughter is attacked, and there's nothing better to do than slump in a deckchair on the beach. It would be going too far to advise people to stay at home, I've got to get by but I can't make head or tail of it. East, west, home is best, I always say.' He thought the name of his travel agency was a good joke.

David had inherited his father's lack of desire for displacement. A year after they had arrived, you could say with certainty that they would never leave, and that in three hundred years' time, the tenth generation of Castelens would still be living quite contentedly in the town.

When David was 17, he worked out that it was time to sell what he called 'Adventure Trips'. The first Adventure Trip that the East-West Travel Agency offered was to Lapland. There, the holidaymakers had to trudge for days from hut to hut while being bitten to death by mosquitoes and surviving on berries and whatever provisions they had brought with them.

At first, old Castelen couldn't see the point. 'You might as well start selling torture.' But David maintained stubbornly that, on the contrary, people needed a portion of real misery. As long as they could see an end to it, and could come home again safely after a short while and tell heroic tales. Finally, his father agreed.

David wrote an advertisement for the local paper about the Adventure Trip to the Far North, in which he described 'the bellowing of the elks', 'the fascinating Northern Lights' and 'the age-old customs and richly coloured splendour of the Lapps.' The trip was booked up within six days.

Castelen Senior found it irresistibly funny that his customers would soon simply bump into their neighbours instead of a bellowing elk.

'All the better,' said David. 'People like that.'

'They've all gone crazy. But they're getting what they want.'

And so East-West Travel Agency acquired another arm, Eastwest Adventures, headed by the world's biggest homebody, David Castelen.

I didn't have to look up David on a university website or use a lawyer. I saw him whenever I was in Zutphen, about three times a year, to visit my father when he was still alive, or when I was in the area for the paper.

After an hour or so I could hear my Eastern accent re-emerging, as if my tongue was glad to be able to form the innate sounds once more. Every so often the thought of returning resurfaced. Like the Greek emigrant who has made a pile in America and, after completing the task, returns to his village on an island in the Ionian Sea. Old Hoffman, who has seen the world, has become wise and returns to his roots. It would be nice if André and Joost did the same, then we could play cards in Annie & Wim's café.

In the thirty-five years that David had lived in the town, he had succeeded in becoming a full-blooded Easterner. He spoke to the people who came to his travel agency in faultless dialect and no one thought it was odd.

He still lived above the shop, and the Adventure Trips were his best-selling line. He had profited from growing prosperity and boredom. One of his most successful trips was a two-week trek through Suriname, with overnight accommodation in bushmen's huts and including a day's piranha fishing. He also dropped people off in the Alaskan wilderness. Oddly enough, the demand for that trip had increased after one of his customers had only just survived an attack by a grizzly bear.

'People are getting more and more demanding,' he said. 'It's no longer enough to give them a walk through a desert full of scorpions or a survival trail through the jungle with rickety hanging bridges over crocodile-infested rivers. These days, they find that on the dreary side. Hanggliding at the North Pole, a voyage to the Canaries in a leaky WWII German submarine, that's the kind of thing you've got to come up with. There was someone here the other day who had read *Moby Dick*. Wanted to go whale hunting, expense no object. So I follow it up, and three weeks ago the guy flew to Japan and is now on one of those ships. He said he was going to bring me back a piece of whale meat.'

David has always remained unmarried. We never talk about it. He never asked about my marriage and afterward never about my divorce; I don't pester him with questions about his bachelor status. We have enough other things to talk about. He is a reader who single-handedly keeps the bookshop of Zutphen in business, and his tastes are diverse. He praises the débuts of writers I have never heard of, and he also recommends obscure Icelanders and biographies of American generals—the Civil War is one of his specialties. He is constantly begging me to read and reread Turgenev. 'Turgenev is the greatest. Certainly Chekhov comes close, he can also make you smell the steppes. But Turgenev is the only one with whom you can hear the people talking. It's almost creepy.'

He is a fervent film buff, and in this area, too, he provides me with valuable tips. How he finds the time to read his way through those piles of books, and meanwhile see all those films, is a mystery to me. He says that he reads a lot when there are no customers. 'Which happens more and more often because of that bloody Internet.'

I had informed David on the phone about my meetings with André and Joost, but he insisted that I come and give him a personal report. 'I feel a reunion in the air. You can't talk about that on the telephone. The Beatles never got back together on the telephone.'

'They never got together again at all.'

'That's what I mean. When shall we meet?'

'Wednesday?'

'Wednesday.'

On Tuesday he sent me an email.

'Dear Bart,' he wrote, 'so as not to give you a shock tomorrow, I must tell you the following. What happened? I've been feeling a bit tired recently, so I figure: let's go and see the doctor. I see Doctor Coomans. He taps my chest, fishes around a bit over my belly and back with his stethoscope: in perfect shape. Blood pressure. Thing round my arm, pumps it up and lets it down again. Much too high. I've got to take medication and lose weight. He asks: do you do any sport? I say: I cycle. No idea why, because I don't cycle at all. Oh, he says, that's nice, I cycle too. Sports bike? I say: yes, a racing bike, a Koga. Only make that comes to mind. Fantastic, says the doctor, Sunday morning at 9.30 on 's Gravenhof in front of Hotel Eden. I go straight to Van Spankeren: I need a Koga. Must it be a Koga? Yes, a Koga. He points to a Koga. Fine, I take that one. Pay out twelve hundred euros and walk out of the shop with a Koga. Plus an outfit. Sunday is the day, I'm dreading it.'

'Dear David,' I emailed back, 'I would have been less surprised if you had acquired a Thai wife. Christ Almighty, the champion of Suriname. We'll go out for a spin soon.'

'Definitely,' he replied. 'With Joost and André along. Team ride. Ordered a Rapha jersey. Do you know it? Brilliant, absolutely brilliant. Merino wool. And a silk bandana. If I'm going cycling, of course I want to look well groomed. That's what they call it, isn't it?'

I forward the email exchange to Joost and André.

I went into the Italian restaurant on the Houtmarkt, where David eats three times a week. He is a man of fixed habits; I didn't have to look for where he was sitting. He was wearing a light-blue shirt, which combined elegantly with a pair of black trousers and shoes that looked as if they were woven. David orders his shirts from Italy, as well as his handmade shoes. He even travelled especially to Italy to have himself measured to the millimetre, one of the few foreign trips he has made in the last few decades.

'Bart!' He got up to shake hands and thump me on the shoulders. 'Bart, man! A great pleasure to see you here again. This town is a rootless place when you're not here. When are you coming back for good? Life would gain enormously in quality! Why don't you set up here as a writer; that would also be very good for the fame of the town.'

David's words of welcome were lectures, spoken in an Eastern dialect doused with vague memories of Paramaribo, which he laid on extra thick because he knew that it gave me great pleasure.

'Friend David!' I said, true to habit. 'Cycling legend, in what exclusive eatery do we have the pleasure of dining this evening? Do you come here often?'

'Only three or four times a week,' he said, beckoning the waiter. 'Today happens to be my thousandth visit, so I think we shall be lavishly fêted by the owner, who has made a packet off me.'

He ordered a bottle of white house wine. 'Stick with what you like, is my motto. What do you think?'

'You're right.'

He asked me if I had already read Roland Barthes on the Tour de France. I said I had *Mythologies* on the to-read pile. Apart from Anna, David was the only one who knew I was working on a book in which I wanted to link cycling and philosophy. To give it a working title, I called it *Spinoza on the Bike*. I had already read a lot about Spinoza and his views. I had also tried to work my way through the *Ethics*, but had unfortunately become bogged down.

David had once actually sent me chapter headings: 1. The Bike, Philosophically Analyzed; 2. Philosophizing on the Bike; 3. The Greek Philosophers on the Bike; 4. Kant on the Bike; 5. Merckx's Tour Victories, Philosophically Analyzed; 6. Armstrong the Philosopher; 7. The Bike as a Means of Transport to the Truth; 8. Sex, Philosophy, and the Bike (plus a Large Beer); 9. How to Seduce Women with Philosophy and the Bike; 10. Reading Hands Free; 11. Nietzsche was a Doper.

With David, you never know if he means something, or if it's a joke. This was somewhere in the middle, probably. He bombarded me with reading tips for the project. I had the impression that he spent half his time in the travel agency on research for my book.

'How's your French? You've *got* to read the new biography of Anquetil. You'll see the link between behaviour on the bike and view of life brilliantly illustrated. Do you know that Anquetil was disappointed when he won a time trial by twelve seconds? He thought it was eleven seconds too much. Brilliant, isn't it? You can use that, or can't you? Or else there are his views on love and sexuality? Haha! And then there's Peter Sloterdijk, the German philosopher. He's written *very* interesting things about ...'

'David, listen. I'm frightened I'll never get round to writing if I read all these books you're recommending first. I'll die reading in bed without having put a single word down on paper.'

He looked at me in disappointment for a moment. Then he turned to the waiter who came to the table to take our order.

'Two Wednesday, Henk.'

'Wednesday?', I asked.

'Great. You'll see. I don't think we've ever eaten here on a Wednesday, or have we?'

David picked up the napkin from the table, laid it on his lap, leaned forward slightly, and looked at me. He was already over the disappointment.

'Bart, you'll never guess. Who suddenly walked into my place last week? Well?'

'No idea.'

'Marga Sap. Marga Sap! An American lady comes into the office, you know, heavy make-up, Botox, and I'm thinking: now what? And suddenly I see it. Marga Sap. Guess what she's called now?'

'Haven't got a clue. Marga Juice?'

'Marge Armstrong. I swear. Marge Armstrong. Haha!'

'You're kidding!'

'True!'

'And?'

'We went for a meal. Here.'

'Original.'

'Before that we walked through the town for two hours. She hadn't been back for at least twenty-five years. She was all eyes.'

'And then?'

'After dinner I took her back to her hotel, and she told me what she thought when I came into your class for the first time.'

'Well?'

'She'd heard that all black guys have an enormous dong and she thought: there's one.'

'Cut it out, David.'

'So, yes ...'

'No!'

'Yes. Marga Sap. Finally.'

'And now?'

'Now she's gone back to Jack in Lansing, Michigan. She sends you her best wishes.'

VII

The day Hinke and I got married was also the day when my friendship with Joost and André was put on ice. In the preceding years the contact had already become much less intensive, and now came the separation.

During the dinner, Joost stood on his chair and started holding forth. When he dropped the name Laura in his slurred speech, I knew it was going to end in tears. He talked of 'Bart's great love,' the woman 'who should have been here this evening, perhaps at Bart's side.' Or, he added, 'at mine.' People looked up in surprise and couldn't understand a word. The speech was meant for my ears only. It was as if he had waited for this moment to pay me back.

'Get him to stop,' hissed Hinke. 'I'm so ashamed. I don't want to hear all this, make him stop!' She shook my shoulder. I made a few vague hand gestures to Joost, but he was unstoppable. It went embarrassingly quiet; I could see a disaster looming, but I wasn't capable of taking appropriate measures.

Joost had just launched into a detailed description of Laura's appearance when David got up, walked over to him, whispered something in his ear, grabbed him by the waist, and threw him over his shoulder. He set him on a stool at the bar, spoke forcefully to him, and came back to the table as if nothing had happened.

I spent my wedding night on an airbed in the living room. I could understand why—after all, Joost was my friend.

André turned up at the wedding in the brand-new Porsche. He had brought a blond girlfriend with him who seemed to come from a different universe. André didn't say much, not even to his parents. There were scores of people he knew, but he moved through the company like a ghost. He wore a white suit and snakeskin shoes. When he left, he hugged me and said: 'Sorry, Bart.' For a long time those were the last words I heard from his mouth.

VIII

If you walk from the Groenmarkt to the Marspoortstraat in Zutphen, after a couple of hundred metres you reach the river. On the other side are the river floodplains, which flood in winter and sometimes freeze over so that you can skate.

One warm July evening in 1980, David, André, and I were sitting on a low wall on the town side, looking out over the water. Joost was missing, as he'd gone to a summer camp for young astronomers in Drenthe.

We watched the ships sailing past. André checked whether there were any pretty women at the helm. He was talking about a TV series in which a mysterious water gypsy had arrived in her boat at a little village on the river. There, she had initiated a boy into the secrets of love. 'Could happen here, too,' he said. 'She could moor here any day. And I'll be at the head of the queue.'

I asked what that meant, being initiated into love.

'Screwing for the first time.'

'Yes, I get that. But what's so secret about that?'

'That's a secret.'

David was throwing pebbles in the water. For my Dutch

exam, I had just read a story about a moped going to sea, and I imagined one zooming over the water from the direction of Kampen, right under the old steel bridge, on the way to the Rhine.

'Ridiculous,' said André. He jumped off the wall to go home. At that moment, David pointed downstream. 'Look at that!' he shouted. We saw a huge black shoebox coming our way. The monster towered high above the water, and was being pushed along by a small boat with a long chimney from which came puffs of smoke. It was as if a little yapping dog was snuffling at a black Dobermann with its snout. André stood up and started waving. The tug ploughed slowly on with its heavy load and shifted course towards the quay. We could see a small man with a large moustache at the helm. Suddenly a hatch opened on the flat roof of the black box. A boy with blond curly hair climbed out. He stood on the roof, like a field marshal following the course of a battle from a hilltop. He raised his hand. To us, or perhaps it was a sign to the man in the tug, who pointed in our direction.

'Ahoy, steady as she goes!' shouted André. The boy and the man did not react. It took about another fifteen minutes before the captain managed to manoeuvre his way to the quay. 'Hey!' he shouted in our direction. 'H-h-help us a minute!'

We ran to the quay. The boy was still standing on the roof. The captain, who was wearing overalls covered in oil stains, had climbed from the pushing boat onto the gangway of the black box, and threw a thick rope towards the shore. André, who had been to sailing camp, grabbed the rope and wound it around a bollard.

'M-m-mind your f-f-fingers,' shouted the captain. Meanwhile, he had gone aft and jumped ashore with a second rope in his hand. After he had secured it, he came over to us. 'Thanks a lot, l-l-lads. My name is Seegers, W-w-willem Seegers. And up there on the roof is my s-son Peter.'

'Hello,' said Peter.

The tug still puffed out the occasional plume of smoke, as if still panting from the effort. Captain Seegers checked the mooring lines. 'Otherwise I'll have to pick it up in K-k-kampen tomorrow. And we've just come from there. And they don't like our kind of b-b-boat there.' He pointed to a couple of nasty marks on the side of the vessel. 'Do you see w-w-what I m-m-mean?'

'Paint and eggs,' shouted Peter from the roof. Captain Willem started hooting with laughter. He turned a winch, which lowered a gangplank hanging upright against the boat. Next, the door hidden behind the gangplank opened. A woman of about 40 walked ashore down the plank in high heels. She was wearing sunglasses. Captain Willem disappeared inside through the door.

André nudged me and grinned. 'Here she comes.'

The woman looked around her as if she had just stepped ashore on an island inhabited by savages. I saw that the tug was called Little Red Rooster, while the big box had no name. Meanwhile, some more people had gathered on the quay.

No one said anything. We were all waiting for an explanation from one of the three people on the boat. Captain Willem Seegers reappeared. He had changed his clothes, and now looked like a waiter in a chic restaurant. He had exactly the same kind of bow tie as Karel Giesma. He fixed a sign next to the door. SWEET LADY JANE, it said, and underneath: FLOATING SAUNA, with the opening hours.

'R-r-right,' said captain Willem. 'Th-th-that's up.' Peter disappeared inside through the hatch.

A little later we found ourselves in the bar of the *Sweet*

Lady Jane. There *were* windows on the side of the boat facing the water. There were red curtains in front of them, through which you could see the vague contours of the other side of the river. There was soft pink carpeting on the floor, and a couple of comfortable sofas were placed around gold-coloured side tables. Captain Willem pointed to the woman behind the bar. 'Madame Olga,' he said. The woman had kept on her sunglasses and greeted us with a barely perceptible nod. 'My mother,' said Peter.

'What would the gentlemen like to dr-dr-drink?'

'A beer for me, captain,' said André.

'Yes, we'll have a beer, too,' I said, pointing to David. We didn't feel at ease. Madame Olga opened a fridge.

'You may be thinking: what a funny b-boat this is,' said Captain Willem, to break the silence. 'Well, the g-g-girls will be here tomorrow.'

Peter smiled. He was roughly the same age as us.

'We'll be moored here for a week or so,' he said. 'That's for publicity. Usually we're in the paper after about three days. Then everyone knows we're here, and we move to a spot approved by the council. And then the men come.'

'The men?' asked David. 'Your father said: the women.'

'Yes. To the brothel.' Peter's father stood nodding in assent. 'Peter has the gift of the g-g-gab. I don't kn-kn-know who he gets it from. Not from m-me, in any case.'

'So it's not a sauna,' I concluded. André looked at me reproachfully.

'A kind of sauna,' said Peter. 'We've got a kind of sweatbox and a Turkish bath.'

'It's a sauna for fucking.' André said it as if that was a generally recognized kind of sauna. Peter's mother looked angrily at him and put three bottles of beer and glasses on the bar. She now said something for the first time, in a language we couldn't understand.

'That's Russian,' said Peter. 'She says it's the first and last time we shall see you here, as the Sweet Lady is only for men over 21.'

'Shame,' said André.

Peter told us that he would be going to school in Zutphen. In Kampen he had been in the fourth year of high school.

'Great, then you'll be in our class. At least if you're coming to Baudartius.'

'Of course he isn't,' declared André. 'It's a Christian school.' Madame Olga nodded to indicate that he *was*.

'We have another friend,' said David, after he had explained to Peter where our school was. 'Joost. He's not here at the moment, he's stargazing on the heath. His father's a doctor.'

'A d-doctor,' cried Captain Willem. 'We n-need one here for the girls.' He said something in Russian to his wife, who nodded in agreement.

David grabbed a pen from the bar and wrote something on a beer mat. 'Perhaps it will be better if you call yourself. This is the number.'

Captain Willem nodded. 'If you lads will excuse me, then I'll g-g-get to work for a bit, because everything must b-b-be ready by tomorrow. Peter will stay with you for a bit. He's a poet. I'm very proud of him.' Those last words came out without a stutter. For the first time, Peter looked a bit embarrassed. 'He's a b-bit ashamed of it, but that's non-non-nonsense. His poems are won-won-won-derful.'

We looked at Peter.

'It's true,' he said.

Peter had something serene about him. He did not seem to belong in a floating brothel, which, come to that, applied to his father and mother, too. They were more like an extravagant, gallery-owning couple, specializing in Russian art.

When we had finished our beers, Madame Olga gave Peter a nod. He nodded back. On board *Sweet Lady Jane*, there was a lot of communication with short nods.

We climbed onto the roof.

'So, tomorrow the whores will arrive,' said André.

'The girls,' said Peter. 'We never call them whores. It doesn't sound nice, my father thinks.'

'How many of them are there, actually?' asked André.

'Four.'

'Are they pretty?'

'We wouldn't get any customers if they weren't.'

André thought for a moment. 'And do you get a free turn?'

Peter looked at him. Then he started laughing. At first a short hiccup, which turned into longer howls and ended with a regular shaking, as if he had convulsions.

'Sorry,' said Peter, when he came to his senses a little. 'But I thought it was a funny question. No, I'm not allowed any turns at all.' He threatened to fall into a coma of laughter again.

'Is that so funny? It's not all that odd, is it? If your father has a garage, you're allowed to drive the cars, aren't you?'

'Drop by once we have our permanent mooring. If you stand in the wardrobe in my room, you can hear the noises from Cabin 3 with a glass. It's amusing.'

'Okay,' said André. 'Amusing. You're on.' Peter climbed back down, and we followed. 'Amusing,' André repeated again.

In the bar, Madame Olga polished the gold tables until they shone. She said something to Peter.

'She says I must ask if I can be your friend,' he said, in a tone as if the question, besides being quite normal, was totally superfluous.

'That's fine,' said David. André and I nodded to indicate it really was fine. Peter nodded to his mother. She nodded to Captain Willem, who was standing on some steps, replacing a light bulb above a sofa.

'I'm v-v-very happy about that. Friendship is the most beautiful thing in the world.'

A week later, Peter joined our class. He was modest and calm, but also had a self-confidence you wouldn't immediately expect in a boy of 16. It was striking that he got on just as well with the girls as with the boys. The girls behaved as if they had known him for years. Peter was the natural leader who didn't have to do anything to win and retain his leadership.

And yes, he was a poet. Odd poems, we thought. They were so full of wild leaps and associations. Sometimes they were four lines long, sometimes a hundred. In the bookcase in his room, besides scores of videos, there was also a whole row of poetry collections. He could recite poems by heart, even very long ones. As he stood there declaiming, you could see how he seemed to disappear into another world. How the words and images seemed to take possession of him. Sometimes a look came into his eyes that struck fear into me.

Close friendship is a rainbow. The rational spirit of Joost, the emotional one of André, the romantic one of Peter, and the stoical one of David fit together well. It is always difficult to analyze oneself, but I think I had something of everyone in me. You may find that a lack of a personality on my part, but also the binding force of the modest ego. If they formed the different colours, I was the reverse prism that merged the beams of light.

Peter left the PR for his poetry to us, and to his father, who had asked Hein Broekhuis of the Modern Fashion Store to make copies of Peter's poems in calligraphy on handmade paper. Calligraphy was Hein's great hobby, and Peter's father paid him in kind. Captain Willem framed them nicely and hung them on the wall of the *Sweet Lady Jane*.

Peter himself was modest about his poems. When he got a letter telling him that work of his was to be included in a literary magazine, he gave it to us to read without saying anything.

'Congratulations!' cried Joost. 'You're going to be famous, man!'

'I want a signed copy,' said André. 'They'll be worth a fortune later.'

'It's a magazine,' Peter corrected him, 'not a collection. That will come later.'

We were proud that such a great poetic talent wanted to be our friend, even though we were not capable of properly judging his talent. 'That lad over there is Peter Seegers,' Joost said one evening in the Talk of the Town disco to a guy at least two metres tall, wearing an earring. He pointed in our direction. 'You know, from the *Sweet Lady Jane*. He's a poet. The writer Gerrit Komrij has called him a great talent.' Joost had had too much to drink.

'Who?'

'Gerrit Komrij! Christ, man. Surely you know who Gerrit Komrij is? Comes from these parts, too. When he says you're a great talent, then you are one. You can be sure of that.'

The guy looked at him with contempt. 'Get lost man, with your Gerrit complex.' He stood up and pushed Joost aside. 'Whore chaser.'

'Yokels,' said Joost, when he came back with a tray of beers. 'Haven't got a clue about art.'

IX

We first saw her on 14 July 1981. The five of us were at the swimming pool, under the oak trees, our regular spot, where there was a slight grassy slope. We were doing what we always did: playing football, eating ice cream, catching wasps in a bottle, talking nonsense, and putting David in a double nelson. From my transistor radio came the voice of the motorbike commentator on the Tour de France. Today's stage was over the Alpe d'Huez, and I didn't want to miss it.

Joost was just subjecting David to what he called the diabolical punishment of Sodomites—he had read Gerard Reve's *The Language of Love* for his literature exam, and that book had made as big an impression on him as *The Rider* had on me. He was hitting David's light-coloured soles viciously with a branch. 'You like it, you old fairy.' Ever since David's admission to the club, he had been our resident gay. It was because of his way of dressing, but also because he never took the trouble to deny that he was. He let us get on with it. He didn't bother in the slightest about the resulting teasing by other people. Other people didn't matter. In fact, we didn't much care whether David really was gay or not.

'And shortly I shall have to whip your tight boy's ass,' cried Joost. David went on calmly reading *Huckleberry Finn*. Peter had an exercise book and was making notes.

André kept the ball in the air and counted. It was actually unnecessary, because if he had to, he could go on till closing time. With his left or his right foot, with his head, or with a combination of all three.

I did nothing. Well, I looked at the others.

Then she came floating along. André stopped counting, let the ball roll away, and turned round. Joost interrupted his torture activities and looked in the same direction as André, while his mouth fell open and his tongue appeared. David closed his book and looked, too. Peter stopped writing and turned his head to the right.

She was radiant. She drew all the energy of the swimming pool to herself and seemed unaware of the havoc she was causing. She laid a towel on the grass, sank down like a leaf on a breath of wind in late summer, turned onto her back, drew up her right leg, and closed her eyes.

Joost was the first to pull himself together. He stammered, made speech movements without saying anything, which for him meant that there were still powerful and unassimilated experiences spinning around in his brain.

'Did you see that?' he asked in a whisper, as if it had been a mirage. 'Did you see that? Christ. I mean, can you see that?'

'What do you mean?' said David.

Joost was too flabbergasted to react to the joke. He stared at the creature open-mouthed.

'Who is that?' I asked.

No one answered. It was a stupid question, anyway. Peter had stood up. He was quite experienced when it came to beautiful women, but this was a special apparition for him, too.

André grabbed his ball, kept it in the air ten or so times, and deliberately let it bounce off his instep, toward the girl. It was perfectly executed: the ball rolled gently in her direction, touched her hip, and came to a halt next to her. The girl looked up. She smiled.

André went over to her. As he picked up the ball, he said: 'Hello.' He said 'Hello' to a holy angel or a film star or God knows what it was.

'Hello,' said the girl.

'Sorry about the ball. It shot off my foot.'

'Doesn't matter.'

André hesitated a moment. He bounced the ball once. 'Do you want an ice cream?' he asked, as if she were his sister.

'That would be nice.'

There was something about that voice. It was rather sing-song, and it was warm. It was a voice that massaged your soul. André pointed to the four of us. 'Come and join us. That dark-brown guy was just going to get ice creams.'

The goddess got lithely to her feet, picked up her book, her bag, and her towel, and came toward us.

She had blond, shoulder-length hair, which framed her face in long locks. Her eyes were blue—not hard, Germanic blue, but the blue you see on houses on the Greek islands. Her skin was golden silk.

'David, your turn.' André said it again with a boldness that I could not remember having noticed before.

David got up and gave the girl a look that suggested he probably wasn't gay after all. She smiled at him, and a wave of jealousy went through me. I should have gone to get the ice creams.

'Chocolate?' he asked the girl.

'Yes, great.'

While David trotted off, she sat down, pulled her knees

up, and then said: 'I'm Laura.'

Peter looked at her for a long time without saying anything. 'Peter,' he said. 'I'm Peter. Her eyes rested on him longer than any of us, but that was the same with all girls.

'Peter, you beauty, Peter, you beauty!' cried the Tour de France commentator on the radio. Peter Winnen had won the stage.

X

I was immediately obsessed with Laura van Bemmel. Of course it wasn't the first time I had been in love; I had been infatuated with a French student teacher of 23, a young neighbour in my street who always came cycling past in tight jeans, a checkout girl in the supermarket, and three or so girls from the class above ours. They were easily interchangeable crushes that appeared as fast as they evaporated again, driven by hormones and a longing for the unknown, with anyone as a guide. But with Laura it was different. For the first time I experienced love as a form of madness. I discovered primeval desire and recognized an almost irrepressible urge in myself. I also knew immediately that it was dangerous, and felt intuitively that it could destroy you.

I wasn't the only one. From the moment that André shot that ball toward her, a dimension was added to the relationship between the five of us—that of jealousy. It is desire that tolerates no rivals, a life-and-death struggle of untameable instincts. Each of us poured it into his own mould: André, Joost, and I into that of yearning and desire, while David tried to keep control by assuming his stoical attitude, and actually Peter seemed to be the only one to withdraw from the fray. And then there were those other insufferable assholes who were always hanging around her.

With great love comes fear, the fear that the object will remain eternally unattainable, and should that prove not to be the case, the eternal fear of losing her. That does strange things to you.

Laura joined our group from the day she walked into the swimming pool. It was as if she had come especially to the pool to meet us. Our quintet became a sextet, a special group of five guys and a beautiful girl, the siren of a tightly knit band.

We didn't go to her place. I went into Joost or André's living room as naturally as our own, and I plundered David's parents' fridge without problems. The *Sweet Lady Jane* was common ground, although Madame Olga grumbled.

But we never went to Laura's, even though she lived near André and me. 'My parents prefer not,' she said. Probably her parents were not even aware of our existence. She didn't tell us how she managed to get away in the evenings when we went out, or to come swimming or skating or just hanging around with us on Saturdays.

When you saw her father and mother walking next to each other on Sunday morning on their way to their little church, you would never have imagined that they had a perfect daughter. The girl was so different from her parents that she must have been adopted or exchanged in the cradle.

Cor van Bemmel was a bookkeeper at Van Deutekom's brickworks, just outside town. He had a funny walk. It was as if his left leg kept getting the signals from his brain a fraction late. Laura's mother, small and rotund, always walked obliquely behind him, as if ready to catch him if he were to fall backward. The look in their eyes betrayed nothing of what was going on inside them, except that all cheerfulness was banished. They spoke to other people only when there was no alternative. According to Laura, they lived in virtual silence at home, too.

Laura's parents belonged to a small religious community that met twice every Sunday in an unobtrusive building in the Kuiperstraat. Laura had not gone to services there since she was 13. She didn't want to talk about what that had meant for her relationship with her parents. 'They can't beat faith into you,' she said. I suspected that Cor van Bemmel had tried.

Once, on the boat with Peter, after we had watched a film about a boy who had been brought up among the Amish, she said a little more about it. 'Suddenly I was so full of guilt, it overflowed. Having it drummed into you every Sunday how bad and rotten you are, at a certain moment you've had enough.' She said she did not understand why she always had to ask for forgiveness. And then, without any further explanation: 'It's as if you're growing up in a concentration camp where you're allowed to think only one thing, and if you don't, you're threatened with eternal damnation.'

'Brainwashed,' said Peter.

The rivalry crept up on us and was not explicit. It would not have struck an outsider, but I noticed it from casual sentences and glances, sideswipes that were never dished out before, little digs. Suddenly someone underlined another person's weakness; the laughter at a stupid remark sounded just a little different. Suddenly André was wearing different trousers from his worn-out jeans, and Joost had bought Spanish riding boots after Laura had once let slip that she thought they were cool. Something happened to the loyalty between the five of us—it was no longer as absolute and it was replaced by distrust. David did not take part in all the macho behaviour and tried to keep us together. He saw before we did how jealousy would drive us apart—and he did his best to stop it. 'You lot are horny apes,' he said. 'Eager beavers.' David already knew that everything we call romantic is, in fact, the destroyer of romanticism, or in any case of unselfish boyhood romanticism.

'So you wouldn't like to fuck her?' said Joost. David shrugged his shoulders in irritation. 'You don't say you'd like to screw André, do you?' he said. 'You don't talk like that about your friends.'

'But I don't want to,' said Joost. 'That's the difference between women and friends.'

Laura knew what her effect on us was, but at the beginning she showed no sign of favouritism, as if she knew that that would mean the immediate end of her place in our group. She balanced like a ballerina on pointe and divided her attention between the five of us as if she were keeping an account in which she maintained an accurate record of the distribution of her sympathy.

I don't know exactly what it was about us that attracted her. Perhaps it was our closeness that gave her a safe feeling; perhaps together we formed a protective wall against everything she had grown up with. Together, we were sensitive, well read, intelligent, funny, and sporty. Peter quoted from world literature, André was the star player on his local football team, Joost could explain relativity theory or point out the constellations in the sky. You played him ten seconds of a saxophone solo and he knew who it was. David was the understanding listener who never interrupted you or brought up his own worries. But with every day that she was with us, every word that she spoke, every look, and every touch, it became clearer that this *ménage à six* could not last forever.

She was a year younger than us, born on 21 April 1965. The reason that she was in our class was because she had skipped a year. She was better than us in almost all subjects—perhaps Joost had a little more scientific precision, but she could sometimes amaze even him with the speed at which she got to the bottom of mathematical problems. Her great love was poetry in English, and Emily Dickinson in particular. And she loved the plays of Ionesco and Pinter. In the fifth year, we performed Pinter's *Birthday Party*. Joost was Stanley, the main part; André and I played Goldberg and McCann. Our acting talent was sadly wanting, and the fact that the performance was a great success was due entirely to her role as director.

Quite soon, something grew between Laura and Peter that was different from the relationship André, Joost, David, and I had with her. Peter had found a soulmate. From the beginning, Laura clearly felt a deep admiration for Peter's talent. She was fascinated by what she immediately recognized as something exceptional. We also saw that Peter could do things we couldn't cope with, but when he became too airy-fairy, we could just as easily put him down as a facile versifier-to-order.

When Peter and Laura talked about poems, they were way above our heads. We didn't mind, and when we had had enough, we said so. Joost, in particular, didn't beat about the bush. 'Crooner and Swooner', he once called them.

Peter gave a new poem to her to read first. He handed it to her and followed her eye movements as she read it. Then he hung on her every word as she gave her judgement.

Usually she thought for a moment, then came out with a review you could have put straight in the paper. All the references, all the images, all the associations—she combined them all into an opinion that was, by the way, invariably positive, with occasional suggestions for a slight improvement or adjustment. Peter always accepted them, at least at first.

'Sometimes she finds something that I haven't consciously put in myself at all,' he said. 'That happens a lot with poems, of course. My father also interprets for all he's worth. Sometimes he creases me up with all the things he reads into it. But with her, there's something strange going on. It's not her interpretations, it's my encoding that she unravels. She tells me why I've written things in a certain way, and she's very often right. Sometimes she gives me a nasty fright, because she says things I would have preferred not to know.'

Peter's talent blossomed when Laura started to become involved. He was still very young, and she was younger still, but she seemed to make him mature as a poet in a short space of time. Sometimes they went to Amsterdam to comb the bookshops—and he made passionate use of her suggestions. They were mainly English-language poets like Thomas, Hughes, and Heaney.

She was subservient to Peter's talent, as if he were the one who could put her own ineffable longings and pain into words, if only she fed his soul enough. Inevitably, she figured more and more in the poems he wrote, until, almost as a natural progression, he began a cycle that revolved completely around her. To avoid direct association, the girl in the poems was called Anna, but it was clear enough that it was about Laura. Of course she saw that herself, too, but it did not change her attitude. She gave him the beads to make the necklace that was intended for herself.

Peter's message was not: I love you. It was about surrender, about a person he could give himself to heart and soul, and from whom he demanded complete surrender.

We did not see immediately that there was a direct line from Peter's poetry to reality. For us, a poem was something that was far removed from everyday life. We understood that the Anna of his poetry was the same as Laura, but at the same time, the poems were about a Laura we did not know, who was perhaps a little like Laura, but seen through the eyes of a poet, and poets simply looked completely differently, and disguised reality until it was unrecognizable.

We did wonder exactly what their relationship was like. We could also see that the dynamic between the two was changing, that, after a while, Peter reacted differently to Laura's comments than he did at the beginning, and that he paid less attention to them and corrected her more often. Once they had an argument when Peter called her a 'prudish cow' because she criticized a couple of sentences in which he was sexually very explicit and said she found them 'vulgar'.

However, there seemed to be no question of any physical attraction between Peter and Laura—that made the intimacy between the two of them bearable for us. They seemed to translate everything into poetry, including the possible love that they felt for each other.

'Why don't you write some poems yourself?' André asked her once.

'Poets live in another world, and I don't.'

'And Peter?'

'Peter does.'

One evening, when we were sitting on the roof of the *Sweet Lady Jane,* Peter announced that he had finished the last poem in his collection. He got up and started reading it. I looked at Laura to see how she reacted—after all, the collection was for her. I had expected her to be moved, proud, perhaps, and she was, but for the first time I also saw fear.

XI

In March, a few days before the presentation of the Spinoza Prize, I received a friendship request and a message on Facebook from Laura Guazzi. I looked at it as if it were a message from a dead person. She wrote a few short sentences. 'Dear Bart, I'd really love to meet up with all of you. I'll be in Avignon in July, for the theatre festival. Can we organize something then? Much love, Laura.'

I wrote back to say how glad I was that she had made contact, and that I would love to see her, too. I wasn't capable of writing any more. All the words got stuck.

Then I called David. 'I know what you're phoning about,' was all he said. 'I've been sitting here for an hour staring into space. And I've already checked out a few things in Provence. God Almighty.'

I drove to The Hague and arrived at a building with a sign saying MUSEON. People were already going in, but we had arranged that I would wait for David at the entrance. He had to take the train from Zutphen. I had emailed André, but heard nothing from him.

I was beginning to wonder if David hadn't perhaps gone

to the wrong town, and I was about to text him when I saw him getting out of a taxi. He raised his hand. 'Sorry,' he said, 'you said recently that time didn't exist, but it certainly does, for our trains at least. They don't always arrive on time, but they always leave on the dot. The despairing traveller wanders in the no-man's-land between the two.'

He looked glorious in his Italian made-to-measure suit. André had expensive suits, too, but in his case you could tell he hadn't grown up with them. His father only wore a suit for weddings and funerals, the same suit he wore for his own wedding, and in his coffin. André seemed determined at all costs to make up for the age-old inferiority of the Tankink family in relation to the suit-wearing classes.

David had the natural aura of the film star who, in the morning, pulls a Corneliani suit out of the wardrobe without thinking and drapes it over his perfect body— fits like a glove, in a superior display of precision measurement and material management. He belonged on the catwalk, as the perfect symbiosis between man and suit that God must once have meant when He showed Adam his nakedness and laid the foundation of the textile industry.

I tapped David on his paunch.

'It'll be gone shortly,' he assured me. 'Have a good look.'

'Shame about that nice suit.'

'You can have this. Take it in a bit, and there you are. That C&A special you're wearing just won't do.'

'Gap. Cost a tidy sum, too.'

He looked at me with feigned contempt. 'Pauper.'

We went to the entrance; the ceremony was due to start in two minutes, and we didn't want Joost to have to apologize for his boorish friends coming in late. We walked down a flight of steps and entered an auditorium that was already pretty full.

On the platform, a man was getting ready to start his speech. The front row was still empty.

Someone shut the doors. The man on the platform drank a mouthful of water. From a door on the right of the auditorium came the nominees for the Spinoza Prize, with Joost bringing up the rear. As he went to his chair, the door opened again. It was André. He raised his hand jovially to the great physicist. The latter looked in utter amazement in his direction, as if he saw in the man with the glistening bald skull, Paul Smith suit, and white crocodile-leather shoes an alien who knocked all his theories sideways.

André looked around the auditorium with his hand over his eyes, to see if he could spot us. 'André!' shouted David. 'Over here!' He pointed to the seat we had kept free.

André hugged David and gave me a hearty slap on the shoulders. The man on the platform cleared his throat and once more smoothed out the piece of paper with his speech on it. At that moment, Joost turned around and looked in our direction. 'Are you finally sitting comfortably, Tankink? Then we can begin!' Everyone laughed, but only we recognized that Joost's imitation of Karel Giesma was still pretty good.

'Go ahead and start, Karel,' André answered. The chairman began. We didn't listen; we were sitting at our desks in maths again like three adolescents.

'Listen,' said André softly. 'You'll never guess. I was looking at my friendship requests on Facebook last week and ...'

'Laura,' said David and I, together. André looked disappointed for a moment, but then excited again. 'Un-bel-lievable!'

A lady with grey hair sitting in front of us looked around angrily.

'Shh.' David pointed to the speaker.

'I was totally wired for at least ten minutes,' said André, before leaning back and pretending to listen to the speaker. A little later he bent over to us again. 'Don't say anything to Joost yet. What a joke. The guy isn't on Facebook, I don't think. At least, I couldn't find him.'

The man at the lectern announced the names of the winners: Joost was among them. After his name had been read out, he looked in our direction and beamed. André gave him the thumbs up. Only when, half an hour later, Joost came forward in order to make a speech of thanks in turn, did we focus our full attention on the platform again. Joost, as always, did up the middle button of his sports jacket.

'How much is the prize, anyway?' asked André.

'One and a half million,' I said. André whistled through his teeth. 'And he can keep all of it for himself?' Joost thanked a long list of people, and said he hoped that the money from the Spinoza Prize would contribute to the unlocking of 'the great mystery.' When he had almost finished, he looked emphatically in our direction.

'At the deepest levels,' he said, 'space and time no longer exist. That is the fascinating and, at the same time, incomprehensible thing about string theory. But sometimes that deeper reality touches our own. I would ask you all not to look around, because they are no vision of beauty, but at the back of the auditorium on the right are my three oldest friends. Their names are David, André, and Bart, and with them during my childhood in the East of the country I laid the first building blocks of my future career. In the construction corner with Miss Hospes. I'm glad they are here and have built a bridge in time, as if it really doesn't exist. Thank you.'

There had been no applause for the previous speakers,

but André began clapping enthusiastically. Joost gave an almost imperceptible bow, and here and there, people joined in with André.

'I was actually at nursery school in Suriname,' said David.

When the reception was almost over, Joost's wife and two teenage daughters left. I had seen Valery once before, before there were any daughters. I don't think she recognized me, but the meeting was too brief to make sure. Their departure seemed to be a relief to Joost. He had already recovered from his surprise at our presence. We behaved as if, because of his research, we were trying to prove that time is an illusion and hence cannot elapse.

Just when André asked what Joost was going to invest his newly acquired capital in, the latter was tapped on the arm by a woman of about 30. He looked her up and down for a moment and went with her into a corner of the auditorium, where it was quiet. She looked familiar to me, but I couldn't place her.

'His bit on the side,' said André. 'He was already undressing her with his eyes. I can imagine that when you've got such a miserable wife. Christ, she looked at me as if I'd crawled straight out of the gutter.'

'American women think bald men are unreliable,' explained David. 'Sociological research. That's why the men wear toupees. Except for blacks, because they, on the contrary, *are* considered attractive when bald. It's because of Michael Jordan and all those other black baldies. All very complicated.'

André looked at him hollow-eyed. In the corner, Joost was gesticulating wildly.

'They've fallen out,' said André. 'She's giving him the choice of moving in together or she's going to finish it once and for all.' The girl took out a notebook. 'Writing down everything he says, so she can use it against him later. Christ, what a woman.'

'Journalist,' I said. 'Can't remember her name right now.'

'Sonja van Vleteren,' said David. 'I recognize her from the photo above her stories. Bits on the side don't write things in notebooks. Maybe in your case, because you're bald.'

'Shame,' said André. 'I thought my theory was much more interesting.'

A little later, Joost came back. The girl was walking to the exit.

'Bloody hell,' said Joost.

'Journalist, eh?' said André.

'Yes. Do you know her?'

'Fucking journalists.' André gave me such a bang on the back that I dropped the hot croquette in my fingers into my beer glass.

A couple of hours later we were sitting in a restaurant.

'Christ, guys,' said Joost, 'this is better than that whole damned prize. It's going to cause a lot of headaches. It attracts bluebottles.'

André asked how things were going between him and Valery.

'Can't stand Holland. Thinks it's a narrow-minded swamp full of croaking frogs and plebs. She has a point. But, well, what are you supposed to do? All that intercontinental marriage, Christ.'

'The whole marrying thing is absurd,' I said. 'Absurd invention.'

'American women ... Don't get me started on that,' said André. 'Tell us what the sex is like, Joost. Don't keep beating about the bush.'

'Moderate to very moderate, André. Approaching zero.'

'Joost is wanking again, like he always did,' concluded André. 'Or were those your students I saw sitting in the second row this afternoon? If so, there's still hope. They looked at you as if they were really in love.'

We didn't talk about Peter. He was with us at table; there was even an empty chair, but we did not involve him in the conversation. We avoided him, as we had avoided him for a long time—actually, since he was buried. We denied his death, or rather we confirmed it by denying he had ever existed.

The only one of us who had ever broken the taboo was David. At his mother's funeral, he ended his address with a quotation from a poem by 'a friend of ours'.

> Go and sleep, on the desolate plain,
> On your side, on her side,
> Till the morning flushes you open.

Sometimes Peter dropped by almost imperceptibly, when one of us used phrases that belonged to his permanent jargon. Expressions from comics, quotes from poems, phrases from the TV series *Soap*—they referred inevitably to Peter Seegers, they adapted to his voice, to the look in his eyes, to the grin on his lips. When one of us had a try, you didn't hear the imitation of the original, but the imitation of Peter's imitation of the original. When Joost talked about 'stewing the plums in their juice', his Amsterdam accent changed to Peter's Nijmegen one, and the phrase danced as it had danced thirty years before. For those who could hear.

But his name was never mentioned.

André stood up to get beer; David went for a pee. Joost opened a message on his iPhone. His expression hardened. The American wife, of course, asking where he was. He typed a reply, very short. Get lost, or something. Go fuck yourself.

André put four beers and a bowl of nibbles on the table. Joost slipped his iPhone gloomily into the inside pocket of his sports jacket.

'Your journalist girlfriend of this afternoon, I expect,' said André, pointing at Joost's chest. 'Did she have some more questions?'

Joost looked at André as if he were a clairvoyant.

'Yes. She wanted to know what André T. is doing in my entourage.'

Joost's telephone rang again. 'That'll be her again, dammit. When those people think they've got a bite, they don't let go. Bloody woman.'

'Whatever it is, keep on denying it,' said André.

Joost looked at the screen. From the way his eyes were widening, you could tell the message was a surprise. 'For Christ's sake, shut up. Jesus! Just shut up a minute! This is a highly significant moment. God Almighty! Listen!'

André winked at me. 'Unbelievable! I'll read it out. Quiet!!'

He cleared his throat. 'Dear Joost. Congratulations on the Spinoza Prize. I can still see us sitting in physics with Maaskant. You were always better than anyone else, I'm proud of you. I hope to see you soon. X Laura.'

He was confused, but at the same time looked at us triumphantly. He had received a text from Laura, who had disappeared without trace. We pretended to be surprised.

'God Almighty!' cried Joost. 'Laura. Laura! A text from Laura!'

'From whom?' asked André. 'What Laura?'

Joost became suspicious.

'From Laura,' he said, 'Laura van Bemmel.'

'Oh, her,' said André.

Joost's mouth dropped open. 'Fuck me. Shitty one, guys.' He put his mobile on the table with a bang. It listed another message, but he didn't look at it. 'Jesus, guys, I thought for a moment it really was from Laura.'

'That text really is from Laura.' André sounded as neutral as possible. 'I passed on your phone number to her yesterday.' Joost looked around the table and studied our faces in an attempt to work out whether he was being set up.

'That's what you get when you're not on Facebook,' said André. 'You may do quite advanced stuff with that string theory of yours, but as far as social media are concerned, you're basically a kind of Papuan. If you want to write her a letter, it's Via Bicchieraia 71, Arezzo. Please make sure you put enough stamps on.'

'So, you mean to say ...' Joost picked up his mobile. After a glance at the screen, his mouth fell open again. He showed us what had come in: the photo of the six of us on the summit of Mont Ventoux. 'It means I'll be with you, too, in a way' it said in the message window. 'Love, Laura.'

'Good photo,' said André. 'Happens to be hanging above my desk, too.'

'Look at him, in those ridiculous gym shorts,' said Joost. 'Good poet, lousy descender.' He drank a mouthful and held the photo close to his face, as if he wanted to crawl inside it and use timelessness to return to June 1982.

'That red Raleigh,' he asked then, 'what happened to that red Raleigh of your Dad's, André?'

'It's hanging in my basement. The name 'Jan Raas' is engraved under the crankset. Worth a fortune, of course.'

'You should have worn helmets,' said David.

Joost was still staring at his mobile. 'Laura! Incredible!'

'She'll be in Avignon in July,' I said, 'for the theatre festival. She's a director. And she wrote that she would really like to see us. Not here, but there. I don't know why. So, eh ...'

Joost made a dismissive gesture. 'Very bad play, this.'

'Villa's reserved,' said David. 'Just outside Bédoin. Camping is very 1982, and we're not 18 anymore. Racing bikes compulsory. Get your diaries, I've booked it from 13 July ...'

Joost banged his fist on the table, as if he were a chairman declaring the final decision of a meeting. 'Okay. We're going back in time. Exciting. I can use a secret address for the time being.'

We hadn't yet lost our ability to come to an agreement quickly. It was already like that when we were at nursery school, and Joost told us in two words what we were going to do. 'Sandpit. Racetrack.' Later we could lie bored to death on the roof of the *Sweet Lady Jane* for whole Sunday afternoons, until someone said: 'Amsterdam.' And half an hour later we would be on the train to Amsterdam.

'We'll take our bikes with us, up Mont Ventoux.' The lack of Facebook had put Joost at a momentary disadvantage, but now he took control of the tiller. 'André will provide the dope.'

'Shut up, prat,' replied André. 'Fucking mountain. I should have stayed nice and cozy in prison. Anyway, I'm going to ride you into the ground.'

'No screwing before the race,' said Joost, looking at me.

XII

When Peter was not writing or reading, he watched films. In his room he had a big television and a video recorder, a Philips N1700. Above it, on two bookshelves, were dozens of videos.

Peter's collection consisted solely of Italian films. In his view, Italian directors were the only ones who created filmed literature. He thought Hollywood movies were pulp, and you shouldn't even mention Dutch films, because then he would start swearing. We thought the occasional Dutch film was okay, but according to Peter that only went to show our lack of taste. 'The director is a vulgar pleb with a camera. And why, in every Dutch film, is any woman who appears in the shot fucked within five minutes?'

He recorded films from TV, but in some way or other he was able to get hold of original videos, too. During that time, I saw every Italian film released in Holland. Peter's room was big enough to serve as a mini cinema for six people. *Last Tango in Paris* and *Novecento* by Bertolucci, the *Canterbury Tales*, the *Decamerone*, and *Salò* by Pasolini, Fellini, Visconti, De Sica, Antonioni, Bolognini, Scola, the

Taviani brothers, and Olmi—thanks to Peter, we developed at lightning speed into connoisseurs of Italian cinema. There was a screening at least once a week, which was mostly introduced by Peter with facts about the film, the director, or the actors and actresses.

On the walls of his room hung film posters that he bought in a specialty shop in Amsterdam. There was Visconti's *L'innocente*, showing a man with two women. He also had the poster of De Sica's *Il giardino dei Finzi-Contini*: a man resting his head on a woman's shoulder.

On one of the evenings, André brought along *Once Upon a Time in the West*.

'That's not an Italian film,' said Peter.

'Yes it is. It's no accident it's called a spaghetti Western. And is Sergio Leone Italian, or isn't he? Terrific film, man, and everything you see is real. Leone doesn't imitate water with blue agricultural plastic, like that Fellini of yours.' A couple of weeks before, André had walked out of the screening of *Casanova*, when the hero was in a rowing boat on a plastic sea.

'*Once Upon a Time* is Hollywood shit. All false sentiment, and also fairly improbable.' The only American films that Peter found acceptable were *The Godfather*, parts one and two, and *Apocalypse Now*, because in his view they were actually Italian films.

One Sunday, Peter invited us over to view his new discovery. It was the end of October, and that afternoon, Jan Raas had won the Paris-Tours. He produced a postal tube and pulled out a poster for *L'eredità Ferramonti* by Bolognini. It showed a woman in a mask. The film meant nothing to us. 'That woman,' he said, when he had rolled out the poster completely, 'is Dominique Sanda. She was in *Il giardino dei Finzi-Contini*.' He paused for a moment, and pulled a smaller roll out of the tube. 'And Dominique Sanda,' he said, rolling it open in our direction, 'is like someone.' He laughed in anticipation of our reaction.

'Laura!' said Joost, like in a quiz. He was right. It was as if Peter were showing us a glamour shot of Laura. The dreamy eyes with the large irises, the nose, and the sharply drawn mouth, the dark-blond hair: Laura.

Laura herself was the only one who was not convinced of the striking resemblance to Sanda. 'I'm not as beautiful as that.'

'You're even more beautiful.' Peter said it in a tone that brooked no contradiction. 'Sanda is 19, here,' he went on. 'She played the lead in *Il conformista* by Bertolucci.'

'What film will it be tonight?' André pointed to the plastic bag on the floor. 'Something with Laura naked in an artistic Italian porn movie?'

'André.'

'Sorry, Laura.'

Peter produced two cassettes and held them in the air. 'Both by the same female director. I looked for them for ages, but this time they finally had them. By Liliana Cavani. We'll begin this evening with *Il portiere di notte*, or *The Night Porter*. I've already seen it, but I was 15 at the time. You don't understand films like that at that age.'

'I can't wait,' said André.

'There's sex in it, so you're bound to think it's a great film.' Peter put the cassette in the video recorder. 'Everyone here over 18?'

Of all the films we saw on the *Sweet Lady Jane*, *The Night Porter* left the greatest impression, with the possible exception of *The Godfather*. I can still recall certain scenes vividly.

The pathological passion between the former ss man

Maximilian and the Jewish Lucia staggered me. I didn't yet know that submission could go hand in hand with love, or that pain could be part of it. I couldn't understand the woman, or the man, either.

'Such are human beings,' said Peter, when the film was over. 'Such is love. Good sex, André?'

André was staring pensively ahead of him. He did not hear the question.

Laura looked wide-eyed at Peter.

A week later we saw the other film he had brought with him, *Beyond Good and Evil*, about a love triangle between an artist I didn't know, a female artist I didn't know, either, and Friedrich Nietzsche. In the opening scene, the two artists made love while Nietzsche sat watching.

I didn't think it was that great a film, much to Peter's irritation. He called it a masterpiece. Later, he told us that he had seen *The Night Porter* three more times, and *Beyond Good and Evil* four times. He did that quite often, and usually you saw elements of the films recurring in his poems.

The female artist, whose name was Lou Salomé, was played by Dominique Sanda.

A little later, in November 1981, Peter's collection *Poems for Anna* appeared. There was a launch party at the publisher's in Amsterdam. We drove there in Peter's father's Chevrolet Impala; with Laura and Peter on the front seat next to Captain Willem and the four of us crammed in the back.

Madame Olga stayed at home, because she wouldn't understand a word, anyway, and besides, you couldn't close the sauna for the launch of a poetry collection. Captain Willem did his best, hanging those poems on the wall, but the customers weren't interested in poetry.

Something else that lessened Madame Olga's desire to

come with us was the problem in her left eye that had been diagnosed a month and a half earlier. According to Peter, it was a hereditary problem, which had already caused a number of her Russian family to go blind. 'She's depressed,' he said. 'She wants us to sell the boat.'

Peter's fame had preceded him on the Amsterdam scene. The beautiful room in the canal-side mansion that was the headquarters of the publishing house was pretty full. Joost, André, David, and I positioned ourselves strategically by the beer tap, and tried to drink our sense of intimidation under the table as quickly as possible. We saw poets who had been on our list for the literature exam, and even a few people we had occasionally seen on television. It took a while for the beer to make it all bearable.

At the request of the publisher, Laura stood next to Peter. On the other side, Captain Willem stood and beamed. It struck the publisher as a good idea to make it clear that there was a real person behind the Anna from the collection, that her name was Laura, and that she was stunningly beautiful. Peter had written a modern twentieth-century poem cycle about Laura—what could be better?

Peter read a few poems. After each one, Joost, who had drunk far too much beer on an empty stomach, cried 'Olé!' The publisher made a speech in which he called Peter a representative of the best in Dutch poetry. After this, Peter presented the first copy to his father, who was overcome, and with his captain's cap in hand had to wipe the tears from his eyes. Everyone in the room was moved, although it had meanwhile become known that the old salt was the captain of an Ark of Delight.

After the official part, a man with black glasses and a beard came up to Peter. He introduced himself and said that he wrote reviews of poetry. 'So the Anna of the poems is an actual woman,' he observed.

'She is an actual woman who is probably the product of my imagination.'

The man nodded slowly. 'Yes, yes,' he said. 'I understand. The word has become flesh. And is it true that you grew up in a brothel?'

'That's correct. A floating brothel.'

The reviewer looked at Laura, who was listening to the conversation with a smile. That smile had a disruptive effect. The man went red, pushed the glasses more firmly on his nose, and asked: 'Are you Peter's girlfriend?'

'I'm his muse.' Laura suddenly seemed to have become a different person. Not the Laura we knew, with her self-confident, retiring attitude. She had a challenging air about her, something I had never seen before.

'I try to live his poems,' she said. 'I take it to the limit. Actually, there are no moral boundaries.' Around her mouth, the haughty smile formed itself with which she kept pathetic male specimens with seduction plans at a distance. She saw that this was one. 'You can't break with the conventions of poetry and maintain them elsewhere. Don't you agree?'

The man nodded. 'Of course, art can only be liberating when it is itself consistent and faithful to its own truth, in all its facets. I believe that Neruda writes that some-where.'

'That's what I mean,' said Peter. 'Neruda, that's right. Old Pablo.'

'I confess that I have lived,' Laura added helpfully.

'So it's not without reason that the collection is dedicated to you,' said the man.

'That's difficult to say myself, but had you noticed that the collection is called *Poems for Anna*, and my name is Laura?'

'Anna is your, ehhh, let's say, literary name?'
'He finds it exciting to call me Anna, I don't know why.'
Who had influenced him, the man asked Peter.
'Liliana Cavani,' he said.

On the way back, Joost imitated the reviewer. 'Art can only be liberating when it is consistent in itself,' he said. 'Don't you agree, Captain Seegers?' Captain Willem laughed so much that he pulled out too far left. An oncoming truck thundered past, hooting.

Peter put an arm around Laura and pulled her towards him. It was a gesture that we saw quite often, the seal on their special poetic bond. We had tacitly agreed that no sex was taking place, that their relationship was a purely spiritual one, and that, hence, our position wasn't hopeless.

The reviews of the collection were ecstatic. The general opinion was that Holland had a new, very young but great poetic talent. There was an article in a national weekly about the thriving poetic scene in the provinces, with Peter Seegers as its standard-bearer. Laura was quoted. 'The new poetry cannot tolerate morality.' Fortunately, Laura's parents didn't read any quality weeklies, otherwise they would probably have crashed their DAF into the slow train to Arnhem.

XIII

One Thursday evening, I cycled over to Joost's. We had a biology exam the next day, and he needed to explain something to me. I went into the big kitchen through the back door. There was no one there. From Joost's room came the sound of Elvis Costello singing 'Oliver's Army'. In three bounds I was up the stairs, banged on the door, and opened it. It was dim inside. On the little side table in the middle of the room, a dripping candle flickered.

Because Joost's bed was opposite the door, I saw her first. She was lying on her front on the bed, reading a book. She was wearing a short dress I had never seen before. It was tight round her bottom and had crept up a little, revealing a large part of her thighs. She had spread her legs a little. Joost was sitting at his desk with his camera in front of him. Photography was his new hobby, and he had even installed a darkroom.

It wasn't seeing Laura that made me feel sick. It was the domesticity of the scene, the calm, the impression that they both found it nice and cozy being together—and the fact that I knew nothing about it, so that, for me it acquired a furtive overtone.

'Oh, sorry,' I said, slammed the door, and rattled down the stairs. A little later I was cycling home at full speed. 'Bastard,' I muttered. 'Fucking bitch. Damned traitors. Whore.'

Two days later, I was walking along the river with David. He liked it, as it reminded him of how he used to walk along the Suriname River when he was little. I brought up the subject of Laura.

'She was lying on his bed, with a sexy dress on.'

'I'm sure it looked good on her.'

'Are they having a thing?' I asked. Perhaps David knew more than I did.

'Not that I'm aware of. But I never talk to him about it. She's at your place sometimes, too, isn't she? André's been to Arnhem with her.'

I didn't know that. So, André as well. I must talk to him about it. You could do that with him, better than with Joost. Shitty that he hadn't said anything to me about it.

'To Arnhem?'

'Yes. To something in Musis Sacrum. Music, I think. Not exactly sure.'

Lying on Joost's bed, going to jazz with André—where did that leave me?

'I've got to tell you something that must stay between us.' I saw a flat stone, picked it up, and made it skim the water. It bounced four times.

'Okay,' said David.

'I'm in love with Laura.'

David started laughing. 'Then I've got news for you. Joost is in love with Laura. So is André, and Peter, in his way. And I'm only mentioning friends and acquaintances in the first degree.'

'And you?'

'Me, too. But I don't know how badly. I know precisely

how bad it is with the others, but not with myself. I don't think I'm as much of a romantic as you guys.'

'Do you ever talk to her about it? About yourself, or about one of us?'

'Never,' said David. 'We talk about everything, but never about love. I don't think she likes talking about that, at all.'

'How do you know?'

'Otherwise she'd do it.'

XIV

André's father stood at the back of the house, cleaning the Raleigh he had bought from the Peter Post team at the end of the season. The bike had belonged to Jan Raas. He was wiping a cloth soaked in benzene along the chain to get rid of the oil and dirt. 'Problem with the autumn,' he said. 'After every ride you're cleaning your bike. Do you still cycle a bit?'

I gave a non-committal nod. 'Sometimes. Not much, recently. André home?'

'Upstairs. Spends a lot of time alone in his room these days. Looks awful. You lot aren't doing stupid things, are you?'

'No.' I went through the kitchen and the hall, and in three strides I was at the top of the stairs. 'André!' There was no answer, and all I heard was 'Another Brick in the Wall' by Pink Floyd. I opened the door. André was sitting in the only chair in the room, with his back to the door and his legs on the bed.

The window was open, and I could easily smell why. André had been smoking for quite a while. He talked about Red Lebanon as if he imported the stuff himself, and meanwhile there was pot growing in a corner of his room. You couldn't notice anything special about him, except that he started speaking more slowly when he'd smoked a joint.

The biggest change was that he had stopped playing football. The screaming of the trainer began to get on his nerves. Even the club chairman had called round to try to get him to change his mind—he had already made his first team début and was regarded as the club's major talent. Scouts from professional teams had already been spotted. But André didn't feel like it, anymore.

'Hey, Bart. Old wanker!'

'André, pothead.'

'Very good grey Afghan,' he said. 'Gives a terrific hit, wow.'

I never went to the café where André got his hash; I didn't like that dark atmosphere that was supposed to be cozy and the vague types who scratched around there.

'For God's sake, give it up, man. They say it can drive you mad.'

'That can happen without this stuff. Anything is possible.'

'Hey, André, listen. I heard from David that you went to Arnhem with Laura.' I tried to sound relaxed.

'That's right. We went to see the Willem Breuker Collective. Do you know them? Experimental jazz, you could say. Not for you. Last Saturday, didn't I tell you? Thought I'd said.'

'No.'

'Well. It was amazing.'

'Oh.'

'Really very special. Blowing and tooting from all sides. It really cheered me up.'

'And eh ... Laura?'

'She was the same. Very cheerful. Loved it, too.'

'Did you go on the train?'

'Yes, how else? On the bike?'

'Next time, I want to go with you. Perhaps I'll like it too. Live is always different from a record.'

'Jealous?' he asked. He laid Hesse's *Beneath the Wheel* on the floor.

'Yes,' I said.

'Jesus, man. We went into Musis Sacrum and half the audience turned around. Not for me.'

'No.'

'Same thing on the train. And on the platform. It's like being out with a celebrity film star.'

'Yes.'

'I pretended not to notice anything, and so did she.'

'Hm.'

'On the way home, we had a compartment to ourselves. Luckily.'

'All to yourselves?'

'Yes, just the two of us. Then we kissed.' He looked at me curiously, as if he wanted to see the effect his words had on me.

'Oh,' I said. 'Kissed. Really kissed, I mean ...'

'Yes, really.'

'And then?'

'Then nothing. The train pulled in and she went home on her bike and so did I.'

I didn't dare ask if anything else had happened since then between him and Laura.

'For the sake of clarity, Bart, we're not going out. I can see you thinking it, so I'll just say it. If you'd gone to Willem Breuker with her, you would have kissed her, too. It was completely normal, it felt as if ...'

'As if what?'

'I don't know, exactly.'

'What felt different, then?'

'Okay, relax, I'm searching for words. I've never felt it before, so it's quite difficult to describe.'

'Yes.'

'It was soft, sweet.'

'Hm.' I must be careful not to start imitating him, with his soft and sweet.

'She also told me that Peter's been acting funny, recently.'

'In what way?'

'She wouldn't say. She said it, and then she started crying. Though a moment before she'd been very cheerful.'

I went home and called Joost.

'Are you still angry?' he asked.

'No, sorry I was so uncool.'

'There was nothing going on. You thought of course: she's lying on his bed in that sexy dress, so he's probably put it in there, that great dong of his. But no. Although I would have had no objection.' He stopped talking in anticipation of further questions.

'I didn't think anything.'

'Of course you did. But I'll tell you what happened.'

'Yes.'

'Right. You come in, you see her lying there, and you leave. I look at her, she looks at me. We both know what's going on. She gets up and starts crying.'

'Crying?'

'Well, not out loud, with that screeching, but just crying quietly. I sit down next to her and put my arm around her.'

'And then?'

'Then she says: "I went to Musis Sacrum with André to see the Breukink collective." I say "Breuker". "Yes, Breuker," she says. Afterward we went for a quick drink, and then we caught the last train.'

'I know.'

'But you don't know this yet,' said Joost. 'Because she was making out with André, in the compartment.'

'I knew that, too.'

'Oh. Why are you calling, then?'

'Did she talk to you about Peter, too?'

'No. She just said she was frightened.'

'Of what?'

'I don't know. She didn't say. She was frightened, she said.'

There was a silence on the other end of the line.

'Bart?'

'Yes.'

'I'm sitting there, with my arm around her, and suddenly she kisses me. Full on the mouth; I feel her tongue slipping in.'

'Christ, Joost. So ...'

'Nothing else. Just for a moment. She wipes her tears away, gets up, and leaves. It was, how shall I put it, it was ...'

'Sweet and soft.'

'Something like that.'

I took a deep breath.

'Did she say anything else before she left?'

'She said: 'I wish I was ordinary. Something like Marga Sap. And I wish Peter was ordinary too. Something like you.'

'Did she say that, something like you?'

'No, I made that up.'

I didn't sleep that night. I just lay and thought of Laura. I had the feeling things were happening that were not normal. That made me afraid, even though I had no idea exactly what those things were. I had lost my handle on things. For a long time, I had had the idea that, in our little world, I saw what happened, and that I could interpret events, but I'd lost that and it made me insecure.

I wrote her a long letter. I wrote down everything I felt and held nothing back. As I stood at the postbox with the letter in my hands, I considered tearing it up. I knew I was on the point of doing something irreversible. I heard the envelope plop into the box, onto other people's cards and letters.

On Monday, the first period was Dutch. In the playground, I looked out for her, feeling very tense, but she was late. I was sitting next to André in the classroom when she came in. I could see from her eyes that she had read my letter. She walked past me and ran her finger almost imperceptibly across my shoulder.

Once she had sat next to Marga Sap, I glanced round. She had her green army shoulder bag lying on the desk in front of her. She had written 'WBK' on it in red pen. She looked at me and smiled. I suddenly felt very happy. She made a writing motion with her hand.

I never got a reply.

XV

One afternoon at the beginning of January 1982, he came riding onto the pavement outside our house like a kind of apparition. Joost on a racing bike, a white and blue Gazelle. I looked as if I were witnessing Our Lord's resurrection. Clouds of steam were coming out of his mouth, as it was only a few degrees above freezing. He was wearing a white Peugeot jersey, and grinned at me when he saw my flabbergasted expression.

Then I suddenly saw panic in his eyes, desperate movements with his legs and one arm, and then he fell over. It was the familiar helpless fall of the cycling beginner who has pulled his toe-clip straps too tight. The first fall, and the most stupid one in the repertoire—the fall that shows you up as a dumb novice.

I went out. 'Fucking things,' said Joost, undoing the straps. 'You break your legs before you've ridden a kilometre.'

I helped him up. He rubbed his knee. 'What d'you think?'

'Nice bike. Did you get any scratches?'

'Champion Mondial.' He pointed to the rainbow stripes on the tube. 'One year old, scarcely ridden.' The blue brake cables came high above the handlebars. Joost pointed to a lever at the end. 'No more controls on the tube; you change gear with your hands on the handlebars. A lot safer.' I had never talked to Joost about a bike before. I had, though, talked about *The Rider*, which he had read at my recommendation. Certainly a nice book, he thought, but it hadn't awakened the urge to sit on a racing bike himself. Joost was too tall and gangling to be a racer. Or even to play at being a racer. He had long, thin legs, which had often provoked the mockery of André when we played tree football in the park. Joost was the easiest victim of André's dribbling techniques.

When we occasionally talked about football, or about cycling, Joost's favourite quote was: 'Sport is a danger to society. Sport is a conspiracy designed to keep people away from what really matters.'

'Christ Almighty, Joost, a bike. I thought cycling maintained injustice in the world.'

'I've changed my mind. Someone who never changes his mind is either stupid or dead. Churchill. There's a need for intellect in the peloton.'

He said it in complete seriousness.

'Did you hear Hennie Kuiper on the radio?' he asked. 'On New Year's Eve. They asked him what his greatest wish for the New Year was.'

'And?'

'To win the Tour de France.'

'Yes, stands to reason.'

He looked at me. 'And then I thought: what is my greatest wish?'

'Well?'

'Also to win the Tour de France.' He seemed to mean it. 'So I decided to become a racing cyclist. It's an experiment.'

Of course it was an experiment. The aspiring physicist Joost Walvoort was crazy about experiments. At home he had boxes full of chemicals, experimental boxes of electronics, and in the attic of the doctor's house, he had built installations whose purpose completely escaped us, but which according to Joost clarified much about the operation of natural laws. And now he had discovered the bike, and himself, as an experiment.

'Mont Ventoux,' said Joost.

'Tommy Simpson,' I said. 'Tim Krabbé rode up it in one hour twenty-one minutes and ...'

'No, but okay,' said Joost, as if he didn't consider my answer important. 'We all die one day.' He took a piece of paper from one of the pockets on the back of the Peugeot jersey and unfolded it.

'Listen, good friend and fellow cyclist,' he said portentously. 'What do we have to cope with in the way of forces while we're cycling?'

'Headwind.'

'Among other things. But that's not the only thing. We are dealing with the following resistances that have to be overcome: apart from the resistance of the air, as you say, there is also the slope resistance, rolling resistance, and mechanical resistance. I've got the formulas for the various resistances here. Interested?'

I saw a host of letters and squares. 'No.'

'I thought not. Spends hours on his bike, but is totally uninterested in what he is doing. Just stupid pedalling, and nothing else. Okay, suit yourself. I will make great strides. In overcoming the various resistances it's a matter of work done in joules and power generated in watts. Yes? If we know the various values, of the resistances and the work and power generated, we can work out how long it will take us to climb Mont Ventoux.'

I suspected what he was driving at.

'Calculated from the hamlet of Bédoin, the altitude difference to the summit that has to be overcome is 1600 metres. The distance to the top is twenty-one kilometres. I have just weighed my bike, and it weighs eleven-point-five kilos. I myself weighed seventy-five kilos this morning ...'

'Come on, Joost.'

'Taking rolling resistance, slope resistance, air resistance, and mechanical resistance into consideration, plus the average gradient, I can now work out how long it will take me to reach the summit, at least I could if I knew how much power I can generate. And I don't know that, unfortunately. Yet.'

'No.'

'But I shall find out.'

'Yes.'

'I've drawn up a training schedule, and you and I are going to get down to work in the weeks ahead. Then we're going to Mont Ventoux. What do you say? The diploma ceremony is on 11 June; a bit of partying, and we'll leave on 16 June, a Wednesday.' The whole schedule was worked out.

'I'm a bad climber. Even short climbs make me feel ill.'

'I know,' said Joost. 'The tone of your muscles is unsuitable for mountains. My legs are longer, and probably my muscles are also more suitable. But with training, you can compensate for a lot. Apart from that, cycling is a battle against yourself, Gerrie Knetemann said the other day.' He sounded like a cycling trainer, and he knew who Gerrie Knetemann was.

In the following weeks, we trained three times a week, with Joost indicating the purpose. He talked about playing for time, and intervals, and after we had done the local climb, the Peeske hill, for the first time, he knew how many watts he had generated by pedalling. He rode up a lot faster than I did. 'You're on the heavy side,' he said at the top. 'In a little while, you'll have to hoist every kilo up 1600 metres. Do you know how much energy that costs? As much as it costs to lift 1600 kilos one metre in the air. Just imagine!'

I was standing there shivering, because it wasn't even February and it was pretty cold.

He had worked out that he would do the climb in one hour and fifty-two minutes. 'And I'm afraid that you'll be around two hours ten.'

After the third training ride, I said to my mother that I was going to eat less. She looked at me with concern. 'You've got to think of your exams, and not only of that mountain. You've got to eat properly, otherwise, in a while, your brain will be short of energy.'

XVI

I cycled to the *Sweet Lady Jane*. On Thursdays, the floating brothel was closed. It was moored at a spot outside town, easily accessible for the valued customers, and with sufficient privacy.

'Hey, Bart,' said Peter from the roof, when I had leaned the bike against one of the willows nearby. He had recently acquired a guitar. 'Listen to this.' He struck a couple of vague chords and started singing, or actually, it was more like shouting. 'And the torture never stops, the torture never stops! Torture, the torture never stops, the torture never stops!' He had been into Frank Zappa for a while, alone among the six of us. I put my index fingers in my ears. 'Stop!' I shouted. 'Fucking Zappa!' He put down the guitar with a grin, got up, and disappeared through the hatch to open the front door.

Peter was home alone. He poured two huge Cokes, added a couple of ice cubes, and climbed ahead of me back to the roof. You could see the skyline of Zutphen, and on the river, the spring light changed the water into liquid crystal.

'My father and mother are giving up the business. It's

because of my mother. She doesn't want to be a madame anymore. She says the types who come here make her sick. Do you know who's a regular customer?'

'Well?'

'Laura's old man.'

'Does she know?'

'No, of course not. And she doesn't need to know.'

'No.'

'And now my father and mother have gone to Amsterdam, because there's someone there who wants to take over the business and the boat.'

'And what will they do then?'

'No idea. They'll manage.'

We were silent again. I didn't know exactly how to start.

'Did you know that Laura was making out with Joost?' I said, coming straight to the point. 'And with André?'

Peter looked at me. I tried to read from his eyes what he was thinking, but that was difficult with him. In the first place because he was wearing sunglasses, and in the second place because he was good at hiding what was going on inside him—he probably learned it from the girls downstairs.

'What is love?' he asked, after a silence of at least two minutes. I looked at him. What kind of a question was that?

'Loving someone.'

'And what's that, then?'

'No idea.'

'Are love, and loving someone, about kissing? Or fucking? Did they also fuck her, by the way?'

'What do you think?'

'I don't think so.'

'You're right.' I couldn't see any reaction.

'Well?'

'What?'

'Is loving someone about kissing and fucking, I asked.'

'I think so.'

'I don't think so.'

'No?'

'Love is about power. Domination.' He said it provocatively.

'Oh.'

'And sex is nothing but chemistry, hormones. Good for providing offspring, and good for my father.'

I decided to ask him straight out. 'So you're not in love with Laura, and you don't want to go to bed with her.'

'I'm not saying that I'm not in love.' He looked at me inquiringly, and I had the feeling that he was playing a game with me, and was winning, that he was playing chess and was thinking two moves ahead of me.

'And don't you want to go to bed with her, despite the hormones? Doesn't sound sexy, hormones.'

'The reward is pleasure,' said Peter. 'I'm only human.'

Laura thought he was behaving strangely. What did she mean by that? I didn't know how to ask, and I didn't want him to know what she had said to André.

'How are things between you and Laura?' I asked.

He looked me straight in the eye and showed no emotion, as if I had asked something very inappropriate. 'How do you mean?'

'I'm just interested.'

'Has she talked to you about me, about us?'

'No, she hasn't.'

'Well, don't talk bullshit. Women can become good friends with a man, but in order to stay friends with them, a slight physical antipathy helps.'

I didn't understand him.

'Nietzsche.'

'And now for something completely different,' he said. He knew whole chunks of *Monty Python* off by heart. 'You're planning to climb mountains with Joost on racing bikes, aren't you?'

'Yes, that's the plan. At least, Joost is planning it, and I'm going with him. Do you feel like coming?'

'Yes,' he said, to my surprise. 'Whenever I give a reading, people bring up Petrarch and his Laura, and of course that's not all that strange, since it's quite obvious, given the stupid coincidence of our names. And then of course they talk about Mont Ventoux.'

'Yes?'

'I thought: perhaps I can come up the mountain with you two.'

'Just like that, without training? You'll never make it.'

'Of course I will. Listen. He got up and started reciting a poem. 'Poetry's cycling up the Mont Ventoux, / where Tommy Simpson wound up dead, / by tragic circumstances led, / the world-beater was dog-tired too.'

'Nice. New work?'

'Quiet. I haven't finished.' He resumed his pose and continued. 'Many up this col have sped, / category one, since then taboo, / it smells of pine, Sunsilk Shampoo, / which below you need for your head.'

I started laughing, and was about to applaud. 'Hold on! Can't you see it's a sonnet? There are six more lines.' He went on. 'Everything's unspeakably wearing, / tackling Ventoux's very tough, / so before you begin, take care. / Yet I make it, though the heat is flaring, / to this summit bare and rough: / vanity and chasing empty air.'

'Brilliant,' I said. 'A poem about cycling—you don't hear that often. But where did you get that from, suddenly?'

'It's not by me. It's Jan Kal. Do you know him?'

'No, never ...'

'I bumped into him recently. Nice guy with long hair. And he told me he'd cycled up Mont Ventoux, and had finished this poem by the time he got to the top. By the way, his heart rate was over two hundred at the summit, since he was untrained and smokes like a chimney. So it's just as well it didn't take much longer, or he wouldn't have survived.'

'And we wouldn't have had this poem.'

'No. But I thought: if Jan Kal can do it, I can do it. And perhaps I'll also have a poem finished by the time I get to the top. Then, if I'm reading somewhere, and they start on about Petrarch and the bare mountain, I can tell everyone to be quiet and read the poem about my climb.'

'Have you got a bike?'

'I'll ask if I can borrow André's father's Raleigh. Raleigh, man, you scarcely need to pedal. If you let me know when you're making the ascent, I'll make sure I'm at the foot of the mountain on that day.'

'Joost wants to train in the Vosges and the Alps first. He wants to go up the Galibier. Perhaps you should come with us.'

'Doesn't interest me at all, the Galibier. What interests me is the Ventoux. I'll follow you on the train.'

We heard the Chevrolet arriving. Peter got up with his hands on his hips. Captain Willem parked the car in one of the spaces in front of the boat and got out. On the other side, Madame Olga did the same.

'And?' cried Peter.

'Sold!'

Peter's mother shouted something in Russian.

'What's she saying?'

'She says she's finally going to be a respectable lady,' said Peter. Down below, Captain Willem put his arm around Madame Olga and led her to the gangplank. Obviously her eyes were not doing too well.

'Oh yes,' said Peter, 'I'll ask Laura if she's coming, too.'

XVII

It was the evening before Joost and I were due to leave. We were sitting in the office of Eastwest Adventures, where we often hung out on the large leather sofa in front of the well-stocked refrigerator. This time, the atmosphere was different: it was the last evening we were together as school pupils.

A few days earlier, we had received our diplomas. Because of their excellent marks, Joost and Laura were addressed separately by Mr Berghout, the head. 'You have done our school a great honour, and now the country expects great things of you.' That day, Laura was on the front page of a national daily because of the six tens and two nines in her results, under the heading 'Genius in the Provinces'. In reply to the question what she was going to do now, she had said that she was going to Perugia for a year to study Italian.

Peter had written a long poem especially for the occasion. Berghout announced him as 'the school's most famous pupil'. He came onto the platform in a pink suit. Next to the microphone was a small table with a cassette recorder on it. This was connected to the sound system in the hall; after Peter had pressed a button, piano music filled the space. It was strange, ethereal music, endlessly repeated. In the auditorium, some people began tittering. Peter stood like a statue in his pink suit in front of the microphone, stared straight into the auditorium, and gradually it went quiet.

I looked at André, but he seemed to be gripped by the music. He was looking into the distance as if he were receiving a secret message. I wondered how long Peter would stand there. At the edge of the platform, Berghout made an apologetic gesture to the audience.

The music seemed to die away, and then turned into a melody that was so strange and wonderful that it brought tears to my eyes. I put my hand on André's shoulder, which seemed the most logical thing to do. Obliquely in front of me stood Joost and Laura, each with a bunch of flowers in their hands. Laura had closed her eyes. Joost played along with his fingers.

I don't know how long it lasted. Suddenly Peter turned down the music and began his poem. It seemed to follow completely naturally; it babbled on in the same rhythm, went up and down, moved from staccato to long sentences that he almost sang, accompanied by notes on the piano. It was about farewells and the stream of time. It was melancholy mixed with hope; he seemed to be in a trance, a magician reciting his magic formulae.

He finished at the same time as the music. There was a silence. Peter wiped the sweat from his forehead. He smiled at the audience and said: 'The poem is called "*Canto Ostinato*", after the music. Thank you.' Laura began clapping, followed by the rest of the audience. André whistled with his fingers, Joost shouted something unintelligible, and people smiled at each other.

'Man, the guy is good,' said André. 'Christ, he really had

me going. I must get that music, I thought I was floating!'
David was wiping tears of emotion out of his eyes.

That evening, we drank far too much beer. Then we cycled to the *Sweet Lady Jane*. Peter dragged a speaker onto the roof, put *Canto Ostinato* in the tape recorder, stripped, and dove into the river, followed a little later by Joost and me. The sounds danced over the waves and swam along with us.

The full moon cast stripes over the surface of the water, and I felt as if I had arrived in heaven. I wanted to stay here forever, in the river, with that music, with my friends. On the roof, David, André, and Laura looked on. All three of them had a glass in their hands. I raised my hand to them. They waved back, and that moved me. Peter swam over to me and grabbed me by my shoulders. He looked at me as if he were going to kiss me on the mouth, and dug his nails into my shoulders. 'Never forget this! You must never forget this. Promise? Promise? Look at me, Bart. Can you see me? Can you hear that music? Christ, man, I could cry my eyes out.'

'I hear it, Peter. I see you. And I shall never forget it.'

'It's over. For Christ's sake, it's over.' He put his hands to his mouth. 'I don't want it to be over,' he shouted across the water. 'It mustn't be over. It must last forever!'

Sometimes I didn't understand what he was trying to say. A little way away, Joost was floating on his back.

'Come in!' Peter called to Laura.

She shook her head.

'Come in!' It sounded almost like an order.

To my amazement, I saw her get undressed, until she had only her panties on. For the first time, I saw her breasts. She hesitated for a moment, then she dove off the roof into the river.

Joost went to Leiden to focus on physics and I went to study Dutch in Amsterdam. All André knew was that he was leaving Zutphen. Peter was going to be a poet, no matter where. 'Perhaps I'll go to Perugia with her,' he said. David was the only one who was staying in Zutphen. His father had offered him a partnership, and David thought that was an excellent plan.

'I must be able to manage another beer,' Joost opened a swing-top bottle of Grolsch. 'This body, honed by training, can easily take it. Bernard Hinault has the occasional beer, too, I read, and he's going to win the Tour again this year.'

I stared straight ahead. I disliked moments like this, when there was sadness hanging in the air.

'Game of Risk?' asked David. No one felt like Risk.

Laura leafed through a travel brochure. 'Do you do trips to Perugia?'

'I think so,' replied David.

'You guys can drop by.'

'I'll certainly stop by,' said Peter. Laura looked at him without saying anything. There were long silences, but no one felt like going home.

'What time are you two leaving?' asked André.

'Ten o'clock. At least if Bart gets packed on time.'

'And then?'

'Then first to Southern Limburg for a short training stint. From there we go on to the Vosges. Then the French Alps, after which it's time for the dreaded Mont Ventoux.'

'And when exactly do you arrive there?' asked André.

'According to Joost's schedule, we arrive in Bédoin on Tuesday,' I said. 'I think I'll be completely shattered by all those mountains, so Wednesday will be a rest day. Thursday we warm up the climbing muscles, and Friday we do the climb.'

'Okay.'

'Fine. Then I'll get the train on Wednesday, and I'll be in good time for the start.' Peter looked at Laura, but she was leafing through a brochure and didn't react. 'There's only one campsite, isn't there, in what's-it-called?'

'Bédoin,' I said. 'Yes, there's only one campsite there. In the centre of the village. La Garenne.'

Laura asked why we actually wanted to cycle up those mountains.

'It's an experiment. At least for Bart and me. To see if theory and practice agree.'

'I'm going for poetry,' said Peter. 'Poetry's cycling up the Mont Ventoux. And because Laura here is called Laura.' He looked at her intensely.

'Perhaps it's something for Eastwest Adventures,' said David. 'Full bus, bicycles on board, and up the Ventoux. I'll be damned.'

Laura said she hadn't felt this sad for ages. 'It's like a funeral.'

With much hooting, Joost drove his mother's black Golf off the pavement in front of our house. André and Laura stood and waved, Peter looked on aimlessly, David wasn't there. 'Those about to die salute you!' shouted Joost from the open window.

I sat with the map of the Netherlands on my lap. Belgium and France were in the glove compartment. I had marked the route to Mechelen in Limburg, the location of our first training camp. Our frames were in the back, on top of each other with a blanket between them. With the four wheels and the tent we had borrowed from David's father, the car was crammed full.

I was sombre. The prospect of having to move to Amsterdam had been keeping me awake for some time. My great love stood on the pavement, waving and blowing me kisses, and next to her was my friend who was in love with her and with whom she had made out, and my friend who wrote poems for her and with whom she had a relationship I didn't understand.

'And we're off, Pol,' said Joost. 'The champions are underway. What direction do we need?'

'Nijmegen. And then follow Maastricht.'

At two o'clock we drove into Mechelen in Southern Limburg, at three our tent was pitched and we were ready for the ascent of the Camerig, according to Joost 'the best preparation for Mont Ventoux, at least in Holland.'

'It's going nicely,' said Joost, as we rode up the first quite steep section of the climb. 'I think I'm in good shape. We'll have to wait and see.'

'You've shaved your legs, Tuur.' I was panting.

'Of course I have. Good for morale. You should see that tobacco on your legs, man. What a sight, it blocks you.' It was as if he had learned the cycling dictionary off by heart.

'Ridiculous,' I was just able to say. I changed into the lowest gear. Already. On a Dutch hill. It was hopeless. I hated climbing.

Joost stood up on the pedals and danced away from me on the first bend. I pedalled like crazy. Did I have to go twenty kilometres up the Ventoux like this?

We stayed a day in Limburg, and Friday we went on to the Vosges. We pitched our tent in Saint-Maurice-sur-Moselle, at the foot of the Ballon d'Alsace. 'First mountain ever climbed on the Tour.' Joost lay on his airbed, shaving his legs. His pedantic display of cycling knowledge was beginning to get on my nerves. 'Can't you just do that in the shower?'

Joost started to laugh. 'You make a tense impression,

Pol. Why is that? Tell your friend Tuur, Eagle of the Mountains.'

'That racing-cyclist behaviour of yours is making me pretty nervous. That bike isn't six months old yet, and you scarcely know how to tighten your toe clips, but you do know how to shave your legs and play the expert.'

'"Good things come quickly," said a great sports journalist.'

'Joost, what do you think of Laura?' We were lying in the tent; it was raining outside. There were only a couple of tents on the campsite. I hoped it would go on raining, then I would have an excuse to forego the ascent that was on the training schedule for the next day.

'How do you mean: what do I think of Laura?'

'What's going on with her?'

'No idea. Is something going on with her, then?'

'The way she was so sad, on Monday.'

'She loves us,' said Joost.

'Us?'

'Yes. Us. And now you're going to Amsterdam, I'm going to Leiden, she's going to Perugia, and André's going to an unknown place to live or stay. What Peter does, we shall have to wait and see. Only David is staying put. For her, everything is falling to pieces. That's what she meant by that funeral, I think.'

'That's pretty sad, if you look at it properly.'

'That's how it goes.'

'Do you think she might be in love?'

'No. Or perhaps she may be.'

'Peter's acting oddly, she said to André.'

'That's what you told me, yes. Peter's crazy.'

'How do you mean, crazy?'

'My father said the other day that Peter doesn't quite mesh together.'

'Happens with poets.'

'That lad looks as if the devil is hard on his heels,' my father said.

'I've never noticed.'

'Neither have I.'

'It's raining hard.'

'There'll be lots of oxygen in the air tomorrow.'

I struggled up the Ballon d'Alsace. Joost had long since left me behind, and I didn't care. His words of encouragement just made me feel more despondent. Now I crawled up at my own tempo, in the very lowest gear.

I thought of Laura. It didn't lessen the pain in my legs, but it did make it easier to bear. I could see her face and her lips forming words. I could not see what words.

At the top, Joost stood smugly by his bike. From the look of it, practice had adhered to theory. As I passed him, he shouted 'Great!' and pressed the stopwatch in his hand. 'Brilliant! Exactly right. Sport is completely predictable; all that bullshit from those reporters means nothing. Artificial suspense—the result is fixed from the start.'

We descended, I faster than Joost. I took chances and relished the speed. Below, I waited as pontifically as possible.

'The right result?'

'Yes,' he said. 'You're heavier, so you fall downward faster. Nothing escapes the laws of nature.'

We rode back to the campsite, and I had the feeling that there was something wrong with his scientific approach. But, as usual, it was an intuitive thought, and they didn't get you very far with Joost.

The next day, we drove the five hundred kilometres to the Galibier. I was alarmed when I saw the first Alps. The Vosges still had something human about them, but with these mountains, the possibility of tackling them on the bike seemed ruled out in advance.

'You don't have to go to the summit of a mountain like that. Roads never go to the peak.' Joost seemed to be longing for his first big climbing experience. 'The real thing. What we've done up to now was child's play; now we're going to experience it.'

We went to bed early. 'The Tour is won in bed,' said Joost. 'Joop Zoetemelk.'

From Saint-Michel-de-Maurienne we first had to ascend the Col du Télégraphe, and then from Valloire the monster itself. To my surprise, the climbing was much better than in the Vosges. I didn't have to let Joost go, and cycled on his wheel for the first twelve kilometres to the top of the Télégraphe. Sometimes he glanced back in surprise.

Towards Valloire there is a short descent, and then the long road up to the Galibier begins. After about ten kilometres, Joost turned around and shouted that we were now over two kilometres high. I could see that it wasn't easy for him.

I began to believe in the mysterious forces in sport that André's father sometimes talked about. He said that there were days when he was unbeatable, something inexplicable, days when the strength in his legs seemed to have doubled, and a kind of automatic pilot seemed to take command, straight to first place on the rostrum. Perhaps I had something like that today; in any case, it was as if I had acquired two new legs.

The higher we got, the quieter it became, until no more sounds penetrated through to me. I saw myself pedalling up, as if I were looking at the image of a camera riding next to me. I looked at my front wheel and thought I saw a kink in it. A moment later it had gone again. The colours of Joost's Raleigh jersey seemed to run, as if they had become liquid. I saw that blood was flowing from my knee, but that didn't alarm me.

A voice said that I must not stop, or I would be fined. I saw Joost getting away from me, and he turned around again and grinned. I was shocked by his contorted face. His legs were made of porcelain. I looked right, and down below saw a house, which was more like a palace. There was a river running past it. I looked, and tried to see David and the *Sweet Lady Jane*. Suddenly, I was scared of riding off the road; I steered left as far as possible, but it was as if magnetic forces were sucking me toward the edge. There were names on the road surface, but I was unable to put the letters together.

There was snow in the verge, and arms stuck out that waved at me. Dusk began to fall. I passed a house with a sign in front that lit up as if it were a neon advertisement. LES GRANGES, it said. I cycled on. Joost was nowhere to be seen; he had probably ridden into a ravine.

'Joost!' I yelled. 'Joost!' I had to save him, but I noticed that I wasn't producing any sound. Everything around me became whiter and whiter; I looked at my legs, my arms. White.

I began to feel sorry for myself, and was afraid I was cycling along a road that continued into infinity, upward and upward. I thought of the Flying Dutchman: that was me, the Flying Dutchman. Time is standing still, I thought. I panicked. If time was standing still, everything was finished. I heard the oxygen being pumped in; it was a gurgling sound, and for a moment I was happy. I had been saved, but I didn't know from what.

Then I saw her, on a bend. She smiled at me. I wanted to stop, but I realized that my feet were trapped, and that my pedals went on turning. I couldn't stop. She was standing there at the roadside in a red bikini; I couldn't understand that she wasn't dying of cold. 'Put some clothes on,' I tried to say, and actually managed to say it, but it was more of a mumble that came out. I looked to the right, at that wonderful body, the round breasts and flat tummy. I thought I could see the curves in her bikini bottoms. I noticed she was wearing high heels, and had put her right foot forward provocatively. Everything slowed down, I almost touched her, I was so close that she could whisper in my ear. 'I love you, Pol,' she said, probably because I was on a racing bike.

'I love you,' I wanted to say, but she had vanished; I had passed her. I turned around but couldn't see her anymore; she had dissolved. I felt like crying, but no tears would come.

I passed a long wall of piled stones; it was Joost's house— could he be here? I couldn't see him, and drank a mouthful from my water bottle. There was something strange in it, something I had never tasted before, something that tasted of flat beer. I rode past a supermarket, but someone yelled, 'Go on, we're closed today.' It now began to get very steep, and I was riding up a vertical wall. I would tell Joost that he might have warned me. It became so quiet that it was almost unbearable; the silence weighed on me like a piece of steel sheeting, and I had to let myself fall in order not to be crushed.

'Combination of increasing need for, and decreased availability, of oxygen,' explained Joost. 'And possibly an acute lack of sugar.' We were sitting in a restaurant two kilometres below the summit of the Galibier, in a room full of wooden chairs and tables with blue cloths. There were no other customers. 'Altitude sickness. Normally only occurs over 2500 metres, but some people are especially susceptible. Hallucinations. By the way, you kept pedalling hard, I had to let you go. Today it didn't go exactly as I had calculated. I must check again; perhaps I overlooked some factors.'

I nodded. I was still trying to disentangle my hallucinations from reality.

We had descended like snails, with me shivering on my bike. I couldn't remember having passed the restaurant during the climb. Joost had found me on a low wall, with my bike beside me. I was starting to regain a bit of a grip on reality, and my head was hurting.

'I saw Laura,' was my reply when Joost asked me how I was. 'She was standing by the roadside in a sexy red bikini. I said she should put some clothes on.'

'You should have asked her to take something off.' Joost was hollow-eyed. His first acquaintance with the mountains had not gone too well. 'How did you know you were at the top?'

'I didn't know. I happened to stop. If I had started to descend, I would have crashed.'

We ordered coffee and two toasted sandwiches.

'And now for the good news,' said Joost. 'The Ventoux is half a kilometre lower than the Galibier.'

'I saw the colours of your jersey run like watery ink. And you were riding behind me.'

When we drove to Bédoin via Gap the next day, my whole body hurt. I couldn't see myself riding up another mountain, and certainly not Mont Ventoux, on which people dropped dead.

'We'll take a day off tomorrow,' suggested Joost. 'Just read a bit, eat well, recharge the batteries. And then on Wednesday we'll attack the Ventoux.'

'Stop talking about attacking. I was attacked by the Galibier, and it won.'

'No, you won.'

'That's not what it feels like. More as if I've been run over by a steamroller.'

We passed Bar de l'Observatoire in the centre of Bédoin. 'The bar where Tommy Simpson had his last drink,' said Joost, in the tone of a guide on a cruise boat. 'A calvados.'

La Garenne, the campsite he had looked up in David's father's international camping guide, was on the edge of the village. We stopped at reception. 'Ah, les Hollandais,' said the lady at the counter. 'Ils sont hâtifs cette année.' She was about 50.

'What's she saying?' Joost hadn't studied any French.

'That they're especially horny this year, the Dutch. She means you.'

The woman put a cross by the place where we could pitch our tent. She came outside with us to raise the barrier. 'Ici à gauche,' she said. 'Bon séjour.'

Joost drove along the path in the direction indicated. He stopped by a large bungalow tent. 'Just our luck. Empty campsite, but we're next to howling kids and a croaking granddad. The rest of the family will be shagging all night. There goes our preparation. I'm going to ask if we can't be a bit further apart. For Christ's sake, we're talking about top-level sport.'

'Don't worry about howling kids.' I pointed to the car that was parked half-hidden behind the tent: David's father's van. EASTWEST ADVENTURES was emblazoned on it.

'Good grief!' said Joost. 'Did he always have that on it?'

Grinning broadly, they came out of the tent. First André, then David, and finally Peter. 'Hey, eager beavers,' said André, flicking away a cigarette end. 'Long bike ride?'

'Laura,' called Peter, 'they're here!'

She was wearing a bikini I had seen before, and looked

enchanting. She had a serious look in her eyes.

'Jesus,' said Joost. 'It really is red.'

David wanted to investigate whether Eastwest Adventures could organize anything in the area. André had nothing else to do, and when Peter heard that David was taking the car, it struck him as a better idea than the train. Peter made a gesture and pointed at Laura. I told you so, he meant.

I was glad, but also unsettled. It was as though the six of us had been herded into a boxing ring. There was no more school, no family, all the familiar things were missing, all protection had gone, new rules applied. Just the six of us and two tents.

Laura seemed absent-minded. She looked on from a distance as Joost described our adventures to André and Peter. It scarcely seemed to interest her. I'd never seen her like this before. She had a large blue bruise on her upper arm.

I asked if she had bumped into something.

'I was beaten. My father didn't want me to come here.' She said it coolly, without emotion.

'Christ.'

'I'm not going back. I'm not going to let myself be hit. Not anymore.'

The next morning, we walked down a steep path into Bédoin. It was about eleven o'clock, and the village was deserted. 'Watch this,' said David, as we went into the Bar de l'Observatoire. He said hello to the owner and ordered six coffees. '*Et six pain jambon, monsieur Jean.*' It was as if he had been camping in Bédoin for weeks. We sat at a round table.

Monsieur Jean served us large mugs of weak slop, and

left the bar. 'Now he'll go first to the baker, and then to the butcher,' said David. 'Monsieur Jean doesn't do stocking up. Funny.'

When Jean had set down the hunks of baguette with ham in front of us, Joost took something out of a plastic bag. It was *The Rider*. He drummed his fingers on the table and asked for silence. 'Bart and I are going to climb Mont Ventoux on Wednesday,' he said solemnly. 'For that reason I'd like to read a bit from a book that has been read by me and Bart, called *The Rider*, so that you can understand what we're doing. Okay, here it goes.' He appropriated everything effortlessly, even the book that I had first discovered, and he had only read after long insistence on my part. Now it was suddenly his Bible, too.

'Tour de France 1958,' declaimed Joost. 'A few days before I saw Charly Gaul ride into the Parc des Princes in his yellow jersey, something new was introduced to the Tour: a 21.5-kilometre uphill time trial on Mont Ventoux. I've cycled up Mont Ventoux on seven occasions ...'

I took a bite of my baguette. I had never seen such a thick slice of ham. I felt tired, but happy, too. She was sitting opposite me and looked at me now and then. I tried to read something in her look, tried to see a difference in the way she looked at me and at the others.

'I always take the Bédoin side,' Joost read. He made an unnecessary movement with his arms to indicate he was talking about the same Bédoin. 'The first five kilometres undulate slowly upwards. You cycle away from the summit, which you can see over your left shoulder, a pastel-yellow wasteland with a dot on it: the Observatory.'

She had put on a short white dress over her bikini. She had light eye shadow on—I had never noticed before. I must be careful I didn't sit and stare at her—I already was, probably. Peter got up and went to the bar. Joost glanced up in annoyance, but Peter didn't pay any attention. '*Un pastis*', I heard Peter say.

'The Forest is the worst,' Joost went on. 'For more than ten kilometres you climb up slopes of varying gradients, but always more than ten percent.'

David and André looked bored. They felt absolutely no desire to climb Mont Ventoux, and the heroism of our plan escaped them completely. André broke off pieces of his bread, threw them in the air, and tried to catch them in his mouth. David leafed through folders that he had collected from the tourist office. He wanted to explore the surrounding area the next day. Peter had stayed at the bar, so that Joost was actually only reading for Laura and himself. My thoughts were elsewhere.

The doctor's son went on reading imperturbably. He saw the smile around Laura's mouth, and that was obviously enough inspiration to lay it on even thicker. 'The reason I always choose the Bédoin side is not because of Simpson.' Joost said it in a tone that suggested that he, and not Krabbé, always chose the Bédoin side. 'But because that 1958 time trial began there as well.'

At first I thought it was an accidental touch, but when her foot stroked my shin, I knew that she was doing it on purpose. I looked at her and saw a slight blush. I was wearing flat Jesus sandals. She went on with her secret caresses. I let the right-hand sandal slide off my foot and touched her leg. She did not withdraw her leg, and I could see from her eyes that I had done what she expected, and perhaps hoped for. I slid my foot upward along her calf, and she stretched it a little, so that I could get higher.

'With my best time, I would have been the last of the non-eliminated riders. Ladies and gentlemen, please note in your programmes: 92. Krabbé, 1.21.50.'

I wanted Joost to go on. I wanted him to begin at the beginning and read us the whole book. But he stopped. The passage on Mont Ventoux had finished. I lifted Laura's lower leg slightly.

'Finally,' sighed André. 'Have you finished? Jesus, man, what a load of waffle. I gave that book to my father for Christmas. Thought: he'll like that, a fellow-cyclist who writes. He still hasn't read it—doesn't trust it, he says. Cyclists don't write, according to him, and writers don't cycle. So, whatever it is, according to my father it's no good.'

Peter came shuffling back from the bar with a glass of pastis in his hand. 'I thought that Krabbé was a chess player, but he's a cyclist.'

'He was a chess player,' said Joost. 'And quite a good one, too. Then he became a writer, and then a writer-cyclist.' When he appropriated something, he did it completely. 'The nicest bit is the beginning of the book, where he prepares for the start of the race. He rides past a terrace, sees people sitting there—types like you lot, say—and the emptiness of those lives shocks him. Wait a minute, I'll read it ...'

'Leave it,' said Peter, by his standards noticeably irritated. 'I don't like all that quoting. Think of something yourself.'

Joost, insulted, stopped talking and started demonstratively reading the relevant passage.

'I could organize a cycling trip to Mont Ventoux,' said David, 'and when we leave, give everyone that book. So they've got something to read on the bus and can get straight in the mood. I could also ask Krabbé to come along. What do you think? Cycle up Mont Ventoux with Tim Krabbé. Oh boy, then I would need to hire a couple of extra buses.'

'Mont Aigoual,' I said. 'The book is more about that. Real

fans of *The Rider* want to go up Mont Aigoual in the Cevennes.' Laura had withdrawn her leg.

David ordered three red wines for himself, André, and Laura, and another pastis for Peter. Joost and I drank water. 'Tommy Simpson died on Mont Ventoux after he'd drunk a calvados here,' said Joost. He let a silence fall, as if he were asking approval for our abstemiousness. No one reacted. Peter emphatically drank a large mouthful from his glass. 'All pretension, Laura,' he said, and gave her an intense look. She said nothing in reply.

A little later, we went to the small supermarket. David had made a list of all the ingredients for a rice dish. While I wandered aimlessly among the shelves, I felt fingers gliding over my back. It was as if she was trying to tell me something with her fingers, and was waiting for an answer. I smiled, but I didn't know what to say.

While we were waiting at the checkout, she came and stood next to me and put her arm around me in a friendly way.

'You've lost weight, Bart. You must eat properly, or you'll blow off the mountain. It's called the windy mountain, you know that, don't you?'

I thought she was such a sweetie. I wanted to hug her and kiss her. I wanted to say that I did not care two hoots about the whole climb, or the Ventoux.

I slept with Joost in the small trekker tent. David's bunga-low tent had two sleeping compartments, with David, Peter, and André sharing one, while Laura had the other to herself. The next day, David said that he was going up Mont Ventoux in the car, and also wanted to explore the surrounding area. He had read that that there was a lot of canoeing, and he thought that also fitted in very well into the travel programme of Eastwest Adventures.

'And today we're going to do a quiet run to loosen our muscles.' Joost had already put on his cycling gear. We had breakfast in silence. Laura had woken up before us, and was lying in the grass some distance away, reading *The Color Purple*.

David got his camera from the tent. 'I think I'll come with you,' said André. 'It will be quite a kick to climb the Ventoux a day earlier than these two racers here. And I've always liked canoeing.' He flicked his cigarette end away, and went over to the car.

'Tonight we're going to try out a local restaurant,' said David. 'On the company.'

A little later, Joost got up, too. 'Okay, Pol, get your cycling kit on, and let's go.'

'I'm not going. My muscles are still hurting. I'm having a rest day.'

'We'll take it easy. Just a few hours to loosen up our legs, not forcing anything.'

'Tuur, I'm not going.'

'I am.' There was irritation in his voice.

'I'll come with you,' said Peter suddenly. 'I should know how it works, changing gear and so on.'

I got up. 'I'm going to read a book, too.' I nodded to Laura.

'Suit yourself,' said Joost. When Peter passed Laura in his shorts and T-shirt, he tapped her on the butt with his right trainer, and when she looked up, he winked at her. 'The champion is off to the start,' he said. She didn't react.

They left the campsite, Peter slightly uncertain on the Raleigh, which was just too small for him. 'Only pull the straps tight when you're out of the village,' I shouted.

'We'll be back in an hour and a half,' said Joost.

I got my book from the tent and sat down in the grass like a yogi. My eyes ran over the letters, but I didn't read anything. I knew she was looking at me. I can't remember exactly how long it went on for. A quarter of an hour, perhaps. I scarcely dared to move. I was scared of what was going to happen, but I was still more scared that it wouldn't happen.

A shadow fell across my book. Laura had stood up and come over to me.

'Bart.' She was standing in front of me; I looked up at her, past her legs, her red bikini bottom, her breasts, at her smiling face.

'Laura,' I said.

She bent over, put her hand in the nape of my neck and kissed me on the mouth. 'Come with me.' She pulled me up and led me to the big tent.

She let me go for a moment in order to close the zip and slide the curtain in front of the plastic windows. Then she turned around and kissed me. I felt her breasts against me, I didn't know what to do with my hands, my eyes filled with tears, I wanted to say something to her, but that was difficult because her tongue was in my mouth.

She gave me a penetrating look, as if she wanted to plumb the depths of my soul with her eyes. She was breathing fast; with her left hand she held my head and with her right she stroked my back. I had only a pair of shorts on and got a hard-on against her belly. She kissed my cheek.

I was lying on her airbed. She stayed standing and smiled at me. I felt I should say something, make a remark that fit the occasion, but I had no idea what that might be. Then, with a single movement of her right hand over her shoulder she undid her bikini top and dropped it on the ground.

There was no affectation in her movement, nor was it an erotic dance. I did not move, not even when she pushed down her bikini bottom and stood naked before me. My heart was in my mouth and I closed my eyes for a moment, as if I could not could bear what I saw, although in my fantasies I had seen her naked in front of me so often.

When I opened them again, she was lying next to me. I didn't know what else to do except to cling to her, hide in her, with my face in her blond hair.

'Laura.' It was the first thing I was able to get out, and it was good. She ran her fingers over my cheek and looked straight at me.

'You're still wearing your shorts.'

'Sorry, but you know I'm the sporty type.' Fortunately she laughed.

'Darling Laura.' I stroked her warm body, her breasts, and her belly. I felt her fingers playing with me and thought I was going to die, but it also seemed the most natural thing in the world.

'I love you,' I said. I hoped that she would understand everything that lay behind those words. She put her hand on my mouth, and we stopped talking.

She got up and put on her bikini. 'Don't talk to anyone about it yet,' she said. She got her book, and I lay down on a towel with my eyes closed. It was as if nothing had happened, or as if we were a couple that had been screwing up a storm for years and didn't bother to talk about it anymore. I caught her once, looking at me seriously. Her sweat was still clinging to my skin, her smell, my ears were filled with the sound of her sighs.

I did not respond to Joost's ambiguous wink when he came back with Peter. Peter was too tired to say anything, put his bike against the fence, and lay down in the grass. Laura bent over him and said something—I couldn't hear what. By the time David and André drove into the campsite at about four o'clock, what had happened had almost become a dream.

David said we should take a photo—that would be nice for later, when we were old and ugly. He got a tripod from the car and mounted the camera on it. Then he looked through the viewfinder and gestured to us, telling us how to stand. He started the self-timer and walked over to us. I thought: so this is happiness. I mustn't forget this moment; this must stay with me for the rest of my life. Peter put on his sunglasses, André blew a cloud of smoke in the direction of the camera, and I put my arm around her.

When we went to the village, I looked at Laura, who was walking in front of me and talking to André. I could scarcely imagine that she was the same person as the woman who had lain naked next to me a few hours before.

A new self-confidence had taken hold of me, the self-confidence of the male who has won the most beautiful female—a primitive, instinctive sort of self-confidence.

André came out of the toilet of Bar de l'Observatoire holding his nose. A little way away was Le Relais du Ventoux, but Joost felt it would be a betrayal of Tommy Simpson to go there. We simply had to take the filthy toilet as part of the bargain. 'There's a good chance that Simpson had his last crap in there. Who says that's not cycling history?'

His drivel about that Simpson was really getting on my nerves. 'English doper,' I said.

'It wouldn't surprise me if that shithole hasn't been cleaned since, and Tommy's turd is still lying there,' said André. 'Perhaps we should ask the owner if he has any more information. We can take the turd with us and offer it to the cycling museum. The last turd of Tommy Simpson.'

Joost raised his hands in despair. 'Cycling barbarians!'

David had been to see the owner of a canoe-hire firm, who had immediately become wildly enthusiastic when

David told him he was director-owner of Eastwest Adventures, and that there was great interest in Holland in canoeing on the Sorgue. 'Canoeing, cycling, I see great possibilities,' said David. 'Plus, of course, the cultural dimension. Avignon, the popes, the festival. And a little way away there's the old chateau of the Marquis de Sade, nice outing. I mean, sport, culture, sex—the ideal mix.'

That evening we ate in a restaurant very close to the Bar de l'Observatoire. There seemed to be a thoughtful pall over the conversation, and not much was said.

XVIII

'Okay, we're off,' said Joost. It was eight o'clock on Friday morning. We wanted to go up early, because we were afraid that otherwise it would get too hot. The previous evening, Joost had shown me the list of the gradients. The first five kilometres weren't too bad, but after that, the Forest started.

'The Forest is hard,' said Joost, as if he had conquered the Ventoux many times before. 'As far as Chalet Reynard, it is always nine or ten percent. Only after that do we reach the real Ventoux. It gets really hard there, guys. Bare, boiling sun, the wind, and diabolical heat.'

Peter stood listening as if it didn't concern him. He had on an old and oversized Raleigh jersey of André's father, faded shorts, and his worn-out Adidas trainers.

'Cut it out, Joost,' I said. 'You're like a sports commentator. It's only a mountain. Just like the Galibier, and we made it up that.'

'Yes, Joost, you're just trying to frighten me.' Peter took a couple of light steps. 'Got to loosen the muscles a bit.'

I rode out of Bédoin at a gentle pace, with Joost and Peter on my wheel. I didn't want us to lose touch with Peter before the real climb began. David drove behind us. Laura was sitting next to him, and André was sitting in the back. 'Going nicely,' yelled Joost. 'Nice stretch to warm up the muscles and raise the heartbeat slowly but surely. After Saint-Estève, it gets difficult.' I went on cycling at the same tempo. We passed a hamlet called Les Bruns and then we made a sharp bend into the Forest: Forêt Domaniale De Beaumont-du-Ventoux, it said on a sign. The road now climbed more steeply.

'Jesus,' said Peter.

'The Forest!' cried Joost. 'Are you two already in your lowest gear?' Peter was struggling desperately with the gear levers, and threatened to fall over in the first few metres of the climb. Just in time, he got the bike moving again. Then his foot slipped out of his left toe clip and he almost fell, after all. He got it back in, and even managed to tighten the straps.

I looked under my arm at my derailleur gear. I had two sprockets left. I saw that Joost was changing down. I knew that Laura was looking at me, and the strength in my legs surprised me. I thought about changing up a gear, but a voice in the back of my head said that I mustn't be rash. There were still another fifteen kilometres to go to the summit. I heard Joost panting on my wheel. I looked around and saw the pleading look in his eyes. He also knew there were spectators. I relaxed, and lowered the tempo.

Peter gestured for us to leave him.

Behind us, André was hanging out of the window. He was imitating a famous commentator with an excited voice. 'And there go the matadors of this Tour de France, side by side up the fearsome Mont Ventoux! It's a majestic sight, listeners, to see these three Dutch lads fighting, here on this French mountain. And it is some mountain, believe me, a monster, a beast, a gruesome pustule. They've shaken off everyone, and not just the old hacks. Where is Hinault? Where is Thévenet? Where is the old Portuguese Joaquim Agostinho? I can't see them. No, I can't see them. There's no sign of them anywhere! Haha!'

I let Joost pass and waited till I was riding alongside the car. I looked at Laura for a moment. She smiled, and it was as if a rush of adrenalin shot up to my thighs. 'You must stay with Peter,' I said to Laura. 'Perhaps you can give him a bit of a tow, now and then.'

'And he's riding alongside us now, listeners,' tooted André into a Coke can. 'I'm going to ask him a few questions. Bart! Bart Hoffman! What is going through your mind?'

'I feel good, and say hello to my parents.'

'He simply says hello to his parents! Hasn't he just stayed a fine, regular guy, this hero of Mont Ventoux? Good luck, Bart.'

David stopped the car to wait for Peter. I rode back to Joost, took the lead, and pushed the tempo up slightly. We rode in silence for a while. Now and then I drank a mouthful from my water bottle. It was hard, but not as hard as the Galibier.

I looked back and could no longer see David's car. 'You okay, Joost?' I tried to sound as relaxed as possible. 'I think that we'll have a slightly easier section in a bit.' I wanted to pep talk him.

Joost looked at the asphalt intensely. 'I'm okay. I think I'm starting to go a bit better. What a bloody mountain.'

We were both in our lowest gear. The signs along the roadside counted off the kilometres. I tried to do what André's father had told me: push and pull, push with the left, pull with the right, push with the right, pull with the left, turn smoothly, don't act as if you're on a delivery bike. I could feel that the temperature was rising, but I did not know whether that was due to my exertions or the sun. 'Another four kilometres to Chalet Reynard,' yelled Joost. I could hear David coming up behind us, and driving alongside us. André wanted to interview Joost, but he made a dismissive gesture.

'And champion Joost Walvoort is having a hard time, listeners in Holland. He goes on pedalling bravely, but the look in his eyes says enough. At the moment he'd rather be at home, solving difficult mathematical problems!'

I let Joost come alongside me. André had observed accurately: he wasn't in very good shape.

'It's hard, eh,' he said, with a tortured expression. 'There's no end to it, that Forest. Think I'm having another bad day.'

I didn't answer. I thought it would be shitty to say I could go at least two kilometres an hour faster.

'Banana?' Laura was holding a banana in her hand. She had already peeled it.

I stuck my arm out, keeping my eyes fixed on the road ahead. I had seen racing cyclists do that when they grabbed something from the car. She took my wrist in one hand and with the other placed the banana in my hand. I thought she was stroking me.

'Do you want a banana, too, Joost?', she yelled.

Joost shook his head.

'You've got to keep eating, otherwise you'll hit the wall,' said André. David parked the car at the roadside. We made the last turn to the right, and saw Chalet Reynard ahead of us. I knew that from here on, it would be a little less steep. You could also see the summit, and that gave you courage.

Once we had passed Chalet Reynard, I accelerated, knowing that I would immediately lose Joost. I'm not sure exactly why I didn't wait any longer. It was to do with Laura, although she could not see what I was doing. I was trying to make the gap as big as possible.

At the monument to Tommy Simpson, a kilometre and a half below the summit, I looked back for the first time. Joost was no longer anywhere to be seen. For a moment I considered waiting and cycling to the summit together, but I decided against it—I wanted to win.

At the top, it was empty. I was completely alone on the summit of Mont Ventoux. Down below I could see Joost, but there was no sign yet of Peter, or of David's car.

It was at least another fifteen minutes before Joost arrived. He passed me hollow-eyed. He got off his bike, laid it flat on the asphalt, and sat down next to it. He put his head on his knees and said nothing. I went over to him and put my hand on his shoulders. He didn't react. 'One forty-eight,' I said.

'I wanted to quit,' he said, when, after a while, he had gathered sufficient strength to raise his head. 'I wanted to turn around and ride back. But then I would have been riding toward David, and I didn't want to do that. I don't know what it is with this mountain. The Galibier is tough, too, but I think this one is terrible. It's a killer. Christ. Have you got anything left to drink?' I gave him my water bottle.

'Wrong gears, too. I needed a 30 or a 32 behind. I have to rely on my suppleness; I don't have your brute strength.' Again, he had a lot to say for himself. 'I burned myself out in the first few kilometres. Then I had a block in the Forest after only five kilometres. I had to force myself, and I paid for it. And perhaps I hadn't eaten enough.'

'It just wasn't your day. Normally, you would have been

able to keep up with me.' I was ashamed of my selfish behaviour. 'I was able to keep going,' I said, 'and didn't have to push it for a moment. I think the ascent of the Galibier did me good. Your training build-up was better for me than for you, if you ask me.'

'That one hour and forty-eight of yours is very different from what I had worked out. And that two hours ten of mine is far below my level. I had calculated that it should be possible in one fifty-two.' Theoretically, he was still the best. We didn't say anything else for a while.

Joost got up laboriously and walked to the edge. 'Here they come,' he said. Peter still had about two kilometres to go. Sometimes it looked as if he was balancing on the spot, so slowly was he hauling himself up the mountain.

'Still an achievement,' I said. 'He's going to make it, too, in his Adidas trainers and without a metre's training.'

'We trained yesterday.' Then he asked: 'Did you fuck Laura?'

'Why do you think that?'

'I think you did. You feel things like that. It hangs in the air for hours. They are certain molecules that you pick up unconsciously, detect, and recognise as sex molecules.'

I didn't say any more. I had promised Laura not say anything to the others, but didn't feel like lying to Joost, either. Fine by me if he thought I had been to bed with her.

'Damn,' said Joost.

Ten minutes later, David's car came around the last sharp bend up to the plateau. Obviously, they had left Peter behind. David stopped by Joost's bike, the door opened, and the driver and his passengers got out. It looked as if they had pushed the car to the top. They were soaked in sweat, and their faces were dangerously red.

'Jesus Christ,' sighed André. 'The bloody heat.' Joost and I looked at him questioningly.

'We couldn't stay with Peter any longer,' said David apologetically. 'The engine was threatening to explode, the temperature gauge was well into red. We had opened all the windows and turned the heating on full, but that no longer helped. That's what happens when you go up a mountain like this so slowly.'

Laura's shirt clung to the contours of her breasts, the most beautiful breasts ever spotted on the summit of Mont Ventoux. We went to the edge to see where Peter was. He still had a couple of hundred metres to climb. 'Come on, Peter!' yelled André. 'You can do it! You're almost there!' You could see that Peter heard, because he looked in our direction for a moment.

'He can really take it,' said André. 'If I had been him, I would have been in the car long ago. But he carried on, the poet did. My appreciation of poetry has increased greatly today.' We walked down a bit toward the bend, to be able to see Peter coming and, if necessary, push him up the last few metres.

'How did you two get on?' asked Laura. I looked at Joost, giving him the honour of announcing the result.

'I was completely wrecked. Bart accelerated after Chalet Reynard, and, normally speaking, I should have been able to follow him, but I tightened up and had to let him go.'

Laura looked at me. I acted as nonchalant as possible. 'I had a good day.'

'I should have had a rest day yesterday, too.' Joost said this with a spiteful smile. 'It clearly gave Bart extra strength.' Laura looked at me. I made an innocent face, as if I had no idea what the hint referred to.

'Rest is the most important thing for a cyclist,' I declared.

'And no sex,' added André. Again, I raised my eyebrows. Had he detected the sex molecules, too, or was he talking off the top of his head? Peter still had two hundred metres to go.

'Come on, Peter!' yelled André.

'No sex?' asked Laura.

'No,' said Joost. 'It's generally known. You waste your precious juices.'

André ran down and pushed Peter up the last fifty metres. 'It's allowed,' yelled André, 'they do it in the Tour, too.' Peter willingly allowed himself to be pushed. His head seemed to be wobbling on his body. At the top, André held him while Joost loosened the straps of his toe clips.

'Wasn't too bad,' said Peter.

'Finish the poem?' I asked, more as a joke than as a serious question.

'Yes. David, have you got pen and paper in the car?'

'Maestro,' I shouted. Perhaps the concentration on the poem helped him up and prevented him from getting off.

'There are some strange conversations going on, here,' said Laura. 'Must be the rarefied air. Sex, juices, poems.' David went over to the car.

'Why didn't you and Joost go up together?' she asked me. 'It wasn't a race, was it?'

'In the mountains, everyone rides at their own speed. It's always like that. I flew up that mountain. I've never had that feeling before, and I thought it was a shame to end it.'

'You just wanted beat him.' She looked at Peter.

'That, too.'

David came back. Besides pen and paper, he was also carrying a bottle of champagne and a box of glasses. He handed over the writing materials to Peter, and everyone was given a glass. André took the bottle and popped the cork. We stood in a circle while André filled the glasses. He had to wait for a bit when he got to Peter, who was standing writing like a man possessed, and he had put his glass on the roof of the car.

'To the Ventoux,' said David, 'and to the heroes who taught it manners! And sorry the champagne isn't cold.'

A little later, we took a group photo with David's self-timer. Peter immediately detached himself from us again and walked away. 'I need a bit of time,' he said. 'But I'd like to read it out here.' He sat down against a low wall.

We looked down. 'I can understand Petrarch,' said Laura. 'It's as if you're looking down from heaven at human plodding and strife. You're no longer part of it. You've raised yourself above it.'

André was standing a little way away with David by the car. They had opened the hood to see whether any damage had been done when they had been crawling up the mountain. Joost was lying behind the car in the shade, on his back on the asphalt, and it looked as if he were asleep. Peter was writing with great concentration.

'Are you sorry?' asked Laura.

'About what?'

'About yesterday.'

I looked at her. What was she getting at? Was *she* sorry?

'No,' I said. 'Of course not. Why do you think that?'

'Sex destroys friendship. Sex destroys love. Sex betrays everything.' She looked intensely sad. I didn't know what she meant, what she was trying to say.

'Joost knows,' I said.

'Did you tell him?'

'No, he knew. We know all about each other, even without words. I think the others know, too. Actually, I think Joost rode up the mountain so badly because he knew about you and me.'

She looked at me. 'Bart.'

'I want to go to Perugia with you.'

She bent over to me, kissed me, and said: 'Don't do that.' There were tears in her eyes. 'Peter knows, too.'

Joost was asleep or pretending to be; David and André topped up the radiator with water from the bottles they had brought with them from the campsite. Peter was writing. The world around me was undulating. I had to grab hold of a post so as not to fall. It was as if I were getting altitude sickness after all. Of course I had to ask Laura what the hell she meant, but I couldn't.

Laura went over to Peter, ran her hands through his curls, and asked something. He nodded without looking at her, raised his hand, and spread his five fingers. She came back to me. André called to Peter that it didn't all have to rhyme.

'Is it because you and Peter ...' I began to ask.

'No,' she said, in a tone that forbade any further questions.

Peter got up and came over to us. Joost looked up sleepily, and David and André hopped off the hood. Peter looked at me, expecting an introduction.

'As you may know,' I said, 'but perhaps not, as recognized cultural barbarians, Jan Kal wrote his famous poem "Poetry's cycling up Mont Ventoux" while riding up this mountain. By the time he got to the top, the sonnet was finished. Some time ago, I was talking about it to Peter, and he thought he could do something similar. Or, actually, things were the other way around. Peter wanted to write a poem while climbing the Ventoux, but to do that he had first to climb the Ventoux. That's right, isn't it, Peter?'

Peter nodded. His face looked serious. 'This isn't a cheerful poem,' he said. 'That may be because climbing isn't a cheerful activity. Or perhaps because of something else.' He looked at Laura. 'The poem is for her. She knows why.'

He wiped the sweat off his face with his T-shirt. His eyes

looked sad. There was no question of euphoria at conquering the Ventoux in a pair of Adidas trainers.

A stream of sentences began flowing, at first slowly, then faster and faster. The themes were nostalgia for the sadness and beauty of unfulfillable wishes, the red Raleigh, and Marlene Dietrich. He had tied everything together at furious speed—images and associations, quotations and experiences of the toiling cyclist.

It was a typical Seegers, a long conversational-style poem, the rough outline of which must have been in his head before the climb, although you never knew for certain with Peter. He could have outbursts of creativity that were so powerful that his thoughts could scarcely keep up. I had experienced that on the roof of the *Sweet Lady Jane*, when we were sitting doing nothing and looking out over the river, and Peter suddenly began writing, in a kind of private shorthand of half-words and half-sentences, hurriedly written down so as not to lose any of the inspiration. Perhaps now the thin air and the intense exertion had accelerated and intensified the processes in his brain, and the whole poem had been created on the side of the mountain.

He celebrated our friendship that here, on Mont Ventoux, had achieved its crowning moment, its climax, too, which was bound to be followed by sadness. He effortlessly juxtaposed the three stripes on his Adidas trainers with quotes from Petrarch's *Canzoniere*. He pulled out all the stops of his rhetorical talent that had grown through all his performances, he whispered and boomed, alternated staccato sentences with fluid strings of words, inserted silences and then accelerated again, went effortlessly from laughter to deep sadness, from euphoria to melancholy. It amazed me that he still had so much energy after his ordeal.

It seemed like a performance for the whole world, as if he were giving his Sermon on the Mount for everyone at his feet. From the top of the mountain, his voice floated in all directions. It was a long poem, and I think that he inserted other sentences that occurred to him on the spur of the moment between the ones he had written down. In line after line, he built up a complex and majestic palace of mirrors in words. He wrote about Gerrit Tankink's Raleigh and combined it with death and love. It all fit; he assembled a mosaic full of surprising colours and strange shapes. He had cycled up the Ventoux in three hours, died, and he now arose, full of life. He quoted a favourite collection, and undoubtedly made lots of other poetry references that escaped me.

It was as if, on the Ventoux he had finally liberated himself, as if the winds around the mountain had cleared his mind of the last petty worries. Everything came together, the small and the large, the sacred and the banal. It was a declaration of love to life, but also a provocative invitation to death.

We stood there and listened, as if rooted to the spot. When he had finished, after ten minutes, a quarter of an hour, half an hour—I couldn't say—he bowed his head. You would have expected him to look at us to see the shattering effect of his words, to receive the admiring looks and hear the cries of disbelief of his friends.

But he bowed his head, as if he were ashamed or submissive. He remained there like that, looking at the ground, probably now genuinely close to total exhaustion. We were silent.

David was the first to go over and put an arm round him. A second later, we were all standing around him, clapping him on the shoulders. He didn't react.

'Peter,' asked Laura, 'what have you done?'

It was, as usual, the most appropriate question. What had he done? What had he done, to himself and to us? What spells had he used, and what was about to happen to us as a result? He looked up and smiled. 'I have said it,' he said. That was all. And probably that was the case: he had said it; he had said everything. He went and stood behind Laura, put his arms around her, laid a hand on her belly, and closed his eyes.

Later, I often talked to David about the minutes during which Peter hypnotized us. We tried to recover what it was; we tried to reconstruct sentences to find out the secret. But we couldn't. Like me, David had a memory of something magical, of a bizarre construction made of countless bizarre elements that nevertheless together formed a completely harmonious whole, a stream of words and sentences that, at some time, had been torn apart, but had now been reunited.

'Come on,' called David, when we had come to our senses a little. 'We're going down. It's a lot quicker than uphill. I feel like some of that filthy coffee at l'Observatoire.'

Joost pulled a face. 'Can my bike go in the car?' he asked. 'I'm trembling all over. I'd rather not make the descent on the bike.' André took Joost's bike and rode it to the van. There, he took off the front wheel, opened the back door, and laid it inside. Joost also walked laboriously to the car, with Laura next to him.

'And what about you two?' David asked Peter and me. 'Can you make it? I don't mind driving back up here in a bit and picking you up.'

'Not necessary for me,' I said. 'I'm crazy about descents.'

'Me, too,' said Peter, although the only descent he had ever made up to then was from the IJssel Bridge. 'I could use a bit of wind in my face.'

'Are you sure?'

'Flying is difficult, Laura, but everyone can fall.'
We waited until the others had taken their seats in the car. I got on and rode after the car. Just before the sharp left bend, I stopped for a moment and motioned Peter to do the same. I said to him that he must stay behind me, about ten metres, and must not brake too abruptly. 'Hands on the handlebars, fingers by the brake. Outer chain wheel at the front, smallest sprocket at the back. Keep control, don't suddenly squeeze hard, because then you'll go over the top or into a skid. On the left is the front brake, on the right is the back. Watch out for oncoming cars. No need to pedal.' Then I put my feet in the toe clips and felt an invisible hand push me forcefully downwards.

I saw David's car driving a little way in front. We quickly caught up with him. I could hear Peter was behind me, less than ten metres, because I could hear him letting out cries now and then. I couldn't tell whether they were cries of excitement, of fear, or something else. In any case, they were a kind of primeval yell. Just past the Simpson Monument, we overtook David. I could see the fear in Laura's eyes. Peter was following me as if I had him on a string. We were doing at least seventy.

I could hear from the diesel sounds of David's car that he was following at not too great a distance. The descent of the Ventoux is smooth, without hairpin bends, and even a cautious driver like David was able to stay close to us. On one of the straighter stretches, I glanced back. Peter was sitting in a strange position on his bike, rather upright, as if he were about to get off. He no longer had his hands in the curve of the handlebars. Chalet Reynard was approaching fast.

Suddenly Peter passed me; he didn't look to the side, just straight ahead. He was pedalling for all he was worth. I estimate that he was going at least eighty, and the distance between the two of us quickly widened. I thought he wanted to be first to reach Chalet Reynard.

Should I have yelled to him not to be so crazy and to brake at once? Should I have hung on to his tail to warn him to moderate his speed? Perhaps, but I didn't. I watched him cycling ahead of me, the poet. Watched him tear down the mountain like a hawk, far too fast, irresponsibly fast, as if there were a 220-volt current in his brakes.

Then his bike made a strange movement. It began with a small lurch, but then the distance to right and left quickly became bigger. I saw that he had lost control, that something was terribly wrong. I saw Peter fall while he was still on the bike; I braked so I could stop next to him even before he was flying through the air. I saw the handlebars wrench themselves out of his hands, saw the front wheel positioned for a fraction of a second at a right angle to the frame, saw the bike rise from behind like a bucking horse and throw its rider out of the saddle. I saw him take off, hit the asphalt, and slide at high speed toward the edge of the mountain. There, it was as if an invisible hand grabbed him by the hair and pushed his head into the ground, so that the rest of his body went on sliding, with his head as the turning point, and then also came to a standstill.

It wasn't a hand, it was a pole.

I braked so hard that I almost skidded. Behind me, I heard David's squealing brakes. We passed the spot where Peter lay; I saw his head, which was going red with blood. I didn't come to a halt until about twenty metres further on. David's car was behind me, askew on the mountain. I loosened my straps and threw the bike on the ground. I ran up, past the car, to the spot where Peter was lying. David and Laura ran after me.

'Peter!' screamed Laura's voice, 'Peter! God, Peter!'

I reached his body and knew at once that he was dead.

He was lying like a baby, on his side, with his knees pulled up. The side of his head had hit the pole so hard that it looked as if part of his skull had been opened with a chisel. His eyes were staring into nothingness. Blood was streaming down his chin; a stream formed on the asphalt. His mouth was open a little, as if he had died with a last word on his lips. 'Oh, God,' cried Laura. 'Do something. Do something! For Christ's sake, do something! He's dying. Peter's dying. That can't happen, that can't happen, that can't happen!' She shouted it out. David had taken off his shirt and was trying to stop the flow of blood with it. He looked at me in bewilderment. André was kneeling on the road. He had covered his eyes with his hands. His father's bike lay some distance further on.

I looked at David, who kept wiping the blood off Peter's face with movements almost like a caress. Laura was kneeling next to him and was holding Peter's head. Her hands were turning red. She was weeping in despair, without a sound. I walked along the road, two metres down and two metres up. I looked down at Provence and I looked up at that damned mountain.

Laura and David had laid Peter on his back and torn open his jersey. Laura pressed on his chest. David made attempts at mouth-to-mouth resuscitation, and Peter's blood stuck to his lips. 'We must put him in the car,' said André. 'We must get him down. Perhaps it's not too late.'

'Clear that back seat!' I shouted to Joost. It only struck me now that he had been sitting in the back of the car the whole time like a mummy. He was staring straight ahead without seeing anything. He didn't react to my words, either. I went over to the car and shouted through the open front door that he must get off the back seat and make room for Peter. 'We've got to take him down,' I yelled, 'come on, get off that seat.' He looked at me and I saw that his eyes were as empty as Peter's. He moved like a zombie, in slow motion. I pulled the seat in front of him forward, grabbed him by the arm, and tugged him toward me. 'Come on, Joost,' I said softly. 'Everything will be all right. I'm sure he's not dead. That's impossible.'

A few minutes later, Peter lay on the back seat. Joost was standing next to the car. Tears were streaming down his cheeks. David got in, and Laura said that Joost must sit next to her. She had taken control. Because Joost's bike was already in the back and André was sitting on top of it, mine would no longer fit in. And even if it could, there would have been no room for me. I could hardly sit on Peter.

I stood by the car, dazed. There was a gentle, warm wind blowing. I could hear the crickets. What time could it be? We had started the climb at nine o'clock. It must be about one. Through the window I saw Peter lying there; someone had closed his eyes. He was lying on his back with his knees pulled up and his head against the door. His chin hung on his chest, the torn jersey was wet through, and a new variant of red had been added to the Raleigh colours.

His father and mother, I thought, as if I suddenly realized that Peter had a father and mother and that they no longer had a son. Laura gave me a worried look.

'Bart!' called David. 'Bart! We're taking him to Bédoin now. There may be an ambulance there that he can be taken to hospital in. You stay here, and I'll come and get you as soon as I can. Got it? And you're not coming down on your bike!'

'Carpentras,' I said. 'He has to go to Carpentras.' Tommy Simpson was taken to Carpentras in 1967. Those killed on the Ventoux had to go to Carpentras. 'First to Bédoin, then perhaps to Carpentras,' said David. Through the back window I saw that Peter's head had slumped to the right and was resting on his shoulder.

They drove off, my friends and my lover. I stayed behind alone on the mountain, walked to Peter's bike, and picked it up. I had to do something, something simple, so as not to go mad. I looked to see if the handlebars were broken. That was not the case. There were some scratches and abrasions on the frame, but apart from that, there was nothing wrong with the bike. The front tyre was flat, that was all. I squeezed the brakes, and the blocks immediately gripped the rim. Then I laid the bike on the verge and went to the spot where I thought Peter had fallen head over heels, to see if there was a stone on the road surface, or something else that had caused him to fall. I couldn't find anything.

I walked back to where he had lain, scooped up a handful of sand, and scattered it over the blood. It was as if the world were growing dark, as if, for a moment, the sun, too, were mourning the death of the poet. Everything around me went grey. A breeze came up that made me shiver. It was as if there were a tennis ball full of water behind my breastbone, a huge tear that threatened to suffocate me. When it came out, through my eyes, my nose, and my mouth, I wanted to scream, but my vocal chords no longer worked. Weakened by tears or paralyzed with emotion.

Only when I had walked to my bike did I finally get some air. The colours returned to the landscape, and something rolled out of my midriff: a deep groan.

It was as if, as he rode behind me, Peter had decided to go in search of death. And he had found it, too—perhaps he had lured it toward him with his poem.

I took hold of my bike and got on it. I wanted to get away from that spot. I descended cautiously, and the speedometer did not go above forty. Now and then I stopped for a while, because I knew the brake blocks were getting red-hot. When I was sitting by the roadside, somewhere half-way through the Forest, I saw David's car coming up. He turned.

'I didn't want to stay there any longer,' I said. André came and sat next to me, and put his arm round my shoulders.

'He's dead,' he said. 'Fucking hell, he's dead. We're such assholes.'

I looked at him.

'We should never have let him do that descent, Bart. The guy had been on a racing bike twice in his life. We should have stopped him. Now he's dead.'

'It's want he wanted,' I said. 'He really wouldn't have let anyone stop him.'

'I should simply have put his bike in the back of the car and told him to get in,' said David. 'Why didn't I do that?'

I stared blankly ahead. 'I told him to stay behind me. And not to brake too suddenly and too abruptly.'

'He kept to that, all right,' said André. 'Not braking, I mean. He suddenly whooshed past you, going like the clappers. What did he do? Did he yell anything as he passed you?'

'No,' I replied. 'He just looked ahead. And he pedalled like crazy to go still faster. It was as if he could see something ahead of him that he absolutely had to grab hold of.'

'The Grim Reaper on a racing bike,' said André. 'That's what he saw. Christ. You must never try to overtake *him*.'

'Joost is lying in the tent,' said David. 'Won't say a word. Shock, I think. He just mumbled that he should have done the descent, not Peter. That it was his fault. The doctor's given him something.'

'Come on,' said André, 'let's go.' I got up while he put my bike in the back of the car.

'Peter's bike!' I said. 'It's still lying there.' I got in, next to André, as I didn't want to sit in the place where Peter had lain. David turned the car again and drove upward until we saw the Raleigh lying on the verge.

'The thing's virtually undamaged,' André noted with surprise.

We drove down in deep silence. I was thinking that we had to inform Peter's parents. As we drove into Bédoin, David asked if I had the phone number of Captain Willem and Madame Olga on me.

Joost was asleep in our tent, having taken the powerful sleeping tablets given to him by Doctor Colmard from the village. Laura, who had gone to Carpentras in the ambulance, was not back yet. We decided to wait for her before calling the Captain. Perhaps she had news. Perhaps Peter had only appeared to be dead, had shown signs of life in Carpentras, and would recover in three days or so.

After an hour and a half, Doctor Colmard's old Citroën drove onto the campsite. Laura sat next to him. He stopped by the bungalow tent.

She got out. She was deathly pale, and said nothing. Doctor Colmard, a thickset man of about 50, walked over to us. He talked about a fracture and shook his head. '*Si jeune,*' he said, and repeated it a couple of times. We understood that the miracle had not happened. Doctor Colmard shook all our hands, and left.

David went to the tent. We heard him talking to Laura in subdued tones. I should have done that, of course, I thought. A little later, he came out. 'Laura has talked to Captain Willem. And she has arranged for Peter's return to Holland.'

She came out. She had packed her rucksack. 'I have to go,' she said calmly. 'David will take me to Avignon, and I'll get the train back from there.' We looked at her. In some way, it made sense that she was going.

She put the rucksack down and made a gesture: we must stand close together. She stood in the middle. We stood with our arms around each other's shoulders. Our heads were touching. All four of us had closed our eyes; I could hear her breathing and felt the warmth of her body.

I don't know what we did, perhaps it was a prayer, perhaps we were crying without noise and tears. It was a farewell, and not just a farewell that would last until we saw one another again in a few days' time at Peter's funeral. It was more final. We let go of one another and Laura kissed us one by one, me last.

'Bye, my dear Bart,' she said, running her hands gently through my hair. The others looked, but she didn't seem to care that everything suddenly became clear. She kissed me on the mouth. 'I'm sorry,' she whispered. Then she got into the car and didn't look back.

Laura was not at Peter's funeral. There was just a huge bunch of white roses on the coffin, with a photo of her and Peter attached to it.

Much later, when I dropped by to see Captain Willem and Madame Olga in their white apartment on the river in Zutphen, I read what she had written on it. '*Wenn ich mir was wünschen dürfte, möchte ich etwas glücklich sein, denn sobald ich gar zu glücklich wär, hätt ich Heimweh nach dem Traurigsein.*' (If I were to wish for something, I'd like to be a little happy, for as soon as I was too happy, I'd be nostalgic for being sad.)

'It's from a song of Marlene D-d-dietrich,' said Captain Willem. They hadn't heard anything from her after the funeral, either. 'Disappeared off the face of the earth. Dissolved. Even her parents don't know where she is. She's alive, that's all they know. Well, still better than d-d-dead.' He was a broken man.

I didn't make any attempt to find her address in Perugia, if she had gone there. I knew that with Peter's death, something else had died. At first, André bluffed that he would go and unearth her, but he didn't take it any further. 'She doesn't want to be found,' he said, 'otherwise she would have left something behind. A couple of crumbs.' Joost went to Leiden.

About four months after Peter's death, a new collection appeared; he had gone on working hard after his début. I read through it, and knew most poems because he had read them out to us. I hoped that, through some strange quirk of fate, 'Mont Ventoux' would also have found a place, but it was not to be—that poem rested somewhere on the mountainside.

XIX

I had rung Anna to say I wanted to speak to her.

'What about?' she asked. 'Is it serious?'

'Very serious.'

'Are you ill?' There was slight panic in her voice. That did me good, although I was now obviously among those in whom a fatal malady could be diagnosed at any moment.

'No, healthier than ever.'

'What's so serious, then? Are you going to remarry?'

'No, never again.'

'What is it, then, Dad?'

'I've got something for you. An early 21st-birthday present. People used not to be considered grown-up till then, that's why.'

'Exciting. Tomorrow evening, seven o'clock, same place?'

'Okay.'

It took me a while to find the collection in the chaotic, towering piles of books that have been erected all over my apartment.

But when I had poured a Belgian beer, sat down in my reading chair, and read the dedication that Peter had written in the front, it was 1982 again. Donald Fagen sang 'Nightfly', I put *Combat Rock* by The Clash on the turntable for the first time, and took *Too-Rye-Ay* by Dexys Midnight Runners out of its sleeve—the LP that I got from Peter for my 18th birthday.

Time is nothing, I thought; time is something we fool ourselves with, a fateful illusion. The proof is that you can return so easily to the past. I saw us sitting there again, with Sting's high-pitched voice ripping through my room, while André went to town on air guitar. Joost maintained that this was a group that was going to be very big, and it was something very different from the punk shit of previous years. Peter said that 'Roxanne' was about a whore. Laura had a pile of records, but no turntable. Her parents wouldn't let her. When we were together she brought them over in a shopping bag. She was crazy about Tom Petty and the Heartbreakers. I think because Petty was very like Peter, with that long face of his, although he had no curls.

Our conversations have always continued. Peter has been dead for thirty years, but he has never fallen silent. I could compile a second posthumous poetry collection from the things he has said to me since 1982.

I was back at the launch of Peter's *Poems for Anna*, when everyone looked at the muse, astonished that such a thing could just grow, deep in the provinces. They may have been even more surprised by that than by the poet who had been inspired by her. His *Posthumous Poems* had confirmed Peter's reputation. He had gained a cult status among young female students of Dutch, ambitious young poets of his generation, and, in Nijmegen, an obscure poetry magazine was even named after him.

About five times in those thirty years, I have been rung up by a journalist working on a portrait of the poet who died young, or a student preparing a dissertation on Peter. I always put them off, as I did not want to become the exegetist of Peter Seegers, and it also felt as if I did not have the right to occupy myself with his life. In those articles, Laura always played a role as the mysterious beauty in the background, but they never managed to speak to her, either. And because André was never in the picture, Joost developed into the most important source of information on the life of Peter Seegers.

Captain Willem had died two years after Peter's death. Anyone who had seen him at his son's funeral was surprised that it had taken so long. His life had ended with Peter's; he was inconsolable and sank into a deep depression. Peter's mother stayed with him until his death and then vanished without a trace. Peter had occasionally talked of a wealthy Russian uncle who was an art dealer in the Rue de Seine in Paris, so perhaps she had gone there. In any case, I never came across her in articles on her son. His Russian blood, though, was always mentioned: melancholy, life as suffering. Sometimes I felt like calling the writer and telling him how far wide of the mark he was. But that wouldn't have been fair, at least not in cases where I had reacted negatively to a request for help.

I read 'Sonnet for Anna' for the second time, and had to cry. They were tears that come when the alcohol has released your feelings, and you sink into self-pity with a certain pleasure. 'Sonnet for Anna' was the poem that I had read aloud at the edge of the bed a quarter of an hour after the birth of my daughter. We hadn't yet discussed a name—my wife because she had already made her choice and assumed it would be honoured, I because I did not want an argument about the name of my child even before she was born. But now that we had to make a decision, I said I would like to call my daughter Anna. My wife knew the poem, of course, but it had never occurred to her for a moment that one could name a child after a poem, or at least after the woman from a poem. She had her grandmother in mind, who was also assuming that the baby would be named after her. In addition, she knew who Anna was, and a bit about my affair with Laura, although I had never told her all the details.

'It's got to be Jildau,' she said.

It was not the moment to fly into a rage. The doctor who had inserted the stitches had only just left the room, and in the cot lay the nameless wonder. But I didn't intend to give in this time.

'I'm registering the birth,' I said, 'and I'm calling her Anna. It's very important to me.'

Perhaps it was because she was exhausted, but my wife did not insist. A moment later, I decided on a compromise. The child must not have the feeling later that she had been born in conflict and dissention. 'Anna Jildau,' I proposed. 'That sounds good, too.' But she was already asleep.

'Come on through, Dad,' said Anna, once she had sat down at the table.

'All well? Money, career, love, all in order?'

'Yep. Yesterday I had my last exam before the summer vacation.'

'What was it on? Poetry, by any chance?'

'No, language usage. Interview technique. Today's special?'

'Today's special. Do you know the poet Peter Seegers?'

'Heard of him, vaguely. He's dead, isn't he?'

'Yes.'

'Ever read anything by him?'

'No.'

I dove under the table to get the package out of my bag. I presented it to her. She took off the gift wrap and examined the book. She looked from the title to me and back again; I said nothing. I wanted her to draw her own conclusions. She read aloud the dedication on the first page: 'For Bart, my friend, with love.'

'Well,' I said.

'I don't understand. Poems for me?'

I laughed. It pleased me that I had been able to wrong-foot her for a moment. She was not omniscient yet.

'The poems are not for you; you were named after the poems. And of course that makes them a little bit for you, after all. I think I can say that.'

She did not react; she read. And was as if what she read pulled her into another world, the world of Peter Seegers, the world of 1982, the world of her father's youth—I hoped. I saw tears in her eyes.

'How beautiful,' she said, after a while. 'And Peter Seegers was your friend?'

'We would sit together for hours on the roof his parents' boat, looking out over the river. The boat was called the *Sweet Lady Jane*, and it was a floating brothel.'

She didn't respond to that.

'But who was Anna, then?'

'Anna was Laura. She was very close to Peter. Closer than to Joost, André, David, and me. In a certain way, that is. She understood more about him than he did himself, I think. She was his, his ...' I searched for the right word.

'Soul sister.'

'Exactly. She was his soul sister.'

'And so why didn't he call the collection *Poems for Laura*?'

'I think they were originally called that, but she didn't want it. It would have brought the poems too close to home, made them vulgar. You should have been there when the collection was launched. Of course, everyone knew that she was Anna, and people were almost more interested in her than in Peter.'

'Complicated, Dad. Poems for Anna, whose name was Laura. You could have called me Laura. We would have skipped a step.'

'That would have brought it all too close. And I don't think your mother would have been too pleased. Even Anna I had to fight tooth and nail for.'

We ate in silence. After I had paid the bill, she asked if I would put something in the book. 'For Anna, my daughter, with love,' I wrote under Peter's words. When she left, she kissed me and said she loved me.

'I was waiting for that.'

'You're a funny one, Dad. A dead poet, a famous scientist, a criminal, and the director of a travel agency. They do say you can tell a man by his friends, don't they? I think you've got a bit of all of them in you. No wonder you became a journalist. They're chameleons, they say.'

'And a woman who's disappeared,' I said, to complete the set.

'Oh yes,' she said, 'I'm in love, too.' Before I could ask his name, she blew me a kiss and cycled off.

When I got home, I laid the photo from Bédoin on the table and poured some wine. I tried to discover things in the faces; I searched for secret signs, pointers, but I saw six happy young people, friends, unaware of anything, and certainly not of the approaching end—except for one, perhaps.

I thought back to Laura, who in Joost's room had smoked a joint with André and sung 'Army Dreamers' by Kate Bush, in a complete trance, and I remembered the words: 'Mourning in the aerodrome, the weather warmer, he is colder, four men in uniform, to carry home my little soldier.'

'Of course,' said André, when I brought it up later. 'That shit of mine could help you see into the future.'

I remembered how André had climbed on a cow after we had cycled back from a party out of town. He held the animal by the horns as if he were on a bike. The cow mooed plaintively and did not move a muscle. The first morning mists were becoming visible above the meadows, and the five of us sat on a fence. Suddenly the cow started moving and jogged to the ditch at the edge of the meadow, with André on its back. When the animal bent forward to drink, André slid into the ditch, like a ship being launched.

David tipped forward off the fence, Peter had an attack of his exertional asthma, and Laura looked with big astonished eyes at André's head, which stuck out from the waterweeds like a large frog. Joost had jumped off the fence and stood behind us, stamping his feet and producing an indefinable sound, a kind of euphoric lament. I ran through the meadow like a drunken calf to hoist André out of the ditch.

XX

We had drunk coffee and changed at David's. Then, at about ten, we drove southward from Zutphen. It was a mild day in May, with the bright, sharp light that paints a cyclist's body in a single day, the hard white contrasting with the brown.

André had two bikes in his car. He had ridden a circuit around the Zaadmarkt and the Houtmarkt on his father's old Raleigh. 'An important moment,' he said. 'For the first time in thirty years, the tyres kiss the familiar cobbles again.' He pointed to the sky. 'This is the first phase of my personally designed journey of atonement. Old Tank is, of course, looking down the whole time from the bar, and now he sees his old bike riding over the cobbles, with me on it. That'll do him good.'

The evening before, I had eaten with him at the Scholtenhuus restaurant. Joost wasn't yet in Zutphen, and David was at a meeting of local entrepreneurs.

I asked him about his father's death. 'It was strange that I was there, and David, too, and you weren't. David didn't want to say anything about it. Ask André himself sometime, he says.'

First he looked at me in silence for a while. 'My father died alone,' he said. 'I knew the end was near, and wanted to go to him. David calls me. "André," says David, "I've got some pretty bad news for you." I think: old Gerrit's dead. But it wasn't that; not yet, at least. He doesn't want you at his deathbed, says David. At first he beat around the bush a bit. He didn't want people to see him lying there like that, the old racer. I think David was trying to spare my feelings. I say: David, stop bullshitting; a father wants his son to be there when he dies. That's how it's meant to be. Then you can clear things up. You hold each other's hand and forgive each other everything. Okay, André, says David, he doesn't want to. I say: What doesn't he want? He doesn't want to see you again, André. Christ, Bart, I hadn't expected that. He doesn't know exactly what you do, David says, but he knows it's dodgy. I ask: What exactly did he say, David, I mean what did he say, literally? And old Gerrit, my father, said this: I don't want a criminal at my deathbed. Even if it's my very own son.'

For a second, I didn't know what to say, and André was fighting back tears. 'Perhaps my mother might have been able to change his mind, if she had still been alive.'

'Shitty, André.'

'I would rather have been riddled with bullets, Bart. I would rather have been tortured to death by a bunch of Turks. Gerrit, old racer, eh. Those guys know the subtle ways of breaking someone. In his head or in his legs. But I must say, this was his masterpiece. Not to want to see your son, at the cost of a lonely deathbed. That makes you a hard man.'

'Fathers.' I thought of my daughter, of my own father, and of Gerrit Tankink, the king of the criteriums. I didn't know whether to consider it cruel, or the ultimate self-sacrifice. André had chosen the last option.

'Looking back, I think it was his last contribution to my upbringing,' he said. 'A kind of all-or-nothing attempt. From that moment on, I started reflecting. And now it's time for the final reuniting of father and son. I have to do something.'

I admired his radical solutions. His dismissal of conventions, such as the convention of death as the end of everything.

'Death is nothing,' said André. 'Death doesn't exist. All bullshit by people with a lack of imagination.' He ordered another cognac. 'Should be fine. Anquetil did it, too.'

André put the Raleigh back in the boot of his BMW. 'That's for another occasion,' he said. 'It's allowed out for a moment now and then, but not yet for the real work. That will come later.'

David had filled two large bottles with water and grape sugar and put them in the holders. Then he filled the back pockets of his cycling jersey with bars, gels, and two bananas. 'Hitting the wall is the worst thing that can happen to you,' he said.

Joost looked in the reflective window of David's travel agency to check whether his cycling jersey was on straight. It was a nice Bianchi jersey that even met with André's approval. 'It's got style, Joost, I can't deny it. It's great, for an American.' He himself was wearing a marvellous black-and-grey Pegoretti jersey with a yellow collar.

'Do you actually know what that Bianchi green colour is called?' I asked Joost. He had no idea. 'Celeste,' I said.

'Fairy.'

'I thought I was the fairy?' David beat his Rapha jersey ostentatiously. 'All hair, dammit. And sweating already.'

André gave David's belly a friendly pat. 'Come on, let's go. Otherwise David will eat all the goodies before we're out of town.' In fact, David was squeezing the first gel into his mouth.

After about twenty kilometres we got to Bronkhorst. David wanted to have coffee on the terrace of Het Wapen van Bronkhorst, but Joost thought that was ridiculous. He said he was just warming up a bit, and that it was very bad for the muscles to stop again after such a short effort. We rode out of the village over the small cobbles of the Bovenstraat, towards the ferry that would take us across the river.

Before us was the peacefully flowing IJssel, on the other side the first undulations of the Veluwe National Park and the church spire of Brummen. It is a spot where little has changed. We came here a lot in the past. We crossed, cycled north along the river, and then over the bridge back into town. Or we went on, via Voorst, until we could take another ferry to the eastern bank. Sometimes, at Bronkhorst, we immediately took the opposite direction, to Doesburg.

'I propose that, on the way back, we have a beer in Doesburg,' said Joost. Our points of reference were still the same.

I leaned my bike against a bench. On the other side of the river, a car was driving onto the ferry. I could not suppress a melancholy feeling. I realized I was an émigré, and how much I felt at home here. 'I must come back east', I said. 'Every time I'm here, it tugs harder at me. It's as if my genes want to return to their roots. Is that possible, Joost, that there's something deep in your genes that always longs for the place where you were born?'

'It's perfectly possible. Although we haven't found any indications yet. But it makes sense. All that moving about does no good at all. You should simply stay where you are. All the misery in the world is caused by that restlessness, I once read.'

'Nothing has changed; nothing has changed here, for Christ's sake. Except for us, that is.'

'André, let's buy the biggest mansion in Zutphen and live in it together. I'll write, Joost will study string theory, and you the history of the Brothers of the Common Life. David will drop in for coffee every day. We'll cycle a bit, reflect a bit, and let life glide past. Deal?'

'Deal,' said Joost. He drank a mouthful from his water bottle. 'Do you remember, Pol, that we stood here before we went up the Ventoux? And then on to the Posbank. Guys, it moves me, it really does. I should have left the crap alone and not got involved with it.' He suddenly looked intensely sad and kicked a pebble into the river. The ferry was halfway across.

David looked at him seriously. 'Are you okay, Joost? You look bad, man. Or did I run you into the ground on this first stretch already with my fiendish tempo?' Joost gestured as if to fend him off.

'I used to stand here smoking pot,' said André. 'On the ferry. Made me very calm. The thing went back and forth, and I looked out over the river. Everything slowed down. I thought I could touch eternity. I knew the guy who used to run the ferry. He didn't mind. Had the occasional smoke himself. Weak shit, great times. I occasionally considered becoming a ferryman. To and fro. Nice and peaceful.'

'How long is that Posbank climb, actually?' asked David. He popped a bar in his mouth.

The ferry moored, a car and two cyclists moved off, and we put our bikes against the railings. André said hello to the ferryman and asked: 'How's Klaas-Jan? He used to work on this ferry.'

'Dead,' said the ferryman.

André looked surprised. 'Dead?'

'Yes. Must be five years ago.'

'Almost six,' said David. 'December 2006.'

'Okay, six,' admitted the ferryman. 'Six. Time flies. Anyway, it was freezing cold, I remember that. He went down to the ferry in the evening. He took it to the middle of the river and stepped overboard. They found him under the bridge in Zutphen. We had a real job getting the ferry back to shore. Boat traffic was blocked for half a day.'

'Happiness is always on the far shore,' said André. 'You know that, as a ferryman.'

'They'd found a tumour. He had three months to live. So he thought: don't feel like waiting, let's get it over with.'

'Brave,' said Joost. 'It takes balls. And in that icy water, too. Despair breeds heroes.'

I looked downstream. In the distance I saw a small boat approaching, with a big black box behind it. I didn't dare to point it out. André was bending over Joost's bike. He told Joost that he should adjust the derailleur. 'Otherwise you'll pull the chain right over it.' Joost nodded.

We walked onto the quay. I glanced at the river again. Plumes of smoke were coming out of the funnel of the tug. I saw Captain Willem, and on the roof was a blond boy.

David was standing behind me. He was trying to click his shoes into the pedals. He saw me looking at the river. There was obviously more astonishment in my eyes than I intended, because he looked curiously over his shoulder. 'Jesus Christ,' he said. He tipped over to the left, tried to release his foot, and fell helplessly onto the concrete.

A little way off, Joost and André squeezed their brakes. David tried to get free of his bike on the ground. André started guffawing stupidly. 'The initiation ritual,' said Joost. 'I remember falling flat on my face like that outside Bart's door, on that old Gazelle of mine. Just stupidly fell over. Didn't hurt yourself, did you, David?' David shook his head, freed his foot, got up, and set his bike upright. He looked to see if there were any scratches on it. André stood bent over his bike, emitting long howls of laughter. David looked at me.

'Did you see it?' I asked. He nodded.

'Did you see what?' asked Joost.

I pointed over my shoulder at the river. 'A boat.'

'A boat,' said Joost. 'You can tell you've been away quite a while. This is a river and boats sail on it.' The ferry was waiting for a small convoy of a tug towing two flat barges with black oil tanks on them to pass.

'The *Sweet Lady Jane* came by,' said David. 'Willem was at the wheel and Peter was standing on top.' It sounded like an everyday announcement. Joost looked at him with a slight grin. 'It came from the other direction,' he said. 'From K-k-kampen.'

We cycled in single file in the direction of the Veluwe: past Leuvenheim, Dieren, and Ellecom. On the wheel of the three men in front of me, I was taken back to the universe of my youth, and I felt safe.

André rode in front. He had made it clear to David, with a brief gesture, that he must follow on his wheel. Behind David came Joost. On stretches of new asphalt, you heard only the hum of the tyres, a sound that normally evokes a blissful feeling in me, but that today caused a feeling of loss. We did not speak, apart from the odd warning about other traffic. Four guys, cycling. Nowhere is the feeling of friendship and loyalty so strong as with a group of men on bikes. You look out for one another; the strongest does the most work and keeps the others out of the wind. As you pass you touch a back, like a brief caress. You feel the concentration, the attempt to become a single cycling beast, one body, one mind.

Joost turned round. 'Great, eh? Back to the primeval fount of male existence. Hunting together, ahead of us the prey. One for all, all for one.' We were already more advanced in unification than I had suspected: Joost's thoughts and mine had already merged.

I was happy to go on cycling forever like that, at about thirty kilometres an hour. Joost's bum ahead of me, slightly too fat, but that had already been the case when he was 18. The light fell through the tall trees along the road to Arnhem. There was a gentle easterly breeze, so that you had the feeling you were in brilliant form and could ride effortlessly at thirty-five. On the cycle path to Rheden, I moved alongside Joost.

'Any news from your lady journalist?' I asked.

'Are you asking as a journalist?' He kept looking straight ahead.

'I'm your friend, and the one who, in a little while, will take you to the foot of the Posbank. After that, you'll have to do it by yourself.'

Now he did look at me.

'The girl was tipped off about a research project of mine from 1999. I'm supposed to have copied stuff without crediting a source.'

'And?'

'Nonsense, of course. Bullshit from a jealous asshole.'

'And now?'

'Now I've hired an expensive lawyer. I have to do something. The suspicion alone is almost fatal. The tables have been turned. I have to prove my innocence.'

Ahead of us, André looked around. 'You did that back in chemistry class, Joost. With me, the experiments always went wrong, but with you everything was always bang on. I always thought that was suspicious.' He moved to Joost's other side and put his hand on his shoulder.

David did his old Marlon Brando imitation. 'This man, my frrriend, who told lies about you, tonight he sleeps with the fishes.'

Friends.

At the pancake restaurant on the roundabout, André stood on the pedals. 'He's off at once, Tankink the born climber,' he cried. 'He can't curb his urge to attack.' Joost went in pursuit. 'Dammit, David,' I said, 'I'd hoped that we'd cycle up nice and calmly.'

David laughed. 'And you'd really counted on that? With those two? Off you go; you must always go up at your own tempo.'

I accelerated. I saw Joost going around the first bend. Halfway up, after about a kilometre, I caught him. He was pedalling far too hard. André was nowhere to be seen. His training sessions on the Erasmus Bridge were bearing fruit. When I got to the top, he was already waiting by the pavilion, looking relaxed. 'The form is there, you see,' he said. 'Now I've simply got to ask Ludmilla to cook with a little less fat, screw a little more, lose a few kilos, and then this gentleman will go up the Ventoux in under one forty. You didn't do that, Bart, when you were 20.'

'That's true.'

'Great, isn't it? There are not many things you can do better at 50 than at 20, but cycling is one—at least if you smoke and drink a lot when you're 20 and live like a monk when you're 50.'

After a few minutes, Joost reached the top. His face was red. 'Derailleur fucked. Right away. I couldn't change down. And I'm a supple climber, you know that. I have to keep rolling, otherwise I wear myself out. Anyway, better for it to happen here than on the Ventoux. Then you'd be done for.'

It was a long time before David arrived. André was just about to go down to see if he might be lying on the verge somewhere with heart failure, when he came toiling along.

'I don't know,' said David, after he had caught his breath a bit. 'I hoped I had a natural talent for climbing, but that turns out not to be the case. The prospect of the Ventoux fills me with great trepidation.'

'Train, David,' said André. 'And bloody hell, you've got to do something about that paunch. You've got to lose at least fifteen kilos. Starting tomorrow you must go on a strict diet. Otherwise it'll be no good. And you need to get hold of some dope.'

Joost was fiddling with his gears. 'If necessary, I'll buy a new bike,' he said. 'It can't ever be a problem of the equipment. That must be in top condition.' He gave the impression of being more cut up about his derailleur than about the accusations of fraud.

That evening, we ate in David's Italian restaurant on the Houtmarkt. The bottles of wine followed one another in quick succession. 'This was the nicest day since my acquittal,' said André.

Joost raised his glass to Peter. 'To the man who descended quicker than his shadow.'

'Last week I gave Anna his *Poems for Anna*,' I said. 'And I told her she was named after a poetry collection.'

'Bullshit, Bart,' said André. 'She was named after Laura, except that you didn't feel like having to call out "My lovely Laura" all day long. That didn't attract you. And why Peter called her Anna, God only knows.'

Joost had no idea why, either. 'Poets. Never say what they mean. I suspect he found it slightly cheap. Petrarch already had a Laura, and now he would be coming along with another one. Anyway, he said something about it, in his great and mysteriously vanished mountain poem.'

'Floated away on the stream of blood,' said André. 'It's now a paper boat, somewhere on the ocean.'

'I've always thought that Laura has it,' I said. 'There was only one person who, at that moment, must have realized that it had to be preserved, and that was her. I wasn't thinking of poetry, then. I was in a panic. And so were all of you.'

'I was in shock,' said Joost. 'But why didn't she do something with it, then? She could at least have sent it to his publisher, or to Captain Willem.'

'Perhaps because of what was in it,' I said. 'He said it was for her. I thought that was a bit shitty. He could have dedicated it to all of us. But perhaps there were things in it that were meant for her alone, which only she understood.'

'I think she wants us to come to Provence to answer all the questions at last,' said Joost. 'She knows it wasn't right, what she did. Just vanishing into thin air isn't right.'

Laura was back, and we could talk about her in a relaxed way. That's what the day had done. It surprised me.

'Little Laura,' said Joost. I couldn't remember us ever calling her that, but perhaps that was how he addressed her in his mind. 'She was beautiful. I stayed in love with her for the rest of my life. That seems to be normal. Your first great love sets the tone for the rest of your love life. Pretty shitty, actually.'

'She had those real climber's legs,' said André. 'Or am I wrong, Bart?'

'Definitely.'

'Did she wrap them around you?'

'I was just going to ask,' said Joost, with a malicious smile.

'Guys,' said David.

'No, she didn't wrap them around me. She sat on me.'

'I've tried to imagine for thirty years what it would be like to fuck her,' declared Joost. 'But it's difficult; you lack the necessary details. How she feels, how she looks when she comes. And his lordship here knows. Apart from that coming, of course. But as for telling, oh no.'

'And he's right,' said David.

I said nothing.

'I'm still terribly jealous, retrospectively,' said André. 'How was it? Hot? Speak up, man. We're your friends, aren't we?'

'Did Peter know?' asked Joost. 'I've always wondered. Whether he knew.'

'He knew.'

André looked at me. 'Had you told him? Laura?'

'Not me. But he knew.'

'How do you know?'

'I knew immediately,' said Joost, without waiting for my reply. 'The moment I got back to the campsite and saw the two of you, I knew. You can simply see it, in a woman, and in a man, too, for that matter. A rather languorous, self-satisfied look. And Peter was a poet, so he was much more sensitive to those sorts of signals. He of course smelled immediately that his muse had just been thoroughly woofed up and down by his lordship here.'

'She said it to me on the top of the Ventoux. That Peter knew.'

André started laughing. Joost looked at him and joined in. David could no longer stop himself, and slapped André on the shoulders. They seemed relieved that we were finally talking about it, thirty years later. 'Woofed up and down,' sobbed André. 'I haven't heard that one in a long time.'

I got up, walked over to the waiter, asked if he had a cigarette for me, and went outside. A little later, André came and stood beside me.

'Sorry, Bart. In the last few years I've gotten the giggles about much worse things. It's my way; I'm sorry.' I put my arm around his shoulder. 'Doesn't matter, André. I just didn't feel like joining in.'

'Why does she want to see us, Bart? I've asked, but she doesn't reply. She doesn't reply to anything. Does she do the same with you?'

'Yes. I mean no.'

'Christ, Bart.' André took a long draw on his Marlboro and began coughing unstoppably. I slapped him on his back. It took a while before he was able to speak again.

'What was it: did you seize your chance, or was there more to it? Had her choice finally fallen on you?'

'I don't know. I've wondered for a very long time, but I don't know. All I know is that that Platonic bullshit of Peter's was nonsense. A poetic pose. He'd been fucking his muse for at least a year. Actually, it began very soon after she moved here.'

He gave me a long look. 'Do you mean that?'

'I mean it.'

'But how do you know?'

'Madame Olga. I was with them in their apartment, a month before Captain Willem died. We were talking about Peter and his muse. Muse, she said, haha. And the rest, like rabbits.'

'Did she use that phrase, like rabbits?'

'No. She used a Russian saying. According to Captain Willem, it meant something like: his sex lived inside her.'

'I must ask Ludmilla. Were we blind, back then?'

'I think so. Or we couldn't see. Too young.'

We went back inside and joined the others at the table. Joost was already on the whisky. André looked around solemnly. 'Guys,' he began. I looked at him, and he knew what I was about to say: leave it for a bit. 'Life is full of surprises. I just wanted to state that.'

Joost knocked back his whisky. 'Glad you're back, friends,' he said. 'Haven't laughed so much for ages.'

The next day I walked from the Eden Hotel to David's travel agency. He was sitting at his computer. 'Kazakhstan,' said David, pointing to the screen. 'It's the next big thing. Trekking through Kazakhstan, mountain biking through Kazakhstan, on the back of a weird animal through Kazakhstan, you name it.' His lack of understanding for the holidaymaker had only increased over the years. 'There's now someone who organizes a winter's stay in Siberia. He's put up a couple of wooden huts, and you can simulate the winter of the stranded Nova Zembla expedition.'

'With real polar bears?'

'Of course there'll be someone along with a Kalashnikov. And the huts are bear-proof. The bears are expected to show themselves, though, so that they can be photographed. Fully booked for next winter, I kid you not.' He shook his head. 'It's becoming a madhouse, Bart. It already is a madhouse.'

'Thirty years ago, you investigated whether bus trips to the Ventoux might be an idea. Now a couple of thousand people go up every day. You had a good nose for that.'

David shut down the computer, looked at his watch and then outside. A BMW X3 turned onto the pavement in front of the travel agency.

'That'll be them,' said David. André sounded the horn a couple of times, and Joost gestured that we had to hurry.

'Take it easy,' said David, 'he won't run away.' André had leapt out of the car with a supermarket bag in his hand.

Joost was in shorts. After he had got out, he grabbed something off the back seat. It was a white Stetson. David got up and went to the door. 'Jesus Christ. Dr Livingstone, I presume?' He welcomed them warmly.

'It was my father's,' said Joost. 'I thought: I'll just drop by his grave in a bit, and I can take off his own hat to him. The old man appreciates things like that. Good afternoon, anyway, friends.'

André kissed David and me on the cheek. André is the most modern of the four of us, although it may also be the influence of his Russian girlfriend. He laid the bag on David's desk.

'Did you bring biscuits?' asked David,

'You'll see in a bit what's inside,' said André. 'You'll have a surprise. So will the people walking in the cemetery tomorrow.'

'There's a shovel in it,' said Joost. 'André is going to desecrate the grave.'

We went outside. David locked the door, after first turning the sign around to say FERMÉ. We walked across the square, past the church, in the direction of the cemetery. I had walked the route frequently, always behind a hearse driving at walking speed. The first time was almost thirty years ago.

Although Peter's parents were not religious, there was a funeral service. Captain Willem thought that his son had been a spiritual person, and so considered it appropriate to say farewell to him in church. In addition, the thought that Peter might be living on somewhere, and might even be happy, prevented him from going crazy with grief before the burial.

In the first few rows, the prostitutes who had worked on the *Sweet Lady Jane* sat and listened piously to Rev. Hespels, a broad-minded man, who delicately pointed out that the Son of Mankind had had as one of his most beloved followers 'the woman of loose morals', Mary Magdalene. At those words, Sonja, who sometimes sat with us up on the roof when things were quiet, and who had studied biology very briefly, let out a little sob.

The fact that they were there said enough about the special character of the brothel. The girls loved Captain Willem and Madame Olga, and they adored Peter. Some of them had known him since he was 10. The women were well-treated on Willem's boat, and every month Joost's father came by to check them for sexually transmitted diseases, a ritual that was always concluded with the drinking of an expensive bottle of champagne to celebrate the fact that all employees had again received a clean bill of health. If one of them had picked something up, then they drank to the timely discovery.

Peter's publisher spoke of the immense loss for Dutch poetry. Madame Olga had asked if one of us would like to say something. 'Perhaps Laura would like to,' she suggested. 'Peter used to say that she always knew his poems before he had written them.'

David stood in for Laura. He did so in simple words that he had shown us in advance. Because he was speaking on behalf of us, he said. We approved of what he was going to say; only Joost had a small addition. David said somewhere that Peter's ascent of Mont Ventoux had been his last poem, and that he had read that poem aloud at the top of the mountain. He quoted one sentence that had stayed in his mind: 'Life flies past, and never stands still for an hour.'

'That was a quote from Petrarch's *Canzoniere*,' said Joost. 'Perhaps it would be right to mention that.'

'Come on, Joost,' said André. 'You can't tell a Christmas poem from a Shakespeare sonnet. So this is either bullshit, or you heard it from someone. And I've got a suspicion from whom.'

That turned out to be right: Laura had whispered it in Joost's ear, on the mountain, while Peter was reading. 'Playing the Smart Alec while your friend is being buried,' I said. 'Petrarch isn't some minor Dutch poet, just so you know.' When David got to the quote in his address, he pinched his nose for a moment to suppress a laugh.

Peter's funeral procession made scarcely any headway. It crawled through the town, as if a strong hand were holding it back, and with the slow movement of the Oldsmobile from Complete Funeral Directors, time also slowed. It was as if Peter's sojourn above the earth had to be extended for as long as possible.

His father and mother walked immediately behind the hearse; after them came André, David, Joost, and I; and, following us, the sound of the prostitutes' high heels rang out on the cobbles. Peter's father was crying with long sobs, and his mother was probably so full of sedatives from Dr Walvoort that she looked ahead as if she were on the bridge of a freighter in calm seas. She focused on the horizon and saw nothing. She was moving, because the distance between her and the hearse did not increase, but it was scarcely perceptible.

It would not have been so strange if Captain Willem had blamed his son's death on us. We had gone to the Ventoux, we had allowed Peter to climb up it, and much worse, to come down again. And without a scrap of experience. But neither Captain Willem nor Madame Olga mentioned guilt. They did not accept the drama: they cursed fate, but they had no need of scapegoats.

Later, at his request, I gave Peter's father as detailed as possible an account of how the accident had happened. He wanted to know in the minutest detail what had happened, what Peter's last words were, how he lay. I still remember one question: whether there had been a smile playing around his lips, on the verge on the Ventoux.

'I think so,' I said.

We were walking a lot faster to the cemetery than in 1982. Joost tried to pinpoint what had changed in those years, what shops had disappeared, where a new house had been built. I couldn't help him. As soon as I go somewhere where something new has appeared, my head immediately ousts the memory of what was there before. Joost obviously didn't have that problem: he effortlessly summed up the names of vanished shops and occupants, and as soon as he named them, I remembered them, too.

After a few hundred metres, André turned left and we followed. It was not the way to the cemetery, but the Berkelsingel, which led to the Kleine Omlegging. Via the Leeuweriklaan we came to the neighbourhood where André and I had grown up, and to our street, the Gasthuiskamp. Joost had stopped invoking the past; it was as if we were back in 1970, 1975, 1982. Time seemed to merge. André stopped for a moment outside the house where he had been born and considered ringing the bell. Three houses further on—Tankink, Van Vliet, Lammers, Reusink, Hoffman—I thought of the same thing, but didn't do it, either.

We made it into a reunion with time: we peered through the windows of our primary school, we went past Laura's house in the Heetijzerstraat. David said that her parents still lived there—they must be over 80 by now.

'Shall we ring the bell?' asked Joost. He made as if to step over the fence that had lost all his paint. David stopped him. 'Better not,' he said. 'They didn't want to see us before, and now probably less than ever. They've lost their only daughter, and that was our doing. They're complete odd-balls; no one ever sees them anymore. How they stay alive is a mystery.'

'Perhaps they're already dead,' said Joost. 'Let me have a sniff through the letterbox. I recognize the smell of corpses immediately.' We walked on, and came to a small football pitch with miniature goals. André did a sprint and executed the move that, over thirty years before, had made him famous: feint inside, a double scissors, and then around the outside, with the ball at his feet. 'Give me the ball!' he yelled, 'and I'll put it right in the top corner.'

At our secondary school in the Isendoornstraat, Joost went across the playground to the main entrance. We followed him. The door was open and we went in, upstairs to the right, through the hall, past the cloakroom, into the corridor with the classrooms. Pupils were sitting in some of them, but we probably looked like civil servants from the Ministry of Education, as they paid no further attention to us.

Karel Giesma's classroom was empty. We went in. The desks were arranged neatly in rows. Joost sat down in the second from the front, I in the seat next to him. André sat in the back desk of the row on the window side. David waited a moment until we were sitting down, and then swung into the classroom so brilliantly, with lots of soul, that it became 1978 once and for all.

'He's black,' whispered Marga Sap.

'Do you think he's gay?' I asked.

'Blacks are never gay,' said Joost.

'Have a seat next to Mr Tankink,' said Giesma. David went to the spot at the back of the class and sat next to André. A deep silence fell. I wanted to grab hold of time. I knew that I was only a snap of the fingers away from the deep secret that we are constantly shifting through unknown dimensions, and that the past is tangible. Then a man of our age walked past the room and looked inside with surprise. He opened the door and said hello: 'Gentlemen!'

'Hey, Dirk,' said André. 'Long time no see.' It was Dirk Brood, the goalkeeper of André's championship team. 'André!' he cried in amazement. Then he looked at us, and gradually, recognition appeared in his eyes: we had often stood behind his goal.

'What's this, Dirk?' asked André. 'Did you have to keep on repeating years?'

'Caretaker,' replied the man. 'Your father's job. Nice and relaxed.'

'How did you know it was Dirk?' I asked, as we walked back across the playground to the Isendoornstraat.

'Facebook. Everyone's on Facebook. Except Professor Walvoort.'

Two hours later than intended, we reached the cemetery on the Warnsveldseweg. We walked past the grave of my father and mother, Joost stopped by his old man's, and André looked for old Gerrit's headstone. It was a kind of death march. David pointed to the grave of a classmate.

'Leave it, David,' said Joost. 'That affects my feeling of immortality. I prefer all my classmates to go on living for all eternity.' David stopped at the grave we were looking for. 'And what about this, then?'

'That's different,' replied Joost. 'That is a poet who died young. Separate category.'

Peter's grave consisted of a marble slab, on top of which rested a pillar as wide as a pair of shoulders, with his name and dates on it. PETER SEEGERS, POET, it said. NIJMEGEN 24-12-1963—MONT VENTOUX 25-6-1982. His Petrarch quote was engraved underneath.

'I didn't know he was born in Nijmegen,' said David.

'Christmas baby,' said Joost, 'a kind of Jesus.'

'The whores' boat was lying there in the Waal, of course,' said André.

'In 1963 there weren't any whores' boats. He was born in Nijmegen because his mother worked in the theatre there.' Joost looked as if he had revealed an important secret.

'As an actress?' asked André.

'No, smartass. Did you ever hear her speak Dutch? She designed sets. That's why that boat looked so immaculate. She stayed behind on a Bolshoi Ballet tour in Holland and never went back.'

'I never knew that,' I said.

'I heard it from my father. He was on that boat so often that, one day, my mother maintained that of course he was paid in kind for his services. They had a huge fight about it.'

André asked for silence. 'Peter!' he said then. 'Old giant! How's it going?'

A gust of wind moved through the chestnut trees. 'Good, from the sound of it,' said Joost.

'We're standing here,' André went on, 'at your grave. Thirty years ago we were here, too, almost thirty years, I should say, and then you had just died. That stands to reason, because it was your funeral. You may wonder: why are these guys coming to my grave now, when it was so nice and peaceful here just now? Well, we want to share something with you. That's what it's called nowadays. As you will remember, you had an accident on Mont Ventoux. It's on your gravestone, for that matter. You went too fast on the descent, and whoops, that was it. The bike belonged to my father, whose grave is a little further on, God rest his soul. Fortunately there was no damage. A few scratches and a punctured front tyre, that was all ...'

'Don't digress, André,' said Joost. 'Otherwise we'll still be here tomorrow.'

'Peter, old wanker, what is the point? This: in an attack of madness, we—David, Joost, Bart, and I—have decided to set out again for Mont Ventoux. At the invitation of Laura, well known to you ...' He looked at me and I saw that he could not restrain himself. 'Laura, your muse and lover.'

Joost raised an eyebrow, but André simply went on. 'We are going to commemorate the thirtieth anniversary of your death. Instead of just doing that on a terrace in Bédoin, someone came up with the idea of climbing the Ventoux again. And, more relevantly for you, of descending it again, too. Meanwhile, David and I have also become cyclists, so it will be a peloton that ascends and descends, with all the attendant risks. We're sincerely sorry that you can't be with us. It would have been nice if all five of us had been able to repeat the heroic ascent of 1982. But it is not possible.'

'Wind it up!' Joost seemed irritated.

André picked up his shopping bag and resumed his speech.

'Peter, dear rhymester of ours, we'd like you to be a part of this in some way. So I've brought something for you.' He produced an old Raleigh jersey from the bag. 'Don't be alarmed', said André, 'this is not the jersey in which you had your fatal crash. That had to be thrown away, as it was covered in blood, and you know bloodstains are very stubborn. Come to that, it was torn, too. I picked this jersey up cheap online.'

André took a step forward and stood on the marble. He unfolded the jersey and started pulling it over the stone. It was the right size. He pulled it down so far that the narrow top section of the pillar stuck through the neck opening. André rummaged in his bag again and retrieved a pair of sunglasses and a racing cap. The sunglasses fitted exactly over the narrow section, and when he had put the cap on the stone, there was a racing cyclist on the grave of the poet Peter Seegers.

'You were here before,' I said. 'You knew this was possible. And if not, it's creepy.'

'I haven't finished yet,' said André. He took a camera from the bag, and a small tripod.

'No.' Joost looked at him with horror.

'I'm afraid he's going to do it,' said David.

'I certainly am.' André opened the tripod and screwed the camera onto it, facing the gravestone. He bent down to look through the lens and adjusted the focus.

'Come on,' he said. He pushed us toward the stone racing cyclist. A moment later, we were in position: Joost, Bart, Peter, André, and David. Exactly as on the photo on the Ventoux—only Laura was missing. André went over to the camera, pressed a button, and positioned himself next to us again. 'A nice smile from all of you,' he said, and tapped lovingly on the cycling cap. 'You too, Peter.'

Later, when we were drinking a cup of coffee in David's office—and Joost a beer—Joost asked André what he actually meant by that 'lover'.

'That they were going at it like rabbits. As the Russians say: he lived in her little hut on the taiga. Or how did that saying go again, Bart?'

'Leave it,' I said. 'But it's true. Madame Olga once told me. And why would she lie?'

Joost was too stunned to be able to say anything. David looked at me with big, incredulous eyes.

XXI

I drove into Avenue Barral des Beaux and turned right into the car park. When I opened the door, the languorous warmth of Provence surged into the car. The first thing I saw was a sign saying CAMPING LA GARENNE on a wall at the end of the car park. It was still there.

I grabbed the edge of the roof, stood at an angle, and stretched my legs. I saw it looking down at me, no more than ten kilometres away, twenty-one on the bike: the summit of Mont Ventoux.

After I had locked the car, I crossed the road. Joost was sitting under the red awning of bar-restaurant de l'Observatoire, with his back to me as if he were expecting me from the other side, the direction of Mont Ventoux. His mobile was clamped to his ear, and he was talking excitedly—he gave extra force to his words with angry gestures.

A constant stream of men on racing bikes came past, some heading for the mountain for an evening climb , others in the opposite direction, after a fast descent. In the thirty intervening years, Bédoin had become a Mecca for cyclists.

I went over to the table, pulled a chair out from under it, did not look at Joost, and ordered a beer. 'You too, Joost?' I asked, looking at the waiter. I hoped he would be surprised, but that wasn't the case. Joost gestured for me to be patient for a little while longer.

'Right,' he said, then, 'I've got to hang up, as someone I know has just come onto the terrace. No, it's not coincidence. It was arranged. He's simply an hour or so early. Keep me posted. Not too often, because that will upset me.'

He put down the iPhone and looked at me with a neutral expression. 'My lawyer,' he said, pointing at the phone. He was wearing a light-blue shirt, shorts, and flip-flops. A glass of beer was set down in front of me. Joost pointed to the glass; he fancied another, too.

I drank a mouthful. 'Welcome to Bédoin!' said Joost, as if he were chairman of the welcoming committee. 'Bédoin, place of dreams and illusions, of blood, sweat, and tears. Bédoin, where Tommy Simpson looked his last on civilization—to be precise, here on this terrace—before starting the ascent of Mont Ventoux and dying helplessly.'

He still obviously found it a good story.

'Who?'

'Tom Simpson, world champion. I've just checked whether there is any reference to the dramatic events in this café, but that is unfortunately not the case. Bar de l'Observatoire has fallen into the hands of a bunch of philistines who regard an Olympique Marseille scarf above the bar as more important than a portrait of the late, great cycling hero. A barbarous disregard for cycling culture.'

'Absolutely.'

'Commercially stupid.'

'What was it like thirty years ago, actually?'

'I don't remember. Bart, thirty years ago! Thirty years!

Ronald Reagan still ruled America, the Wall was still firmly in place, we were lads, that lady over there at that table was still a virgin.'

'Perhaps she still is.'

'We were 18. Eighteen. What is it? The most beautiful age? The most tragic?' The waiter brought his glass of beer.

'Cheers. Hallowed ground, Bart. Here we got to know life. Love and death. You found love, we found death. And now we're back, God knows why. Let's say the call of the siren.'

'Something like that, Tuur.'

He took my hand and whispered. 'Did you have a good journey, Bart?'

'Very good. Drove here in one go. I felt like a 30-year-old cycling journalist again. And you?'

'Landed this morning at Avignon airport. It took a while for my cycle case to come out of the plane, but then I hired a car and drove over here. At one o'clock, yours truly was sitting on the terrace with his first pastis in thirty years. Christ, it's wonderful.'

'What did your lawyer want?'

'The man is defending my reputation and good name. I'd told you, hadn't I, that they're busy besmirching it? I'm not going to sit back and let them do it. So I've hired a bloodhound. Expensive, but if all goes well, it'll do the trick.'

He made a grand gesture. 'Paradise, Bart. Can you smell the lavender? Can you feel the hot air of the mistral warming your old body? I'm staying here, I've just decided. We were never meant to settle in northern climes. Far too cold and windy. This is our natural habitat.'

'Then stay and think about string theory here. What difference does it make? Brains work a lot better at higher temperatures.'

'Exactly, none of it makes any difference.' He pointed to the Leffe glass. 'These days, they have Leffe as normal. Thirty years ago, you had to be very posh to find a beer here. Let alone a Belgian beer. It's all turning into one and the same. That's fine, and it'll be the death of us, but how can you stop it?'

I asked if he had had any contact with André and David. David was driving with André, after they had dropped off Ludmilla at a girlfriend's in Paris. Joost looked at his watch. 'Half an hour, and they'll be here,' he pronounced, as if he had a live link with André's TomTom.

Exactly thirty minutes later, André parked his BMW with two wheels on the pavement in front of the terrace and beeped his horn. Because of the tinted windows, he was invisible, but he could see us. There were three racing bikes on a bike rack. The right-hand door opened. David got out, stretched, ran a hand through his hair, and turned in our direction. He looked sharp, in a white linen suit and immaculate white leather shoes. He opened the rear door and took a straw hat off the seat. After he had put it on and had polished his vintage Ray-Ban Wayfarers, he walked towards us.

The whole terrace looked at the black man and his imposing entrance: still supple in the hips, even after twelve hundred and fifty kilometres in a car and thirty years in a travel agency.

'Gentlemen. Here we are, then.' David shook Joost's hand and then mine. Next, he pushed up a chair, wiped the seat with a handkerchief, and sat down. 'It's still a tough drive,' he said, as if he drove from Zutphen to Bédoin every weekend. He dabbed his forehead with the same handkerchief. The waiter took an order for two beers and a white wine. 'André is still changing. And fixing his make-up.' A mysterious grin appeared on his face.

A little later, André got out and left the door open. He was wearing a little hat, a pair of black sunglasses, and a dark suit with a white shirt and a narrow black tie. 'One, two, one two three four,' he yelled, and immediately there followed the pompom-pompom-pompom intro and the punchy brass section of 'Everybody Needs Somebody to Love'. The Blues Brothers had come to Bédoin, this time in a solo version. André had obviously practised, and it was as if John Belushi had risen from the dead after thirty years. He had even taken hold of an old microphone. On the pavement, people stood and watched; everyone began singing along and clapping.

When the number was over and André thanked the audience with one knee on the ground, there was applause. Joost whistled with his fingers. André stood up, bowed again, casually closed the door of his car with the heel of his shoe, and came over to us. 'Phew, hot in a suit like that,' he said, fanning himself. He embraced Joost and me.

'Very good, André,' said Joost, pointing to the spot where André had performed his act.

'I thought: I'll put it all in musical perspective. When David, Laura, and I drove down here back then, David had one cassette tape with him. And this was on it. Just after Lyon it started driving me nuts, and I threw it out of the window. This was a way of making it up to them.'

'"Sweet Home Alabama" was on it, too,' said David. 'By those rednecks, Lynyrd Skynyrd. I just mean, it was a very good tape. Shame.'

'Good, guys, very good,' said André. 'At first I had some misgivings, but now it feels good to be here. But where is the girl? Of course, I'd actually rehearsed that number mainly for her. Bart?'

'Laura didn't know exactly when she could make it. Her

schedule in Avignon is very full. But she's coming. She'll let us know as soon as possible.'

'She'd better. It was her idea.'

'It's always the same with those women, André,' said Joost. 'They lure you somewhere with sweet talk, and when you get there, they give you the cold shoulder. They keep the initiative. And we always fall for it. Beer!'

'Mineral water. I'm down to my ideal weight, and that's how it must stay.'

'Christ, André. That Belushi didn't drink mineral water.'

'That's why he's been dead for thirty years.'

I asked why he had brought three bikes with him. 'One is David's,' said André. 'The Pegoretti is for training. But on the big day, I'm going up on the Raleigh. The old man won't believe his eyes. That bike is the only thing I've inherited from him, and I'm doing the ascent for him. With him, I should say.'

'I hope you've checked the brakes,' said Joost. 'And the tyres.'

'All in order,' said André, giving Joost an irritated look. 'Peter will be sitting at the front on the handlebars, and old Gerrit behind. He's never been to the top. It'll be a hard climb. But all the same, I'll leave you for dead.'

'Have you put on a triple chainwheel?'

'Triples are for fairies, Bart. I'll just use the inner chain-wheel.'

David looked with concern at Mont Ventoux, which luxuriated in the evening sunshine like a cat with a white bib. 'That thing is much too high,' he said. 'If you ask me, it's higher than thirty years ago.'

An hour later, Joost and I followed André out of the village. We had bought three large boxes of groceries in the supermarket next to the car park. The cashier laughed at the large quantities of spaghetti that we put on the conveyor.

'Drop by for a meal,' said Joost, but his French was so appalling that she gave him a puzzled look.

A narrow road through the vineyards ended at a large gate. David got out and pressed a few buttons on a panel, and it opened. The house was called Mas des Chênes.

There were wooden shutters in front of the windows in Bianchi colours. There was a swimming pool, surrounded by a lawn and old oaks. In the shadow of three cherry trees was a wooden dining table, and on the terrace, a bench and two chairs were placed around a barbecue.

'Good work, David,' said André, as we subjected the house and garden to a preliminary inspection. 'You can see we are dealing with an experienced tour organizer. You've brought us to paradise. Shame cyclists aren't allowed to swim.'

From one of the bedrooms came Joost's voice: 'Old-fashioned nonsense. I shall have a dip in a bit. Great bed, so if I come across a pretty woman, you won't hear me complain.'

'Cyclists only fuck in the winter,' called André.

'Well, not this cyclist.'

A little later we went outside again to get our luggage from the cars. It looked as if André had decided to move in permanently. Yoga mats came out of the car, a big box of spare parts, and a toolbox. He had brought various cycling helmets, spare wheels, and four boxes of sports drinks.

'I'm just a control freak,' he said, with a guilty expression. 'The thought of needing something here that I've left at home drives me nuts.' He dove into the car again and carefully lifted out something that had been lying against the side, packed in strips of cardboard. After he had taken them off, I saw what it was: the big photo of the six of us on the Ventoux, from his apartment in Rotterdam.

'Just to make it a bit homelier. I know that these rented

places usually have the most atrocious things on the wall. This seemed appropriate. Means that Peter will be with us, in a sense.' André tapped Peter's head and turned the photo to face the house. 'Well, Peter, what do you think of it? A lot better than a miserable little tent, isn't it?'

'What a handsome guy I was,' said Joost. 'Someone like Laura, you just can't understand it.'

'Gone downhill pretty badly since then,' said André. He went into the house, put the group portrait against the sofa, went back to the car, and returned with a drill. 'That's what I mean. You've got to be ready for anything.' A little later the sound of a heavy-duty hammer drill rang out.

Alarmed by the noise, David half-fell downstairs. 'André!' he shouted above the din. 'What are you doing?' He waved his hands to keep the dust out of his face. 'For Christ's sake, you're just drilling into that wall. That's an absolute no-no in a holiday home. There goes the deposit. Jesus, man.'

André switched off the tool and looked at David. 'I've got filler with me. Afterward, you won't see a thing.' He took a Rawlplug and a hook from the toolbox, tapped the plug into the hole, and screwed the hook in. Then he picked up the photo frame, hung it on the wall, and checked at a distance whether it was straight.

'Left-hand side down a bit.' Shaking his head, David opened a cupboard door to see if there was a vacuum cleaner inside.

That evening, David cooked some quick spaghetti with tomato sauce. He had swapped his white suit for jeans, a T-shirt, and a cook's apron. When we were sitting around the table outside, the window of André's room on the first floor opened.

'David, what's the address here?' The voice sounded panicky.

'Why?'

'I've forgotten my father's Caballero jersey. Damn, I just can't understand it. I've got eight sets with me, but the jersey I want to climb the Ventoux in, I leave at home. I've got to have it, otherwise I won't make it. I'll have it delivered by courier. What's the name of this place?'

'I'll give you the address in a bit. But first, come here and carbo-load.'

I lay awake, listening to the strange sounds of the house and the crickets in the garden. In the room next door, I heard André's bed creaking. Downstairs, the door of the fridge opened and shut. That was Joost, who didn't feel like going to bed yet.

I was back. For thirty years, I had avoided this spot. When Hinke said she would like to go to Provence on holiday, I discouraged her. When Anna later conceived of the plan of going to France for a year as an au pair, I hoped that she wouldn't end up in Avignon or Aix-en-Provence. Eventually the whole plan fell through, which didn't upset me that much.

I had declared Bédoin, and a wide area around it, a no-go area. In the years when I was a cycling journalist, the Tour went via the Ventoux a couple of times. On those occasions, I drove directly from the start to the finish. Once, the finish was at the summit near the Observatory. That day, I said to a colleague that I wasn't feeling well, and that I was staying in my hotel room to write my piece. I had a tough time following the end of the stage on television.

I knew it was all nonsense, that the Ventoux had nothing to do with death, betrayal, and love, that I was the one who had filled it full of stories, and that there were no guilty places.

I thought of Laura. How often had I played back and

weighed her words of that afternoon? Finally, I no longer knew what she had said literally, and what I had added as an interpretation. What I mainly wondered, without ever having been able to find a satisfactory answer, was why she had gone to bed with me. Perhaps she had suddenly fallen hopelessly in love. Perhaps she was fed up with Peter's live-in cock. Or perhaps one of those strange developments had taken place for which there is no explanation and which we can only gratefully accept.

The following morning, André had bought baguettes and croissants in the village. He had also brought back a newspaper, although iPhones and iPads were charging up all over the house. 'Bloody things kill my feeling of distance,' he said. 'It doesn't matter to an iPad where it is. It will effortlessly retrieve the paper, even if you're at the South Pole. I find that worthless. Wi-Fi makes travel pointless. I would rather have yesterday's news on paper. That gives you the sense of delay you sometimes need.'

Joost asked where he had picked up those ideas.

'In prison. I can recommend three months or so on remand to everyone. You calm down and you start wondering about things. If we were to make it compulsory for everyone to spend three months in jail every five years, the world would be a much better place. Suddenly, you realize that you mostly fill up your time with nonsense, and that there are only a few essential things. That is a rich and liberating insight.'

We decided not to go cycling yet. In Joost's view, it was better to let the body first become accustomed to the changed conditions. In addition, he had a bad hangover after he had made big inroads into the beer supply all by himself. 'Let's go to the campsite,' he suggested, 'and see if

Madame Ginette is still alive.'

André drove down the narrow path to the campsite and parked by reception. Joost pointed to the right, at the swimming pool. 'Decadent. A swimming pool. With a terrace. Look at them with their espressos. Even good old camping is going down the pan. Boiling water on your Campingaz burner stove and making very nasty coffee, which you still drink up very happily, because you made it yourself. Back then they only had *eau non potable* here. You were aware you were doing something very original.'

'If I'd known that, I would have reserved a pitch here,' said David. 'A lot cheaper, too.'

'Come on,' said André. 'Let's get out. In search of lost time.'

'Christ,' said Joost. 'Read the great classics in your cell, too, did you?'

The campsite had become bigger, but it wasn't difficult to find where our tents had been in the early summer of 1982.

'It was here,' said David, pointing, 'on this hillock. We wanted to be able to see Mont Ventoux, although I didn't have the remotest idea then of climbing it. My van was there, here was the bungalow tent, and there that leaky trekker tent of Joost and Bart's.'

'When I stuck my head out of the tent, I could immediately see the Ventoux,' said André. 'And then I thought: better them than me. But, well, I still smoked, then.'

David walked around and took photos. 'I've never understood the love of the Dutch for camping. Those wretched airbeds. Showering in the toilet hut with a German shitting next to you. Killing yourself on the guy ropes when you have to piss at night.'

'I always pissed behind the tent,' I said.

'Then you're now, more or less, standing in your own

piss.' Joost kicked the dusty ground. 'Look, no grass ever grew again. It's clear. Dope. Your victory is annulled retrospectively and you'll disappear from the records. You never climbed the Ventoux, you were never here before, and your whole Ventoux past is one big illusion. Got it?'

I lay down on the ground, approximately on the spot where the bungalow tent had stood back then, and closed my eyes. I was thirty years and sixteen days away in time, but I had filled the gap with space. I felt how she sat on me. I gently stroked a drop of sweat from her breast.

'Time doesn't exist,' I said to Joost. 'I feel it very clearly. I'm a kind of hands-on expert on your string theory.'

'I saw,' he said, glancing at his iPhone. 'Research has shown that the prick, especially, is a very sensitive instrument. Time and space merge in it. The great secret is hanging between your legs. I think that this hypothesis will one day win me the Nobel Prize.'

I had to laugh: we could still see right through each other.

'How long did it take you back then, Bart?' asked David, with a worried look.

'About a minute, I estimate,' said André.

'One hour forty-eight,' I said. 'Joost, two ten. Do you remember, Joost?'

Joost put his iPhone into his trouser pocket and said absent-mindedly that it was right. 'Think so, yes, I lost track for a moment. At any rate, it wasn't in line with my hypotheses.'

'Such was the state of science in 1982,' I said.

'Of course, there weren't any compact cranksets in those days,' said Joost. 'That's a disadvantage for a *coureur* who relies on suppleness, like me. As far as Chalet Reynard, it was reasonable; after that I blew up once and for all. I think I'd eaten something bad.'

We went to reception. A middle-aged man asked what he could do for us.

'Madame Ginette,' asked David, 'is she still alive?'

'My mother,' replied the man. 'No, unfortunately she died in 2002.'

We walked to the narrow path that led to the village. 'I'm becoming 18 again,' said Joost. 'This is a secret path, a hole in time. Can you see a change? Are my black curls coming back? I can see the first adolescent pimples on Bart.'

André gave him a hard thump on the back. 'All I can hear is your big mouth from thirty years ago. With a trace of that shitty Amsterdam accent in it. Is that hard evidence?'

XXII

André had taken the back wheel off his Pegoretti and was moving the loose chain carefully through a dish of paraffin, after which he cleaned it with a brush.

'Important, eh, clean chain. I've seen my father do this a thousand times. When he had lost, it was because he had had no time to clean his chain and grease it again. It ran more heavily,' he said. He sniffed the paraffin fumes voluptuously. 'Marvellous. I get a kick out of it.'

'My bike guy told me it's actually very harmful, that cleaning with paraffin,' said Joost. 'You take the grease out, and you can never get it in again.'

'Typical bullshit.'

'It's not bullshit. Those chains aren't the same as when your father was cycling. It's fifty years ago, dammit. Nowadays, the grease is injected under pressure.'

'Just go on waffling. For all you know about it. With your bloody spoke theory. Right. Completely clean; in a bit you won't hear it anymore. You'll see who'll ride up that col supple and tight. Your chain must ...' He looked at Joost provocatively before finishing his sentence. 'Your chain must make love noiselessly with the sprockets, said my father. That's how it is, you see, cycling wisdom passed on from father to son. No modern bike-builders or phoney racers can compete with that.'

'Stupid prick,' declared Joost, in a tone that I knew André would not be able to take. He went over to Joost and stood in front of him. He was shorter, but there was an intimidating air of menace about him. His eyes forced Joost backwards. His whole body exuded aggression and willingness to suffer pain, but especially to inflict it.

'Repeat that.' André said it very calmly. 'I didn't hear it properly.'

Joost knew it was serious. 'Calm down, André. I didn't mean it like that. I just meant that more than one view is possible about cleaning the bike chain.'

'I want to hear what you said. You sometimes speak so indistinctly. And with such a shitty accent. Sort of Leiden professor.'

'Sorry, André. I apologize.'

André pointed in the direction of the swimming pool. Joost shuffled backward, in the direction of the water. When he got to the edge, he looked at André pleadingly.

'Do you remember what you said?'

'I didn't mean it like that, man! It was a joke!'

André was almost touching Joost by now. He looked deep into his eyes. Then he gave him a push with his fingertips.

'I know what it was!' he cried, when Joost came spluttering to the surface. 'You said, stupid prick! Haha! You always used to say that when you'd run out of answers.' Still laughing, he went back to the bikes and started taking the back wheel of Joost's bike off. When Joost tried to protest from the water, he just made a gesture with his hand. 'Just stay in the pool, Joost. Swimming is the new cycling. Meanwhile, I'll clean up your chain. The thing looks filthy. That guy of yours should be ashamed.'

The next morning, we drove to Sault along the D1 via Mormoiron and Villes-sur-Auzon. There was excitement in the car. We were about to do what we had come here for—the reason we had accepted the invitation to come here, apart from a few more deep-seated motives connected with death and love, which we, as yet, had no idea how to deal with.

Cycling is concrete and manageable. A bike, a road, a man: nothing could be simpler. In cycling you only need call on the top layer of your brain, and introspection is not immediately necessary. Sometimes exhaustion ensures that images rise to the surface that you had forgotten you were carrying with you, but you can always dismiss them as exhaustion-induced hallucinations.

And now we were thinking only of the first careful reconnaissance of the mountain. We were to ride from Sault to Chalet Reynard, a distance of approximately twenty kilometres. Because Sault is already at seven hundred and sixty metres, we did not have to cover so many metres of ascent. 'The muscles have got to accustom themselves to the constant pressure,' said André. 'Climbing is a different way of cycling.'

Joost said nothing, to be on the safe side, although he had undoubtedly read in some academic journal that climbing is not at all a different form of cycling.

'I think that climbing a mountain on a bike is ultimately unnatural,' said David. 'That's intuitive, but you have to be intuitive with these kinds of things. Rationally, there isn't much to say about them. You stand at the foot of a mountain with your bike and you look up: what is your first thought?'

'Let's get to the top!' André hooted at a group of cyclists to warn them that he was going to pass them.

David, who was sitting next to him, looked at him.

'That's a characteristic difference between you and me. You're ambitious, I'm not. You want to prove yourself, I don't. I avoid problems, you tackle them head-on.'

'You're Surinamese, I'm not. They're relaxed. Sometimes I wish I were Surinamese, too. But then we wouldn't have an X3 with silent air conditioning and a Bang & Olufsen Advanced Sound System. But, of course, that's how it is.' He pressed a button, and Lynyrd Skynyrd filled the space.

'Louder!' Joost started playing air guitar to the first notes of 'Free Bird'.

There was a market in Sault, and tourists jostled around the stalls selling regional products. 'That's what you get when you don't like cycling uphill,' said Joost. 'You go from one market to another, lugging all kinds of rubbish that you then have to eat in the evening. And so it goes, from bad to worse.' He pointed to a married couple. 'Look at that poor guy, traipsing behind his wife. He doesn't know it yet, but he's already dead and in hell.' He waved to the man, who gave a friendly wave back.

André put the car on a piece of grassland just outside the village that served as a temporary car park. Everywhere, men in cycling gear were preparing for the climb.

We had already changed into our cycling kit in the villa. David had one of his Rapha ensembles on, a brilliant jersey with three stripes across the chest, and the text L'ETAPE DU TOUR on it. 'Specially designed,' he said. 'Dedicated to Thierry Claveyrolat, winner of the Albertville-La Toussuire Tour stage of 1990. Look, it says so here. It's a training jersey. When we do the actual ascent in a bit, I'll come up with something really special.'

'Nice guy, that Claveyrolat,' I said. 'Committed suicide. Shot himself in the head. About twelve years ago.'

'Bart, do you have to, just before we begin?' David looked

at his jersey as if he were checking it for bullet holes. 'I shall be thinking of that the whole time. It's lousy for your climbing.'

We put on our cycling shoes, and André locked the car. 'Let's go.' We followed the 'Mont Ventoux' signs and wound our way through the market shoppers out of the village. Just outside Sault, the road went sharply downhill. 'Fuck it,' said David, 'we shall have to come up here on the way back.'

The first stretch of the run was flat, and after a few kilometres, we rode into the hills. We didn't say much. Each of us was checking his body, afraid of the first signs of exhaustion, the first sense that we were actually going too fast.

David had a heart monitor. He kept looking at his bike computer, to check that he was not exceeding the maximum levels. 'Dammit, not by a long way,' he said. 'I can go up to a hundred and forty, and I'm only on a hundred and fifteen. But I wouldn't mind going a bit slower.'

'If you absolutely have to get to a hundred and forty, you've got to pedal harder,' said Joost. David shook his head. 'I listen to my body,' he said. 'Those gauges are just an aid.'

We rode up in silence. It was as if we were stalking the Ventoux from a secret side instead of attacking it head-on via the Forest. We were like scouts trying to discover the enemy's weak flank. We cycled to Chalet Reynard and, via a detour, back to 1982. In that way, I was able to tell myself that it was just a mountain we were cycling up, and not the mountain where my friend had died, and which I had avoided for all those years.

'Nice climb!' yelled André. 'None of those crazy gradients. And beautiful views. Guys, this is happiness. Just cycling. Not thinking about anything, and your eyes on the asphalt a metre in front of you.'

'Twenty kilometres, seven hundred metres of ascent, average three-and-a-half percent,' reported Joost. 'Let's not get carried away.'

'Shame,' I said. 'I was just thinking that I'd improved a lot since 1982, it's going so easily. Are you sure about that three-and-a-half?'

'Yes. If we cycle on to the summit, it's four-and-a-half on average. But we won't do that today.'

'Can we have a break?' David was panting. 'Is that allowed?'

We stopped.

Joost put his bike against a tree. 'Actually, you should cycle without stopping, but because today is a training run, a short refreshment break is allowed.'

'Are you doing okay, David?' asked André.

'Okay.'

'What did your GP think about your climbing Mont Ventoux?'

'To be on the safe side, I didn't ask him. I was afraid he would forbid me. I have the occasional heart flutter. It would be good if I could lose a few kilos, he said ...'

Joost interrupted him. 'You're not going to fall off your bike, are you, David? We're here, finally, to come to terms with Peter's death, if I've understood things properly. So if you keel over, we'll have worked through our trauma, but we'll be left with the next one. We'll be back here in another thirty years. I can't handle that.'

'I'll do my best,' said David. 'And should I kick the bucket, I will state in advance that it wasn't your fault, and that you shouldn't feel bad about it. It's just my own fault. And the doctor's. That lot drive you to your grave these days, instead of insisting on as calm and motionless a life as possible.'

Three quarters of an hour later, we were sitting on the terrace of Le Chalet Reynard with a lasagne in front of us. I did not feel any intense emotions or fears. I had made the mountain bigger than it was, and now I was sitting eating halfway up it, no different from eating a large fried-egg sandwich in Bakkum. David had arrived a quarter of an hour after the three of us. 'My own pace,' he said. 'Important. I realized that today. If necessary, I'll crawl up that mountain like a snail. It'll still be a personal best, anyway.'

I looked at the cyclists coming from the direction of Bédoin and going straight on up the Ventoux. I looked for the spot, but the place where Peter had his accident was not visible from the terrace.

'David,' said André, 'I really think you should concentrate on retro travel with that agency of yours. If you ask me, there's a gap in the market. Taking a trip down the Rhine again, with fun dance music on the boat. Or to the waterfalls of Schaffhausen. Back to normal, you know. Not that absurd nonsense with campers at the South Pole. We've seen crazy times, and from now on, it's going to be like it used to be. Just a week with someone in a beach hut at the seaside. Great fun. I'm already looking forward to it.'

'I don't know, André. I'm a bit fed up with that travel agency of mine. Thirty years is a long time. It's time for a change of direction, but I don't yet know what.'

'Your passion, David. Once you've found that, you can change direction before you can say Jack Robinson. I know from experience.'

'You had some help from the justice system,' said Joost.

'Coke was never my passion; it was a source of income. My passion is old books and old cars, for now.'

'And your Russian sweetheart.' Joost was back at it.

'My passion, I'm still thinking about it,' said David.

'Perhaps I'll find out this week. Because of the oxygen debt in my brain, I'll suddenly see the light in a flash.'

Joost looked at the breasts of the little waitress. 'God, it's beautiful here. Is a glass of white possible? Or is that irresponsible, given the descent ahead of us?'

'You must do as you think fit,' said André, 'but I'm sticking with water. I think alcohol shows a lack of respect for the mountain. You saw what happened to Simpson after one drink. The mountain simply won't take it.'

Joost sighed. '*Une bouteille d'eau,*' he said, with a Casanova smile at the waitress. '*Et quatre espressos.*'

'Laura,' said André. 'I'll give her a call. She should know that we're back on the Ventoux. That we've returned to the scene of the disaster. Not quite, but still. She should know.' He looked up her number and held the mobile to his ear. There was a silence. We heard a voice saying something in Italian. We looked at André. 'Laura, André here. Calling from the terrace in Chalet Reynard. I'll call you later.' He laid the phone on the table. 'That was the first time I've heard her voice since she said goodbye to us in Bédoin. Hasn't changed a bit, not even in Italian. Jesus, what did she scream when Peter was lying there?'

All four of us knew, but we didn't feel like repeating the words.

'Lovely voice,' I said. 'Made for Italian.'

Because I couldn't get to sleep that evening, I decided to go downstairs. For a moment I considered cleaning my bike, but that might give the others the idea that I had gone crazy after half an ascent of the Ventoux.

I went into the kitchen and opened the refrigerator to hold a cold beer against my forehead and then drink it. Behind me, I heard footsteps on the stairs. It was Joost. I grabbed another beer and sat down at the kitchen table.

'Can't sleep,' he said. 'It's going around and around in my head. It's better if I don't lie in bed, because then it gets worse and worse, and I won't get any sleep at all.' He put the bottle to his mouth.

'I know that.'

'What time is it?'

'Two-thirty.'

'Not too bad.' I didn't know if he meant that he had expected it to be later, or earlier. 'That book of yours,' he asked, 'when will it be finished?'

'I should actually work at it uninterrupted for a few months, but that's not possible at present. Perhaps in a little while. I've got to buy days off.'

'Absurd.'

'And you?'

'Me?'

'Yes. How are you? Or is that an odd question?'

He picked up his mobile, looked for a moment, and showed me a text. 'This came this evening.'

'Dear Mr Walvoort,' I read. 'From my American source, I hear that an article will shortly appear in an American journal (*Scientific Spectator*, Boston), which is a report on research into your scholarly production. The article will be sent to me next week. According to my source, it is "devastating." Could I call you about this sometime soon? I have not yet contacted the university. Yours sincerely, Deborah.'

He saw the shadow of a smile cross my face.

'I had the same thing. I almost got the giggles from that "Yours sincerely, Deborah." Someone brings the news of your imminent death, blackmails you in passing, and remains sincerely yours.'

'What does this mean, Joost?'

'This means that I'm going to hang.'

'That you're going to hang? But you had a bloodhound of a lawyer, didn't you? Can't he do anything about it? Surely they can't just accuse you of all kinds of things and ruin your reputation?'

'In that article, it says that I have stolen and copied the greater part of my scientific production of the last five years. That's what it boils down to, at any rate. It comes from a guy from Yale. I had a fight with him back in America.'

'Bastard.'

'Science is an ordinary job, Bart. People are jealous.'

'Does he have a point? Is there any truth in it?'

He was silent for a moment.

'Then I expect it will be in your paper tomorrow.'

'Christ, Joost, I'm your friend.'

'True, what's true? They're not research results from which you can reconstruct how they were arrived at. No one knows what's true in string theory. It's a theoretical reality. So what's true in it? Who was the first to formulate new insights? But even the suspicion of fraud is sufficient to put an end to everything. And if those Americans have a chance to fuck over a European, they won't let it pass.'

Joost got up, fetched another beer, and lay down on the sofa.

'Bloody hell, Bart. And meanwhile, there's also that fuss with Valery. She wants a divorce.'

'Because of this?'

'No, she doesn't even know about it yet. No, just because she thinks I'm a prick, and because I screw a student every now and then. I don't understand a thing about women.'

'No man understands women.'

'Compared with women, string theory is child's play, I swear.' He began laughing loudly, with the long and increasingly loud bellows which, at secondary school, had made him the terror of the teaching staff. If Joost Walvoort started laughing, you could forget the rest of your lesson. Joost's laughter caused chaos and anarchy.

It wasn't long before tears of laughter were streaming down my cheeks, too. I didn't know exactly why, but it was connected with the aggrieved tone in which Joost talked about all the disasters that befell him.

'So, Valery wouldn't even let you fuck students,' I said, between two fits of laughter. 'Unbelievably childish. That woman doesn't understand a thing about life.' Joost crashed from the sofa onto the floor and shook with laughter.

'We'll have another beer,' I said, a little later when he had resumed his seat at table. 'This is fun, like the old days. Shall we wake up the others, too?'

XXIII

Joost slumped listlessly on one of the recliners near the swimming pool. He looked ahead gloomily. He was waiting for a call from his lawyer, but it just didn't come. That was bad news, he said. It probably meant that he was unable to prevent the publication in the *Scientific Spectator*. The reporter called three times a day, and that was also bad news.

'Valery is leaving for America with the girls today, to think things over. I don't know why you have to go to America to think things over, but well. I see a man before me: he's lost his job, his reputation has been smashed to smithereens, and his wife and daughters live across the Atlantic. They've already almost forgotten him. Only when the monthly alimony comes in do they think of him for just a moment. The man has had to sell his house, and now he rents a draughty flat above a hairdressing salon in a lugubrious 1960s district. He sits at the kitchen table and drinks that sour three-and-a-half-euro Gewürztraminer. And it's only nine-thirty in the morning. If you're determined to drink yourself to death, you must start early.'

I threw a grape at him. 'Stop it, Joost. In England, they

call that catastrophism. The tendency to worry yourself to death with all kinds of dreadful scenarios. For the time being, nothing's wrong, and perhaps they'll find out that that American motherfucker copied it all from you.'

That morning, we had gone for a short ride along the Gorges de la Nesque. It was far too hot for a longer trip. Apart from that, David dismounted after thirty kilometres, feeling dizzy. 'Perhaps you should give your doctor a call after all,' I suggested to him. 'Just to ask him if it's sensible to ride up the Ventoux in a temperature approaching forty degrees, as a moderately trained man in his late forties with a weight problem.'

'It's all or nothing,' said David. 'I've simply got to find my rhythm. I'm not used to this top-class regime. But my heart monitor is still working perfectly, so there's no problem.'

From the distance, on the way to our villa, came the sound of a car. André shot to his feet.

'Saab 96,' he said. 'I'd recognize it anywhere. That tack-tacktack sound. My granddad had one. That was still a two-stroke. This is a four-stroke, but definitely a 96. Must be a real oldie. The last one was made in January 1982.'

We looked at the gate. The villa was at the end of cul-de-sac, so the car would have to come to a halt quickly. It was indeed a green Saab 96. It stopped, the right-hand door opened, and Anna got out.

'Anna!' I called.

'Anna!' I yelled to the others. 'It's Anna!' I jumped up and ran to the gate. 'Code 9999. What a surprise!' Anna stuck her head through the bars to give me a kiss. She looked red, and rivulets of sweat were running down her temples. *'Je suis en vacances avec mon ami Lennard,'* she said. *'Il fait chaud.* We had to turn on the heating to cool the engine, or something.'

She pressed the 9 four times and the gate began opening squeakily. I looked at the driver of the Saab.

'Lennard?'

'We're studying together. I'm in love with him.'

The car drove at a snail's pace onto the gravel drive and stopped next to my Picasso. Lennard got out. He was at least two metres tall, he had blond hair with a hairband, and the face of a film star. He was wearing a Boston Celtics shirt, and with it faded jeans and All Stars.

'Basketball player.'

Lennard walked in our direction and put his hand out about five metres away.

'Lennard Lenstra.'

I was just able to swallow the question whether he was any relation to the football icon Abe Lenstra.

'Nice car. Nice sound.'

'Belonged to my granddad. But the snag is the cooling system. And there's a problem with the starter motor. When it stalls, you can't get it going again, and have to push. Try doing that by yourself.' He lifted up his T-shirt, which was wringing wet with sweat.

Anna pulled a face. 'I thought I was going to die.'

We walked over to the others. 'This is Lennard Lenstra,' I said. 'He's a basketball player, and the starter motor on his Saab 96 is kaput. And the cooling system is up the spout, too. And apart from that, he's the boyfriend of my daughter Anna, on the right.'

Lennard nodded in agreement. He and Anna shook hands with everyone.

'That was always the weak point,' said André. 'In Sweden, they obviously didn't need any cooling. The heating in those Saabs was perfect.'

'That's true,' said Anna. 'Is there anything to drink? I'm totally dehydrated.'

David got up. He kissed Anna and shook hands with Lennard. 'Perhaps you'd like to shower and put on some clean clothes. Come with me.' They followed David to the house.

'A beauty,' said André. 'And with a father like you. That Hinke had strong genes.'

'That lad should go to an American college,' said Joost. 'I can use some of my contacts. I can be his agent. NBA, here we come. A new future dawns.'

André gave him the thumbs-up. 'Sounds a lot better than sour wine in some modern suburb.'

That evening, David had prepared the barbecue. He had bought tuna, prawns, and scores of sardines. There were salads, and he had bought a jerry can of rosé from the local cooperative. 'The best rosé in the world. At least that's what the guy who worked the pump said.'

André had put his dock on the windowsill with the aid of an extension lead and placed his iPad in it. 'You look up something on Spotify,' he said to Lennard. A moment later, Joe Jackson's 'Real Men' washed over the terrace.

André glanced from Lennard to Anna with a questioning look in his eyes, as if he suspected a conspiracy. 'Do you know what year this LP is from?' he asked. He did not wait for the answer. 'Do you know what an LP is?'

Lennard said that he didn't know the date. 'My father's got that record.'

'1982,' said André. 'Came out on 25 June.'

'How come you know that so precisely?' Lennard was surprised.

'Because I know the dates of all Joe Jackson's LPs. And because 25 June 1982 is a special date.'

'Oh,' said Lennard. Anna said that she had, after all, told him why we were here. David laid the tuna on the barbecue. Joost tried to fill the glasses from the jerry can. I looked at my daughter, and wondered how I should assess her relationship.

'On 25 June 1982, a friend of theirs had an accident on the Ventoux,' said Anna. 'That was the guy whose poetry collection I showed you.'

'And what are you all doing here now?' inquired Lennard, after a short silence. 'Are you paying a kind of, er ... tribute? Are you unveiling a monument?'

'They are here at the behest of an old friend.' Anna couldn't help laughing. 'Where is she, Dad?'

'She'll be here later. She's a director, and she's doing something at the Avignon theatre festival. And, of course, we're also here for the Ventoux. We want to see if we can climb it faster than thirty years ago.'

'Except me,' said David, turning the pieces of tuna. 'I'm going to see where I drop dead.'

'And except for me, too,' added André. 'Because in 1982 I was still a long-haired pothead.'

Joe Jackson sang: 'Time to get scared, time to change plan, don't know how to treat a lady, don't know how to be a man.'

Anna was standing in the living room, looking at the big photo of the six of us. 'Nice photo.' I put my arm around her.

'André brought it with him. To cheer the place up. But actually to remind us why we're here.'

'And?'

'It's odd, a photo like that. Confrontational, especially since four of the six people are walking around here. And soon there'll be five. They are the same people, but at the same time, they're different. You see what time does.'

'What does time do?'

'Time wears you down. Time changes you. How shall I put it? Who do you see standing there? Your father?'

'No, that's not my father yet.'

'Yes, I am.'

'But you're not my father yet. I'm nowhere yet.'

'Half of you is in my genes.'

'Half an egg isn't an egg.'

'We're actors. Here I'm playing the high-spirited 18-year-old who is just going to climb Mont Ventoux. Ten years later I played the role of the happy father. Now I present myself as a good-looking 48-year-old, with a daughter of 21.'

'But who are you really, then?'

'You must have a good look at me on my deathbed. Then I'll return to what I really am, stripped of everything, the past forgotten, without a future.'

'I don't think it's a very nice view of human beings, Dad. I don't like the idea that you play at being my father. You are.'

'I'm a method actor. I identify with my role to such a degree that I become it.'

'Dad ...'

'I love you, Anna. Love is not a role, it's real.'

'Fortunately.'

I kissed her and was about to walk into the garden, but she stopped me. She pointed to the photo. 'Do you know what I see?'

'Six people aged 18 on the campsite in Bédoin, on 24 June 1982.'

She pointed to Laura and me. 'I see a guy in love. And a girl. I don't know if she's in love with you, too. She has a funny look.'

'Funny?'

'Yes, funny. Absent.'

I tried to see what she meant, but couldn't.

'What happened?'

I decided to be honest. She was doing her best to understand me, and I must not set her on the wrong track. I must not pull off one blanket from the truth, while leaving three more on. 'It was like this, Anna. Wait a minute, I'll get a glass of water. You, too?' She nodded. I went to the fridge and poured two glasses.

'It was like this. Laura, that girl, was the girlfriend of my great friend Peter, the poet. I thought she had a very special thing with him, something I, or any of the other guys, couldn't compete with. Something higher, something to do with poetry and with words that I didn't understand much about.'

She said nothing.

'But in the days before this photo was taken, something happened that I had never expected. I noticed that she was trying to get closer. We were very good friends, mind you, and I'd been in love with her for a long time, like the others. I was jealous of Peter. But now I noticed that she was coming very close. She touched me when she didn't really need to; she looked at me differently.'

'Perhaps she was just in love with you, or with both of you.'

I hesitated for a moment. I could leave it at that. There were things that were so intimate that you didn't have to share them with everyone, and especially not with your daughter.

'Four hours before this photo was taken, we went to bed together, as they say. Joost was cycling with Peter. André had gone with David to see some canoe-hire place, and the two of us were left alone on the campsite. The campsite here in Bédoin, La Garenne. I can still show you the exact spot.'

'No need.'

'That's where it happened.'

'And Peter?'

'I'd resolved to tell him after the ascent of the Ventoux. By then he was dead, of course. But he knew.'

She ran her hand through her hair.

'There's something else,' I said. 'We thought that Peter and Laura didn't go to bed together. That they had a different kind of relationship, something poetic, platonic. But that wasn't the case.'

She kept looking at me.

'After Peter fell and was killed, she travelled back to Holland. Alone. She wasn't at the funeral. She had vanished without trace. Her parents knew only that she'd gone to Italy and wouldn't be returning for the time being. I knew she intended to study in Perugia for a year. I never saw her again. She completely disappeared from my life, and from that of the others. Until this spring, that is.'

I could see that she was trying to understand Laura, the woman who was named Anna, to whom she owed her name. She was only a couple of years older than Laura was then. 'She was Peter's muse, they went to bed together, and yet this happened between you. And when Peter died, she disappeared. Why?'

'That's been my big question for years, and I hope I'll get an answer here.'

'Something must have happened between her and Peter. Something terrible that meant she had to break irrevocably with him. By going to bed with his best friend, for example.'

'Do women do things like that?' I heard myself put the question to my daughter, of all people. I was getting old.

'Yes, and men, too, for that matter.'

Perhaps she was right.

'Why didn't you go and look for her?'

I said nothing, because I didn't know the real answer. Because I am someone who resigns himself to circumstances, who never disputes the course of events. A fatalist.

'Why did she bring you all here? Come to that, why isn't she here yet?'

'She's directing at the Avignon festival. You can't get away just like that. She'll certainly be coming. And then we'll find out why.'

'Surely you can just give her a call?'

'Do you know what it is, Anna? It's spooky calling your own past. Wait until you're the same age as I am now. Anyway, the past never answers.'

That evening I tried, and suddenly heard her voice. We made a date.

XXIV

My telephone rang, and I saw it was the paper. I knew what they were calling about.

'Yes, I know him,' I said. 'But it's a long time ago. Secondary school. Since then we've lost sight of each other a bit.' I looked at Joost, who was calmly swimming lengths in the pool. 'No idea where he's hanging out now. Nice friends, yes. Coke dealers and scientific charlatans. Anyway, I don't think it would be kosher for me to give you a portrait of him, anyway. Apart from which, I'm on holiday. Who? Okay, tell her to call me if she needs to know anything. A nice anecdote about copying in class, or something.'

'Thanks,' yelled Joost. 'Charlatans, good word.'

'Be grateful I didn't pass the phone straight on to you. Here he is. Ask him yourself.'

'What are they going to do?'

'A big profile of the fallen scientist. With quotes from old friends, who just can't imagine how. And from colleagues who'd had their suspicions all along.'

'They're all disengaging from me. Terrified that they'll be dragged down. They're all checking if they have ever done anything with me, or ever quoted me. I am badly infected. Before the rooster has crowed thrice, they'll all have denied even having known me.' He dove.

Anna came strolling along in a dazzling bikini, and Lennard walked behind her with a basketball in his hand. What he was planning to do with it was not clear to me. There was no basket anywhere. He read my mind.

'To get a feeling for the ball. I have to have the ball in my hands for at least an hour a day. Don't need to do anything with it apart from that. Just feel. My hands and the ball must fuse together.'

'Harvard, Yale, Brown, Princeton, you name it,' cried Joost. 'I think that last year Harvard was basketball champion in the Ivy League. Say the word, and I'll put you in touch with the people you need.' Lennard bounced the ball on the edge of the pool. 'If I go, I won't go to one of those stuck-up universities. For basketball, you need to be elsewhere. Michigan State, North Carolina, Duke.'

'I'll go along,' said Anna. 'Cool!'

Joost lay on his back. 'Anyway, they'll see me coming at Harvard.'

Anna came and sat next to me.

'Have you already been to the scene of the accident?'

'Not yet. We'll do it later.'

'It's why you've come, isn't it?'

'Us coming here is a bright idea of Laura's. But, of course, we also liked the idea of coming back. Perhaps you'll like the idea, too, in thirty years' time.'

'What do you talk about all day?'

'You can hear. Bikes, women, Mont Ventoux, David's travel agency, old cars, coke dealing, Joost's problems, cleaning bike chains ...'

She shook her head impatiently. 'I mean things that matter. The reason you're here.'

'We're here to climb the Ventoux. Among other things, that is.'

'Would you all have been here if Peter hadn't died?'

Joost was sitting dripping on the edge of the pool.

'My daughter never gives up. She doesn't ask, she demands answers.'

'Give them, then,' said Joost.

'Yes, give them, then,' said André.

'Okay. The answer is no.' I immediately began to doubt if that was true. 'Or yes. Yes or no.'

'Dad!'

'Perhaps things would have gone differently,' said André. 'A particular decision, a particular event, which initially you don't even see as that important, may ultimately have great consequences. Where did you meet Lennard?'

'He came and sat next to me in a modern literature lecture.'

'Why?'

'He was late, and there was no room anywhere else.'

'That's what I mean. And now you have a relationship, and perhaps from that relationship will come the man who'll save the world. Just for example. Or who finally triggers its downfall.'

'I sat next to her because I saw an empty place beside a pretty girl. Does that count?'

'No, Lennard, my boy,' said André. 'That's goal-orientated behaviour. I'm talking about small coincidences with big results.'

'Like someone being killed on a mountain,' said Anna. 'Would you not have become a coke dealer if he hadn't fallen?'

I was glad that she was directing her interrogation technique at André, for a change. He looked straight ahead reflectively. 'That would have depended on other small coincidences, in turn. But if Peter hadn't died, that might have had consequences for my choice of profession, certainly.'

'You wanted to study archaeology, didn't you, André?' Joost joined in the conversation.

'Yes, or non-Western anthropology. That was also very popular at the time. I hadn't completely decided. I had given myself a year to think about it calmly. That eventually turned into thirty. I've nearly decided, now.'

'And you, Joost?'

'I would have become the first professional racing cyclist with a doctorate. It's fatal, experiencing something like that so early in your career. I would probably have become a real wimp on descents. That immediately puts you out of contention. Shame.'

'You'd still have started working with vague strings,' I said. 'Even if the whole Ventoux had collapsed. Some lives develop along lines as straight as steel wire.'

'Until they get rusty.'

'I would have become the director of a travel agency,' said David. 'A small travel agency in the east of the country.' He put dishes of small fish in vinegar, sun-dried tomatoes, and roasted peppers on a side table. 'Dig in, friends.'

André had put the Saab on the stone terrace in front of the house and was hanging over the open hood. Lennard was standing there a little awkwardly, handing André tools. 'Open-end spanner eight,' said André. Lennard looked in the toolbox and gave André the spanner. 'That's a ring spanner. Open-end spanner! Never souped up a moped, Lennard?'

'Nope. What's that, a moped?'

'Unbelievable.'

Joost and I were ready for a short training run. David

had taken a day off training, and André wanted to test himself in the Forest. Because we didn't feel like it, he went later in the day by himself. It was hotter then, too, and he could 'go deeper'. Anna was still in bed.

'Cross-head screw,' said André.

Ten minutes later, he started the Saab's engine. He pressed the accelerator a couple of times and let the engine idle. He accelerated hard a couple more times, let the engine cut out, and started again. 'Like a dream,' he said.

XXV

Lennard parked his car in front of Café Le Relais du Ventoux and turned the music down. I bent back and kissed Anna. 'Have a great holiday,' I said. 'It was very sweet of you to drop by.' I put out my hand to Lennard. 'Careful with my daughter, please, I haven't got a spare.'

'Of course, Bart. Thanks for the hospitality. It was cool. Come and see us play.'

'I will. Certainly now that it's your last season in Holland, if I understand Joost correctly.' I got out. Anna sat next to Lennard at the front. She looked at me. 'She's sitting at the second table on the left. I recognize her from the photo. Beautiful woman, Dad.' She pointed past Lennard to the terrace. I bent forward and kissed Anna on the cheek through the window. 'Text me when you're there.' She nodded; Lennard turned up Mumford & Sons and put his foot on the gas.

It was strange to see Laura sitting there. She was reading *La Repubblica*. She hadn't changed in thirty years, an eternal girl of 18, and I hadn't expected ever to see her as an older woman. Her photo on Facebook had prepared me a little, but now that I saw her in the flesh, I was still shocked.

The feeling that I was travelling through my past became even stronger.

She looked up and smiled. I realized she must be thinking exactly the same thing, and that in her mind, too, the young Bart was being replaced by the most recent version. She was wearing a white skirt and a blouse in various shades of red. She was lightly made up, and her hair was exactly the same as thirty years ago: shoulder-length and falling in an elegant wave along her face. I was suddenly very aware of myself, of the way I was looking, of how I moved and how I walked the last few metres toward her. I saw myself in slow motion; I tried to keep myself under control, gave myself director's notes, felt an artificial smile, considered in a split second what my opening words should be—I became, once more, the insecure adolescent greeting the prettiest girl. For a moment it was as if time froze, as if both of us were pausing for a second before the big moment.

'Laura.'

'Bart. Beautiful daughter you've got.'

I embraced her and kissed her on the cheek. She kissed me back, and I felt the shiver that went through her body; I held her by her shoulders and looked into her eyes.

'No tears,' she said. I hadn't realized that tears were running down my cheeks.

'Sorry. Sentimental old fart.'

'You always were. I thought it was sweet.'

'You haven't changed a bit.'

'You mustn't lie to elderly ladies.'

'You're just as beautiful, I mean.' I felt the man of 48 slowly but surely returning to me. We sat down.

'God, I think this is fantastic.' The waiter stood waiting patiently, as if he knew he was a witness to a special reunion. We ordered two cappuccinos, and looked at each other without saying anything.

'I've finished in Avignon.'

'How was it?'

'The audiences are difficult there. We were in the Palais des Papes, the great showcase of the festival. We played in French, but we're Italians. That makes it difficult. On the first night, by halfway through the performance, a third of the audience had left. And they don't do it in polite silence; it's accompanied by a lot of shouting. It's a battle.'

I asked what the play was about. I realized that I could have looked it up on the Internet, and that I was again immediately showing my churlishness, and how interested I really was in what play she had directed.

'Il ritorno,' she said. 'The Return', by Sergio Pierattini, best young playwright in Italy. Great piece. Once a few positive reviews had appeared in the papers, it got better. And at the last performance, we had thunderous applause that lasted for a quarter of an hour.'

'Are you tired, now?'

'A bit.'

'When are you coming to the villa?'

'Tomorrow.'

'Okay.'

'I'm sorry I couldn't come before.'

We drank up our coffee. 'Let's walk a bit,' she said, putting a five-euro note on the table. 'Talking as you walk is easier.' I was glad I sensed uncertainty in her, too.

We crossed the street. I pointed in the direction of the campsite. 'La Garenne', I said. 'We've already been. It's much bigger now. There's even a swimming pool.'

She smiled. 'I don't think I want to see that campsite again. Some things must stay as they are in your memory. That's difficult with people, but with campsites it's possible.'

We walked past the shops. She stopped by a stall, dipped a piece of bread in a dish of oil, sprinkled a little salt over it, and tasted it. The man on the stall gestured for me to taste, too. He refilled the dish.

'*C'est délicieux*,' said Laura. She handed a half-litre bottle to the man and took her purse out of her bag.

'Allow me,' I said, and handed the man another bottle. She gave him a fifty-euro note and said: '*Les deux*.' The man put the bottles in a plastic bag and we walked on.

Suddenly, she put her arm through mine. I was amazed at how quickly intimacy can return. It was as if she were looking for support.

'What did you think when you got my message?'

'News from the other side. She's still alive. It wasn't an illusion; my memory didn't deceive me. Laura exists. But mostly I was poleaxed, to be honest.' She looked at me. 'I thought I had long since disappeared from your life,' I said. 'Forgotten and buried. And the others, too. David was as surprised as me, and André, too. And you should have seen Joost's face when he got your texts. Totally flabbergasted. Started stuttering all over the place.'

'It was impossible to forget all of you, even if I had wanted to.'

'But you didn't give a peep for thirty years?' I did my best not to make it sound reproachful. 'I mean: a message like that, of course, comes as a surprise.'

'I understand that.'

'I didn't know you were called Guazzi.'

'No, you couldn't know that.'

'Laura?'

'Yes.'

She knew what I wanted to ask. A smile played around her lips. I couldn't determine whether it was melancholy or, on the contrary, betrayed some inner amusement.

'Have you ever wondered what happened to the five of us, after Peter's death?'

'I still wonder. Why there suddenly seemed to be no future for the five of us, and why ...' I had to stop for a moment.

'Why I ran away from you.'

'Is that what it was?'

'Yes.'

'Well?'

She didn't reply, and I felt I shouldn't insist. If she had run away from me, she had had a good reason.

I took out my iPhone and searched for a photo. I stopped under the awning of a bakery, as the photos couldn't be seen in full sunlight. When I had found the photo we had taken in the cemetery, I gave the mobile to Laura.

She looked at the photo and then questioningly at me.

'At Peter's grave. We put a cycling jersey and a cap on him. At least, on his gravestone. It came to us when we were cycling. André made a short speech ...'

She looked at the photo again and then she came up to me, put her arm around me, and started crying. Silently, but her whole body was shaking. I stroked her back. I had hoped that she would find it funny, but I had forgotten for a moment that she had not been at Peter's funeral, that she had never seen the grave, and that, for her, Peter was still a young poet and a bleeding corpse on Mont Ventoux.

'Sorry,' I whispered. 'Sorry, that was insensitive of me.'

'No, it doesn't matter,' she said. 'I don't know why I suddenly have to cry. Not because of that photo. Because of us, I think. Because of poor Peter. Because I'm tired. Come on, let's walk a bit further.'

We walked to the spot where she had parked her car. She had one last appointment in Avignon. When we said goodbye, she kissed me. 'I'll see you tomorrow, dear Bart.

Prepare the others for the arrival of an old lady.' It was as if she wanted to say something else, but she said nothing. She started the engine, put her hand up, and drove off. I stood there for at least a minute. A lady coming out of the supermarket with a full trolley asked me if everything was all right.

'*Oui*,' I said, '*oui, ça va.*'

I crossed the street and walked past the shops like a sleepwalker. When I came to a kiosk, I saw a Dutch daily in the rack. It was that day's paper. I took it out and read the main headline. At the bottom of page one was a photo of Joost, and next to it the headline: 'Professor Fraud'.

XXVI

I went into the kitchen. David was topping crackers with *rillettes de veau*. 'Right on time,' he said. 'I'm working on the doping. Just take it and don't ask any questions. You'll fly up that mountain.'

I wanted to say something, but didn't know where to begin.

'Is there something wrong, Bart? You look a bit unhappy, and you've bought a paper.' I shook my head: I had to play for time to think. André and Joost were sitting at the kitchen table, looking at Joost's laptop.

'Citroën DS,' said André, pointing to a photo. 'Built between 1955 and 1975. Launched at the Paris Motor Show in October 1955. In the first quarter of an hour, there were seven hundred and forty-three orders, the first day twelve thousand, and the first week eighty thousand. Total panic at Citroën: they had no idea how they were supposed to produce those kinds of quantities quickly. Success catches you unawares. The thing had been made by technology fetishists and designed by a sculptor, Flaminio Bertoni. Suddenly, they turned out to have created a symbol of beauty, modernity, and innovation. The philosopher Barthes wrote: 'it is as if it has fallen from heaven'. Marvellous car; according to some, the most beautiful ever made. I wanted one from my year of birth, 1963—preferably one made on my birthday. But that is difficult to trace. A French Citroën freak is, at this moment, busy determining the date of manufacture based on chassis numbers.'

Joost looked at him as if he were in a lecture. I popped a cracker in my mouth and listened. I was still holding the paper. It felt like a hand grenade.

'A million and a half were made,' said André. 'Not a particularly large number. But there are still tens of thousands driving around. If you want to show people you're not common, that you have a sense of beauty and tradition, and have a bit to spend, you buy a DS. Preferably a convertible, as they're really rare.' Joost typed in 'Citroën DS convertible' and pictures of open-topped Citroëns appeared.

'The founder of Citroën was André-Gustave Citroën,' I said. 'He was the son of the Amsterdam diamond merchant Levie Citroen. Without the two dots. The grandson of a lemon-seller. In 1873, Levie moved from Amsterdam to Paris. So, actually, Citroën is a Dutch make.' I don't why I said that. Perhaps because it gave me some breathing space.

'Nonsense,' said Joost. 'You might just as well call a department store chain like Vroom & Dreesmann German.'

'So that's why you always drive Citroën,' said André. 'Pure nationalism. If DAF still existed, you'd have come here in a Daffodil. One like Laura's father had. Variomatic.'

'I wonder when she's coming,' said Joost.

'Tomorrow.'

'Have you talked to her?'

'Yes.'

'Christ! Where?'

'Bédoin. So, she's coming tomorrow.'

'Out with it!' Joost sounded excited. 'How does she look? Making secret assignations, are we? Are you at it again?'

'Actually, I should drive a Peugeot,' I said. 'Peugeot is Protestant. Citroën is Jewish, Renault is Catholic.'

'Cars don't have a religion. What did she say?'

I felt sorry for him. He was, once again, the Joost Walvoort of the dinky toys we used to play with in the big living room of the doctor's house on the Jacob Damsingel. It was as if he were making a last-ditch attempt to recover his innocence. The boy's dreams. The carefree air of life without yesterday and tomorrow.

The sword of Damocles was hanging over his head, and I held it in my hands.

'I'm looking for a specimen of this car in good condition,' said André, as if he hadn't heard a thing. 'Peugeot 203. The last one was made on 25 February 1960 in Sochaux. On a Thursday. That's the one that I want. Or, at a pinch, the penultimate one. But, well, try finding it.'

'Fascinating, this,' said Joost. 'I should have gone into drug dealing, too. At least you can afford such a smart hobby. Bart! Don't stand there looking so stupidly at me. Have you been to bed with her *again*?'

I was scared. Joost looked at me inquiringly. 'Hey,' he said, 'you've brought a paper with you. Let's have a look. A real paper makes a nice change, now and then.'

I looked him straight in the eye and laid the paper on the table in such a way that he immediately saw his own photo.

'Fuck.' He said it quite calmly. 'Fuck.'

André had turned the paper towards himself and read the headline. He gave me an angry look. David came to the table and picked up the paper.

Joost got up. He was deathly pale. He looked at us, but

said nothing. Then he went outside. Through the window, we saw him pick up one of the plant pots at the edge of the lawn and smash it on the paving slabs. A little later, he stood shouting into his mobile. He held the phone right in front of him and barked into it as if he were face to face with his rival from Yale. He was silent for a second, probably in order to listen to what was being said on the other end of the line, and then threw the mobile into the pool with a firm baseball pitch.

'They can't take that treatment,' observed David. 'But it's a beautiful, powerful gesture.'

'An old, university-issue phone,' said André. 'He certainly won't throw his own iPhone in the water.'

David went outside and we followed him. Joost looked at us, bewilderment still in his eyes.

'What good is a lawyer like that to me? The guy can't even stop these kinds of stories. It's outrageous, isn't it? I've already been crucified, although nothing has been proven.'

'Joost ...' I could see he was in panic.

'I'm being slaughtered. They're cutting off my balls and letting me bleed to death in the gutter. Bye, Joost, with your big mouth. Nobel Prize Joost. I'm nothing, anymore. In Japan, I would have to commit hara-kiri now.'

'Hara-kiri is not necessary here,' said André. 'Which is one piece of luck.' No one laughed.

'How is it possible, Joost?' I asked.

'How is what possible?'

'This.'

Joost looked at me despairingly. So despairingly that I was immediately sorry I had asked the question. I should have inveighed loyally against the enemies who had been out to get my friend.

'I mean, of course they're all bastards, but ...'

Joost spread his arms in a gesture halfway between an apology and an admission of guilt.

'Shit.'

David gave him the coffee he had left in the kitchen. 'Surely they can't just crucify someone?'

'Happens.' André started tapping his mobile. 'I've got a really good lawyer for you. Not some weak bungler.'

'I'm going to hang, André. I took risks, and now I'm going to pay for it.'

'Joost, man, you're simply admitting your guilt. What you have to do is deny it until your last breath. Here, do you have a pen?'

'Leave it, André.'

We looked questioningly at him. 'It's cheating until you get caught.' He put the coffee on the table and went away, into the house.

'I don't understand a thing', said David. 'How is something like this possible?'

'Do you know why racing cyclists use dope?' asked André. 'To win, to become famous and immortal.' He paused for a moment. 'Sucker.'

'It was impossible that he wouldn't get caught,' I said. 'He must have known a moment would come when he would get into trouble.'

'Every person imagines they're invulnerable,' said André. 'Tell me about it. All around me, people were getting caught. By the law, or by the competition. But they won't get me, I thought. Not me. That's what Joost thought, too. You guys would have thought the same. The others, not me.'

'Actually, he's already committed hara-kiri,' said David.

We went inside. Joost was not in the room. We heard a regular 'tock' sound against the wall of his room. Then we heard the sound of a glass smashing on the flagstones. David knocked on the bedroom door. 'Walvoort?' Joost didn't react. We did hear him walking about, though.

'Joost,' said André, 'perhaps you copied a few things. What difference does it make? We all do it, sometimes. For us, it was completely new. And for us, you haven't fallen off your pedestal. You're our friend and you'll always be our friend.' No answer.

We decided to leave him in peace. I got a book, but didn't read anything. André had laid a yoga mat in the grass and was trying to fold himself in two. David was scooping leaves out of the pool. After a few minutes, he retrieved Joost's mobile triumphantly from the net.

'I bet they hung up,' said André, with his head between his thighs.

The next morning, Joost had disappeared. His things were still in his room, but he himself was nowhere to be seen. We couldn't call him, either. His bike was still in the shed.

'Should we be worried?' asked David.

'Joost isn't the sort of guy who jumps in front of a train.'

'There isn't a train here, anyway, Bart,' said André.

We went on with breakfast in silence. When we'd finished, André suggested going to Bédoin and having a walk through the village. 'Check the gutters. See if he's in one.'

'Not for too long,' I said. 'Laura's coming this afternoon.'

We walked once up and down the main street of Bédoin, turned without thinking onto the path to the campsite, and did the rounds of the tents and caravans. After a coffee at Le Relais, we went back to the villa.

'You'll see, Joost will be lying nicely by the pool,' I said. But he wasn't.

'Police?' asked David.

'Don't be daft,' said André. 'Next thing, you'll see Joost featuring in some French missing-persons programme on TV. The man left the house in a state of extreme stress. Stay calm. He'll turn up again, soon.' He put the television on. We saw a peloton riding past fields of sunflowers.

'Boring Tour,' I said. 'The Dutch have given up and the Brits have sent a computer-driven team. According to the programme, Wiggins must win, so that's what will happen.' André stood and watched for a moment. 'They don't take enough drugs, nowadays. In the past, they swallowed something and went onto the attack, but that's not allowed anymore. I'm glad my father doesn't have to experience this.'

David was leafing through a telephone book. 'If he's not back before six, I'm calling the police.'

Two hours later, we heard a car arriving. David turned on his recliner; I lowered the sound on the television and got up. André put the cloth he was using to clean his bike on the ground.

It was Laura. Next to her in the convertible sat Joost. We stood there like a three-man reception committee. We were relieved at his return, but did not show it. André and David were looking at Laura with curiosity, though they tried to hide it as best they could.

Joost got out. 'Well, if it isn't Joost,' said André. Joost looked as if he had been run over by a train after all, and raised his hand.

'I brought a hitchhiker,' said Laura.

'I was about to say that I don't get in cars with strangers,' said Joost, 'but then I saw.'

Laura went up to André. 'André, how unbelievably great to see you again.' She hugged him. Then she did the same with David. 'David,' was all she said. 'David.' He held her rather awkwardly. 'Dear Laura,' he said.

'Where have you been, Joost?' asked André. 'We were worried.'

'Sorry,' said Joost. 'I just couldn't stand being here. I had to be alone. I walked for about six hours, and just as I was thinking about going back, a convertible stopped next to me.'

Laura nodded in confirmation. 'I recognized his way of walking—unbelievable, isn't it? I could see only his back, but I knew it was Joost. I stopped, and he says: "Hey, Laura." As if he had expected me to pick him up there.'

'That's how it felt. I saw her and thought, hey, there's Laura. Right on time.'

'Good timing, after thirty years,' said André.

A little later, we were sitting round the table under the grapevine. Laura told us how things had gone in Avignon. André briefly summarized how his life had gone since 1982. David added a few notes on the life of a travel agent. Joost said nothing: he had obviously filled her in during their drive to the villa.

'Now, tell us.' David poured Laura a glass of wine. She looked at him in surprise.

'Yes,' said André, 'exactly what has happened to you since June 25, 1982? You might as well begin with June 26.'

XXVII

We had put on our cycling kit and were getting ready for a short circuit. 'It's important to do a bit every day,' André explained to Laura. 'The muscles must be toned up for climbing. That's how we work our way up to peak form.'

'I'll try to lose another fifteen kilos or so, today,' said David. 'So I can go up the Ventoux later as if I'm on wings.'

Laura had stayed over, having drunk far too much to be able to drive back to her hotel. Besides, the old magic that had brought us together three decades before had taken effect again almost immediately. The circle was closed, we were complete, and it would have been illogical for her to go. In addition, David had already prepared her room that morning. 'Of course it's no accident that I rented such a luxurious villa with six bedrooms.' But she did not need convincing.

David laid bottles of water in the back of Laura's car. 'Great that we finally have a back-up car. Now, at least we have the option of calling it a day.'

We rode to Bédoin, and from there took the Route de Malaucène. Before us lay the Col de la Madeleine, a mere hill compared with the Ventoux, but very suitable for cranking up climbing confidence. That was what Joost said, at least. He seemed to have forgotten his wretched situation temporarily, and was constantly in the lead.

'Take it easy,' yelled David, 'my body warms up slowly.' We reined ourselves in and climbed the hill at a moderate tempo. The climb was about six kilometres long, but never got really steep. Nevertheless, we quickly lost David and our back-up car; after a kilometre's climb at most, David gestured to us to get going. 'If you wait for me, I'll feel pathetic,' he panted. 'Anyway, I *am* pathetic.' Laura stayed with him.

Joost, André, and I rode up calmly. At a viewpoint a kilo-metre from the summit, we waited for Laura and David. David arrived after a few minutes, sweating profusely. 'I was able to resist the siren call of the broom wagon,' he said. 'A terrific achievement, especially considering the driver.'

Laura leaned against the hood of the car and looked at us. She got a camera from the car and took photos. She couldn't help laughing. 'You're a fine bunch. Thirty years later, back in your cycling gear, and up the mountain. Don't give a damn, that's the image you project. Men are funny.'

André had put his arm round Joost and turned to Laura. 'I think that, back then, he was already copying from you in physics, wasn't he?' She laughed.

'Except that Maaskant never caught me.'

'I meant that the cheating was always there. Just as you could already buy bad weed from me. It was all already there.'

'Bart filled the school paper single-handedly, and Peter wrote poems,' said Laura.

'And you were his muse,' said André. 'That's what he called it, at least. What was it like being a muse? And did you go on being a muse afterwards?'

'It wasn't my choice, André. He chose me. I was 16. When Peter died, I stopped being a muse.'

'You understood his poems,' I said. 'We just said: it doesn't rhyme. You saw who Peter was.'

'He was a genius. At the time I felt that intuitively, and now when I read his poems again, I see that I was right.'

Joost looked at her. 'Was he your lover? Muse, muse—I always find it so vague. I could have called Valery my muse for a while. The muse of my scientific work. But she was simply my lover. Bart, was Hinke your muse? Is your little Russian your muse, André?'

'Her name is Ludmilla, Joost, and I believe only poets have muses.'

Laura opened the door of the car. 'Let's go on.'

We stayed together as far as the summit. The descent into Malaucène was an easy one. I changed down to the smallest sprocket and pedalled for all I was worth. The others followed but had to let me go on the winding section, last of all André. I had the feeling that I was flying. To my surprise, I suddenly heard Laura's car coming closer. Just for a second; a couple of sharp bends that I was able to take at full speed forced her to brake.

When I had passed the 'Malaucène' sign, I squeezed the brakes and waited with a glorious feeling.

Laura was the first to stop next to me. As André screeched to a halt behind her car, she came straight toward me. She stood in front of me, gave me a furious look, and hit me in the face. 'Bastard' she said. She went back to her car, got in, and drove off.

I looked at André and shrugged my shoulders. 'Jesus. I descend like a champion, and ...' Joost came along, with David on his wheel. He saw my astonished expression. 'Laura slapped his face,' André explained helpfully, 'and then she drove off.'

XXVIII

I was lying in a deckchair with my eyes closed. David was having a siesta in his room. Laura wasn't back yet. She had rung David and said that, for now, she had other urgent things to do. André and Joost were sitting on the other side of the swimming pool, both in swimming trunks, with their feet dangling in the water.

'How's things, Joost?' asked André.

'I'm denying reality for a little longer, if you don't mind.'

'You're just like me. I deny everything, too. But this is different. I had to.'

'I had to, too. I still have to get used to the fact that my life is over, so for convenience's sake, I'll go on denying for a little longer. I'm living on borrowed time, as it were.'

'You're exaggerating.'

'I was on course for the Nobel Prize. For Christ's sake, it was there in the paper in black-and-white. The Lance Armstrong of physics, they wrote.'

'Nice comparison. That Armstrong, of course, wasn't whiter than white, either. Anyway, I was in all the papers, too. My initials, that is. In retrospect, that would have been better for you, too.'

'Goddammit, André. I'm nothing anymore. The last thirty years have been wiped out at a stroke. This morning, I was suspended by the vice chancellor. That's the preliminary to a dishonourable dismissal.'

'Fuck that prize, Joost,' said André, icily. 'Fuck American women, fuck Professor Ph.D. Spinoza Prick Walvoort. Tell them to stick it all up their ass. Okay?'

'Perhaps I'll be able to do that in a year's time. But now I don't know what to do. I'm deeply ashamed. I want to go and sit in a cave like Saddam Hussein and never come out.'

'Don't do it. You've made a mistake, like me. You haven't played the game entirely according to the rules. You've turned the general public against you. So what? Does that make you a bad human being?'

'That's what it feels like, to tell the truth.'

'Repeat after me,' ordered André. Joost looked at him. 'Stick it all up your ass!'

To my amazement, Joost repeated André's words, if a little timidly. 'Stick it all up your ass!'

'I'm glad I'm rid of it.'

'I'm glad I'm rid of it.'

'Louder! Fuck you all!' screamed André, at the top of his voice.

'Fuck you all!' repeated Joost, almost as loud as André. 'Fuck. You. All!'

André grabbed him and pushed him into the water. 'And now I'm going to baptize the reborn Joost Walvoort,' he said. 'In the name of the father, the son, and the holy beast!'

Joost rose out of the water like a water-polo goalkeeper, and with a wild cry pulled André into the pool.

Laura walked across the grass in her high heels with no apparent effort. She had obviously been to her hotel. She was wearing a dark pencil skirt with a white silk blouse. It gave her an aristocratic look. She came up to me.

She seemed to hesitate for a second. 'Sorry about the slap,' she said. 'I shouldn't have done that. But I was driving behind you, and suddenly everything came back. I ...'

'I know. I wasn't thinking about that at that moment. I had everything under control. That descent is really easy.'

She went over to a deckchair and pulled it next to mine under the parasol. Joost was in his room, André lay on the other side of the pool, reading *The Fifteenth-Century Printing Types of the Low Countries*, which according to him was 'fantastically interesting'. David had gone into the village to do some shopping.

She lay on the recliner with her eyes closed, but I knew she was not asleep. I put my book away and closed my eyes, too. My arm touched hers.

'Funny that that mountain should be called Col de la Madeleine,' she said.

'The real Col de la Madeleine is much higher. It's a famous mountain on the Tour de France route.'

'Do you know *À la recherche du temps perdu?*'

'No. I may have started it once, but I can't even remember.'

We didn't say anything for at least five minutes. Then I asked: 'Why are you here? Reawakening old memories?'

'Not necessary. I could write an hour-by-hour report on those days. A detailed reconstruction.'

'You should do it. I'll do it, too. We can subject the workings of the memory to closer scrutiny. Cup of tea? Mineral water? Cold Sauvignon? Rosé de Provence?'

'It's five o'clock. White.'

I got up and asked André if he wanted anything to drink. From the window came Joost's voice. He could use an ice-cold beer. I went to the kitchen. Joost walked outside. He was wearing only swimming trunks. 'Have you hit her back yet?' he asked. I heard David's car approaching, and poured a glass of Sauvignon.

When I walked into the garden with the tray, André was doing wheelies along the edge of the swimming pool. He was amazingly good at it, and could ride about five metres just on his back wheel with no effort. Laura laughed loudly. Joost did his old swimming-pool trick: a handstand on the edge of the pool, after which he let himself fall flat on his back. David had sat down on my recliner next to Laura, and was dabbing the drops of sweat off his forehead.

'Can you also do it on just your front wheel?' Laura shouted to André. 'I've seen it a few times at the circus.'

'Impossible. But I can do a circuit of the pool standing on my saddle.'

The splashes from a bomb dive by Joost made ripples in the wine. I put the glasses on the ground. 'Come to Mummy if you want a drink.' But André was just climbing onto his saddle, and Joost said he was going to do a forward somersault into the water. 'Laura, come on in! The water's lovely!'

She got up, glass in hand. 'I'll just finish my wine and I'll be there.' I felt a stab of jealousy, and I cursed myself as I used to for my awkwardness in dealing with girls. I should, of course, go and put on my swimming trunks and swim three times from one side to the other underwater. Dive between Laura's legs and lift her up. Play the floating corpse. But I didn't.

'Have you already made a reservation for this evening?' I asked David.

'Just drove past. Nice restaurant by a dry riverbed with a wonderful outside terrace.'

I watched as Laura went inside to put on her swimsuit. She was relaxed and beautiful.

248

XXIX

The restaurant was called Le Four à Chaux, and was on the way from Caromb to Le Barroux. 'Our David has found a very idyllic spot,' was André's reaction. 'I've said so before: ultimately, his talent lies in all-inclusive holidays.'

David gave him the finger.

We sat down at a round table. 'Very good for social interaction,' said Joost. 'A round table has no hierarchy.'

All five of us knew that it was not going to be a light-hearted, fun evening. Laura had invited us to come to Provence, and perhaps she would now make it clear why. But even if that didn't happen, it was inevitable that we would talk about 1982. We had avoided it so far, but we couldn't do so any longer.

After the waiter had brought the aperitifs, a silence fell.

We waited for Laura's opening move.

When the waiter came to take the order, we pointed to her.

'*Crème brûlée de foie gras et pieds et paquets Marseillais*,' she said.

'*Pour moi le même*,' said Joost.

'*Pour moi aussi*,' said André.

'*Et pour moi*,' said David.

I only had to nod. We didn't move a muscle; we knew how this kind of act had to be performed.

'*Du vin?*'

'*Côte de Brouilly.*'

'*Pour moi aussi*,' said Joost.

Laura felt what was expected of her. She had brought us together here, and now she had to explain why. She raised her wine glass. The five glasses hung above the table and tinkled against each other.

'I'm glad that we're together again after thirty years,' she began. 'I've missed you all. That may sound odd, since I haven't given any sign of life. But you must believe me when I say that you haven't been out of my thoughts for so much as a day.'

We said nothing and drank a mouthful of our wine. We believed her. She continued.

'I was divorced a year ago. My ex-husband's name is Fabrizio Guazzi. For a long time, I was happy with him. But in the past few years I noticed that my past was returning, a past that he had no part in, and that he, in a certain sense, had marked the end of. And now it was back, and hence he became a stranger again. I even went back to Zutphen once, alone.'

'You could've dropped by,' said David.

'I didn't dare. It took a long time before I dared to approach you.'

The waiter brought the starter. '*Encore une bouteille*,' said Joost.

'I started dreaming of Peter,' she said. 'Or rather, I started having nightmares. I saw ...'

'... the blood running out of his mouth. His eyes that were still open. His look of astonishment.' I didn't know why I chipped in, perhaps to come to her aid, to let her know that she was not the only one in whose head that film was playing.

'That too, but other images, as well.'

'I've never had nightmares about it,' said Joost, 'but that's because I never have nightmares about anything. I've often blamed myself for his death, though.'

I was glad that he put this on the table. Guilt—it was all about guilt, about death through guilt. For thirty years. It had been the cause of our estrangement; we had avoided one another so as not to have to talk about guilt. We weren't yet 20, and the thought that we were responsible for Peter's death, that one of us was responsible for Peter's death, was too heavy a burden.

'I'll tell you something I heard only recently,' said André. 'Peter was riding that Raleigh of my father's, the bike I've got with me again now. However, at that time it didn't have tyres on, rubber tyres with an inner tube, but so-called tubulars. They were a kind of hose fitted around the rim and glued in position.'

Joost was about to say something, but André gestured to him to shut up.

'Just after Peter's accident, perhaps at his funeral, for all I know, my father speaks to Bart Verhulst—you know, the man who lives in one of those white houses on the IJssel. Verhulst of Verhulst Tiles. The man sponsored an amateur team. He's 90 now. Two months ago, I'm sitting in a restaurant having dinner with Ludmilla. Sitting next to me is Bart Verhulst, with lots of children and grandchildren. He's just spending a year's salary on celebrating his birthday. He sees me, and says: If it isn't Gerrit's son. He gives me a severe reprimand for not having been at my father's funeral. I explain it to him. He says: They should just legalize the stuff. You're quite welcome to come to *my* funeral.'

'André just loves the sound of his own voice,' said Joost.

'Right. And then he suddenly starts talking about Peter's death. He had been a friend of Peter's father. Went screwing on the *Lady Jane*. And he says that old Gerrit told him, at the time, what must have happened. The glue they used for those tubulars was rubbish. And particularly when it got hot, things got dangerous. Heat and braking on a descent made them lethal. The glue melted and the tubulars came off the rim, leaving you flat on your face.'

'Why did your father never tell you?' I asked.

'I don't know. Perhaps he felt guilty and didn't want to shout it from the rooftops. Perhaps because he wasn't sure. But he trusted Verhulst, and he obviously had to unburden himself to someone.'

'Sounds plausible,' said Joost. 'Weird to hear that thirty years later.' He looked relieved.

'Tubes and bad glue are all very well,' said David. 'We should still never have let him ride down that mountain. The guy was on a racing bike for the first time. It was a bloody miracle that he got to the top at all. He should have left it at that.'

'Bart and I were experienced at descents,' said Joost, 'but Peter had never even ridden down a bridge.'

'We'd descended a couple of hills in Limburg: the Posbank and the Galibier. That experience was nothing to write home about.' I found Joost's pose of we-were-experienced-racers rather inappropriate.

'Of course, we'd have had no chance, either, if a tyre had come off like that,' he admitted.

'It's a possibility', said André. 'It isn't certain. Perhaps it was something else. Perhaps the damage could have been contained if he hadn't ridden so damned fast.'

'I shouldn't have descended so fast,' I said. 'I was challenging him. He may have thought it was a race. He was a poet. They think they can fly and walk on water.'

Joost turned to Laura. 'Now that we're on the subject: do you blame yourself for anything?' I saw that she hesitated about what she was going to say. Joost went straight on; the wine was beginning to take effect. 'For example, because the day before the climb, you went to bed with Bart, here. For example.'

Laura gave him a cool look. 'That's true. That happened.' She looked at me.

'It's true,' I said, although everyone at table had known for a long time that it was.

'Did Peter know?'

'Yes.'

'Joost is suggesting suicide,' I said, as flatly as possible. 'Suicide, because of a broken heart or jealousy.'

Laura looked around the table. She seemed suddenly angry. 'I can assure you that it *wasn't* suicide.'

We said nothing. She knew Peter better than we did. 'Do you remember what he read out, on the summit?'

'No,' said André. 'I wasn't that much into poetry, and at that moment I was checking his brakes. It wasn't due to them.'

'I *was* listening,' said David, 'but I have a bad memory for poems.'

'Sadly lost,' declared Joost. 'So we'll never be able to check whether he was trying to tell us something. Something, something ...'

Laura stood up. She took a piece of paper out of her bag, looked around the table, and began to read the poem aloud. It still existed. Peter had given it to her, on the summit of the Ventoux. Or else she had retrieved it from his pocket after the fall. I thought I recognized stanzas, but perhaps it was the typical Seegers style, the images and associations, the staccato sentences alternating with sudden digressions, that made it sound familiar.

It was long poem, and Laura was reading for at least a quarter of an hour. A deep silence had fallen over the terrace, and at other tables, the conversation fell silent. At the phrase, 'Bleeding love in Hotel zur Oper,' her voice faltered and she looked at me almost pleadingly. Hotel zur Oper, I thought, where do I know that from?

When she was finished, she said: 'Not a suicide note.' Her face was deathly pale. She seemed to have migrated to a dreamy region of which we had no notion, and where we would never penetrate. It was as if she had summoned up Peter with an invocatory formula, and he had spoken via her tongue.

Laura sat down and covered her face with her hands. Joost looked shattered. I felt tears running down my cheeks.

'So, what was it?' Joost ventured to ask after a long silence. 'So what happened?'

Laura took her hands away from her face. She had not been crying. The look in her eyes was severe now.

'What does it matter? Recklessness. Bad luck. Bravado. Did anyone at this table deliberately drive him to his death? No? Then you must all draw a line under it. You must finally grant the guy his own death and stop making it yours. Admit there's no guilt, and no guilty party. Feeling guilty is being too cowardly to accept that things happen as they happen, and sometimes go disastrously wrong.'

I knew the moment had now come. But she built it up cleverly. 'The relationship between me and Peter was not what you saw. Or perhaps I should say: I had found out that he was a different person than I thought, at first. Someone other than the gentle-natured poet. He was that, too, but there was another side to him. And you never knew that side.'

The waiter asked if we were ready for the main course. Suddenly it dawned on me. Hotel zur Oper, Dirk Bogarde, Charlotte Rampling, *The Night Porter*.

XXX

We had returned from the restaurant and were sitting by the edge of the pool. André asked whether she remembered her own entrance into our lives.

'Of course,' she said. 'You were keeping a ball in the air. Joost was sitting on David's back, Bart was lying in the grass, and Peter was sitting on a towel writing in an exercise book. I thought from the start that you were a funny lot. You were performing a kind of play. And you went on doing it. You're still doing it.'

'Perhaps that's why you became a director,' said André. 'Since you'd already been mixing with actors for a few years.'

She laughed. 'Peter had written a poem that afternoon—I can still remember it.' She quoted it as if she had it in front of her. 'Go and sleep, on the desolate plain. / On your side, on her side, / Till morning flushes you open ...'

'I read that poem at my mother's funeral,' said David. 'I didn't know he'd written it that afternoon.'

'There was something about him. He seemed absent, yet nothing escaped him.'

'What did you think of him?' asked Joost. She understood what he was driving at.

'I thought that he was a dreamer. Someone who lived in another world. And I also wanted to live in that world. It was as if he had found an extra dimension. He could say things that, at first, I didn't understand at all, but whose meaning later became clear. And then I was amazed.'

'Amazed?'

'Yes. At the way he looked at things.'

'I never saw it.'

André gave her a penetrating look. 'Did you fall for him at once?'

'I don't think I was ever in love with Peter. Perhaps I thought I was, for a while. There was something else, though.'

'He once told me that you two had a platonic relationship,' I said. 'Only much later ...'

Laura laughed sarcastically.

'Do you all remember *The Night Porter?*' she asked. 'From 1974, but I think we saw it in 1981, or thereabouts. *Il portiere di notte* by Liliana Cavani. With Dirk Bogarde.'

'Hotel zur Oper,' I said.

'I remember,' said David. 'Bogarde as an ex-ss man who works as a night porter in a hotel. With what's her name ...'

'Charlotte Rampling.' Images formed in my head that I would have preferred not to see.

'I think that Peter and I must have seen it five or six times. I thought it was a gruesome film, but he was obsessed by it. I was 16, and didn't understand at once what appealed to him so much. Now I do: he recognized something. Something in himself. The Jewess Lucia, who had survived the camp by giving herself to the SS-man Max. It was as if Peter suddenly saw that love and sex are about power. Of course, he could have seen that on that boat of his father's as well, but maybe that was too close to home.'

'Sexy scene,' said Joost, 'when she sits on him in the hotel. Beautiful woman, Rampling. The dream of every 18-year-old, to be initiated by Charlotte Rampling.'

Laura looked at him, and a smile played around her lips. She began to sing softly: '*Wenn ich mir was wünschen dürfte, möchte ich etwas glücklich sein, den sobald ich gar zu glücklich wär, hätt ich Heimweh nach dem Traurigsein.*'

'Beautiful and sad,' said David.

I recognized the words, but did not immediately know where from.

'Marlene Dietrich. Lucia sings it for ss officers, and Max puts a box with a present for her on the table. There's a severed head inside.'

No one said anything. I was afraid of the ominous implication.

'It was as if Peter suddenly realized the nature of our relationship. That he could do what he wanted with me, that I survived the imprisonment with my parents thanks to him. Thanks to all of you, but mainly thanks to him. That I had already subordinated myself completely. It excited him. He became Max, and wanted me to become his Lucia. And I did. On another level, in another world, the world of two adolescents. But we did it, I did it.'

I didn't dare ask her the kind of thing I was supposed to imagine.

'What kind of thing am I supposed to imagine?' asked André.

'A girl of 16, 17. A boy of 18. And both of them derive a perverse kind of pleasure from the balance of power in their relationship, from pain and humiliation. That's about it. Want details?'

'That's okay,' said André, 'I get the picture.'

'You, too?' asked Joost. 'That perverse pleasure, I mean.'

'Me, too. I didn't realize until much later that I had exchanged one form of non-freedom for the other.'

'And what happened then?' Joost had assumed the role of interrogator.

Laura looked straight ahead. 'What I'm going to tell you now is difficult.' She paused and rubbed her hand over her forehead, as if she were in pain. 'Cavani's next film was called *Beyond Good and Evil*. We watched it on the boat. You, once; Peter and I, much more often. It's about the *ménage à trois* between Friedrich Nietzsche, the writer Paul Rée, and Lou Salomé.'

'I think that was on the day of the big cycle race, Bart,' said André.

I didn't think it was funny. I was afraid of what might follow. I could feel panic welling up.

'Peter wanted to be Nietzsche, and I was Lou Salomé, of course. And he felt that Bart was most suited to the role of Paul Rée. In the film, Rée fucks Salomé while Nietzsche holds his hand.'

This was what had been hidden for thirty years.

She looked down, hunched up, as if she expected to be beaten.

Say it's not true, I thought. Please say it's not true.

'The bastard,' said André, 'For Christ's sake, he was manipulating everyone.' Joost sat speechless, looking at Laura. David went to the kitchen, shaking his head.

'I think he was crazy by then,' said Laura. 'Temporarily, or for good. And I think he had taken me with him into his world. It didn't seem particularly strange to involve Bart in our relationship. I think I found it pretty exciting. After all the moralizing in my childhood, it felt like a liberation to transgress boundaries. I only saw later that it wasn't. But I already said that.'

I looked at her. Say something, I thought, say something that makes it a bit bearable.

'Lou Salomé really loved Rée. She lived with him for years, long after Nietzsche had gone mad.' She was now looking me straight in the eye.

'Oh,' was all I could say.

'Fucking hell,' said Joost, when Laura had gone to her room.

André put his hand on my shoulder. 'Now we know why she wanted us to come here. To retouch our image of Peter and her. Shitty, Bart. I can imagine you feel pretty shitty. It's a long time ago, but things like that ...'

I made a gesture: leave it.

'When I get home, I'm going to watch that DVD of *The Night Porter* immediately,' said Joost. 'God Almighty. How does someone of 18 take it into his head to do something like that with a girl of 16? How fucked up can you get?'

'How can you be so close to someone for years, and yet not know what's going on inside him?' I felt as if I'd been run over by a dung cart, despite what Laura had said at the end.

'And why does the bastard kill himself, then?' asked Joost.

'Well, we can cross jealousy off the list. Everything went according to plan. Bart fucked Laura, all that was needed was for the love triangle to be formed. He smashes up on the bike. The girl has had herself fucked for nothing ...'

'Christ, Joost, take it easy,' said André.

'You have to have a guilty party,' I said. 'Preferably me. Because I'm supposed to have betrayed Peter. And now you're lost for an answer. Because the traitor is dead.'

'Not at all,' said Joost. 'I want to know how things happen. For what reason they happen.'

'Perhaps they happen because they have to happen.'

'Spinozan waffle. No good to us. Perhaps old Peter simply wanted to make an impression on you. As a fellow-lover-to-be, for example. Surely he must have had homo-sexual feelings, otherwise you don't dream up something like that.'

I felt it would be better if I left. A black rage was rising. I picked up a couple of glasses and went into the kitchen. Joost followed me; André and David, too, as if they felt that something was about to happen. In the doorway, I turned to face Joost. 'Big mouth. You arrogant big mouth!' I went on and put the glasses on the draining board.

'Be reasonable,' said Joost. 'Peter is dead, so she can explain it all as she likes.'

'Do you know what it is with you, Joost? You're still jealous that she chose me and not you. You would have loved to be part of the trio. You would have loved Peter to hold your hand while you fucked her.'

Joost pointed to Laura's head in the photo on the wall. 'Why shouldn't the reality of 1982 have become distorted in her mind? What's the truth? We haven't come any further at all.' He made for his bedroom. 'Night all,' he said.

I followed him. I saw a grin on his face. He was enjoying my unmasking. It reassured him. He hadn't lost to me—he had lost to Peter, the director of a sick play. Peter had chosen another leading man for the role of the humiliated one, and he could live with that. It was a consolation for the frustration of a failed marriage and the rage at a destroyed career.

He turned around in order to say something else. I pulled the photo off the wall and advanced on Joost. He stood watching, as if rooted to the spot, as if curious to know what was going to happen. I raised the frame and hit him over the head with it. The wood grazed his forehead, and the card on which the photo was mounted tore from the impact. I pulled the photo further over his head, so that the frame formed a grotesque necklace.

'You fucking little doctor's son! Shitty Amsterdammer. Dirty cheat, phoney scientist.' I tried to hurt him however I could.

Joost just looked at the photo around his neck. His lips moved as if to say something, but nothing came. A trickle of blood ran from his forehead down his nose. André and David were also speechless.

Laura stood at the top of the stairs and looked at us, as if we had just performed a fairly intense but also quite crude play.

Joost looked up in fury. He pulled the frame from around his neck and went into his room. When he came back, he was wearing a sports jacket. He pushed his wallet into the inside pocket. He held a handkerchief to the cut on his head. He said nothing more, looked at no one, and went out.

XXXI

Joost had left and not come back. David had gone to his room, shattered. As a boy he hadn't been able to deal with conflict, and he still couldn't. André said that he didn't have a negative of the photo, so that he thought it was pretty shitty of me to have hit Joost with it. 'You could have used a chair.' I said I was sorry.

I went outside and tried to recognize the constellations. The light in David's room went out. In the tree above me, a cricket started chirping. I felt myself calming down. I needed to rewrite my history, but for the moment I didn't feel like it.

How long this went on for, I don't know; perhaps I had dropped off to sleep. The lights in the house had been turned out. I saw her coming out of the kitchen in her white nightdress and with a blanket in her hands. She came over toward me and pushed a recliner next to mine. She pulled the blanket over her and said nothing, but felt for my hand. There was a very long silence.

'Life's a bitch and then you die.'

She gave me a puzzled look. She didn't know the expression.

'Life stinks.'

'What we do with life stinks.' She turned onto her back and looked at the sky.

'Do you know why you did it?'

She didn't reply.

'Do you know why he did it?'

She put her hand on my arm. 'Forgive me,' she said. 'We were young. Forgive him. We lived in a fictional world, as if we were characters in a novel.'

'Strange that you can still feel humiliated thirty years later.'

'It's not that strange.'

'No.'

'When you're young, there's only a tiny distance between play and reality. Perhaps the same was true of Salome and her two lovers.'

'What would have happened if Peter had not had the accident?'

'I don't know. I didn't speak with him alone again. When he came back, he knew what had happened. And I saw fear in his eyes. Do you remember that he lay down in the grass and said nothing for at least half an hour? That wasn't from exhaustion. Perhaps he realized he had gone too far. That he had played a cruel game, with me, with you, and with himself. A little *too* cruel, for a lad of 18.'

'Soon you'll be saying that he committed suicide, after all.'

She was silent for a moment. 'I don't know.'

'This afternoon you said Salomé loved what's-his-name, Rée.'

'I loved you, too. I could never have done it if I hadn't loved you. You must believe me.'

'Why did you go away, then?'

'I had no choice, Bart.'

'I don't understand.'

'Not yet.' She turned onto her side and looked at me. 'After my divorce, I thought: now I can make new choices. Now I'm 17 again. And now I'll make the right choices.'

I stroked her hand gently.

'But it's not true. You can't go back. Ever. You're no longer the same person you were thirty years ago; neither am I. There's not much we can do about it.'

I closed my eyes. 'You can't catch up with time. Sometimes I think I'm very close, but I'm not. Quite tragic, actually. Life is a bad design.'

'But it's good, too. Otherwise there'd be no end to it.'

'I hoped I would get some answers here. But there are just more and more new questions. And the answers I do get, I would rather not have had.'

'You're still here, Bart.'

She threw the blanket over me and looked at me.

I put my arm around her.

The first rays of sunshine had picked me out. How long had I slept? Five hours, four? I looked at my iPhone: 06:07. Today I had to climb Mont Ventoux, after the worst preparation in the history of cycling.

Perhaps it will be called off, I thought. Joost has gone after a terrible fight; everything is ruined, and this time for good. What's the point of pretending? It had been a ridiculous idea to try to conjure up and repair the past.

I looked at Laura's sleeping face. I listened to her breathing. I had never been closer to the past than at this moment. I saw the young woman she had been; I heard the words that had come from her lips. I could touch her as I touched her then. I was master of time.

I stroked her cheek. She opened her eyes, but said nothing. I let my hand glide down her jaw to her neck. She put her hand on my head. My hand slid over her breasts to her belly. She ran her hands through my hair. She looked at me, and I thought I saw tears in her eyes before she closed them. Then she took my hand and held it.

I pushed the blanket off me and stood up. I bent over and kissed her on the mouth. 'I know,' I whispered. 'You can't repair time.' She opened her eyes, and this time a tear ran down her cheek. She gave me an infinitely sad look.

I got up. I saw the summit of the Ventoux, already in full sunlight. I suddenly felt calm and strong.

André was standing by the draining board. 'Good morning. Night under the stars?'

'Yes.'

'Did it happen?'

'No. That's not possible, anymore.'

He gave me a hug. 'Brother, today we're going to have a great ride, and that's all that matters.'

'So, we're going? After that fuss with Joost, I mean.'

'Of course we're going. A quick power breakfast, and we'll be off.'

'I don't know. We were going to do this with the four of us, partly to draw a line under things. Now Joost isn't with us ...'

'We'll do it without Joost. Otherwise I'll go alone. The old Raleigh has to go up. But I think Joost will be coming.' He filled two water bottles and went off.

I got my mobile and called Joost. I got his voicemail. After I had called him a second time, he answered.

'It's Bart.'

'Yes?'

'Are you going up today?'

Silence.

'Last night I slept on a mattress on which three generations of whores have earned a good living,' said Joost. 'So, not a wink of sleep. I've got a headache because my best friend tried to kill me with a photo. And partly from the drink, of course. Apart from that, I doubt everything, feel bilious, know for sure that love doesn't exist, and am contemplating suicide.'

'Joost ...'

'But of *course* I'm going to climb that mountain! What did you think? I'm not here for no reason, am I? Your hitting me last night was pure intimidation, but I'm not going to let that put me off. Don't leave, I'm on my way. It'll be a little while, because I'm on foot.'

'Joost ...'

'Yes?'

'Sorry.'

'Okay. Sorry that I taunted you like that.'

Suddenly I doubted everything that, a minute before, I thought I knew for sure. The four of us going up the mountain seemed to me the only right choice.

Laura came into the kitchen. 'Are you going?' She looked worried.

'Of course,' I said.

'Joost, too?'

'Just had him on the phone. He was up for it. He'll be along shortly.'

'I'm glad.' A weight seemed to lift from her shoulders. 'Could I borrow your phone for a moment? My battery's flat.'

XXXII

An hour later, we were ready to leave. André, besides having his father's bike, and the cycling jersey that had arrived by courier, was wearing old Gerrit's racing shoes to be able to get into the old-fashioned toe clips. He saved the real surprise for last. Once we had all put on our helmets, he took a racing helmet out of his back pocket that must have dated from his father's heyday. He looked pleased. 'Right, like that I reckon Gerrit must be able to recognize me from the back-up car in the sky.'

David was wearing a yellow jersey. Joost felt it and exclaimed: 'Wool! The guy's got a woollen jersey on!'

'Yellow jersey of Eddy Merckx, Tour 1971,' said David. 'Almost ten minutes' lead over Joop Zoetemelk. Need I say more?'

'You're not going to be cold, at any rate,' said Joost.

'Aren't you going to ask how I got hold of it?'

'No; perhaps later, when we're at the top.'

We put some extra water bottles in the car with Laura, applied sun cream, and got going.

'Don't turn it into a boys' race like last time.'

'Of course we won't, Laura,' said Joost. 'We'll just see who gets to the top fastest.'

David said that he was already pretty warm.

'Don't think about it,' said André. 'Think of Eddy Merckx in 1971. Think of what your father said.'

'Of what my father said?'

'The words of a song that's running through my head. "Think of Eddy Merckx, think of what your father said."'

'My father would have said I'd gone crazy.'

'You're from Suriname, so you should find this a nice temperature. Come on, stop whining.'

We rode to Bédoin. Joost insisted that we have a coffee on the terrace of l'Observatoire, as a tribute to Tommy Simpson. 'Actually, we should also have a calvados, but we'll do that later when we come back down again.'

'Caffeine is dope,' said André. 'Let's hope there's no drug-testing station at the summit.'

It was exactly ten o'clock when we turned right at the roundabout at the end of the Avenue Barral des Beaux. A little further on, we started our chronometers: we had begun.

I tried to work out how my legs were feeling. Usually, at the beginning of a day's cycling, the answer was bad. Now I thought I felt energy. I urged myself on: somehow or other I was in top form.

We didn't talk much. The prospect of the Forest and the climb to the top fully occupied us, and none of us felt the need to share his thoughts with the others. We concentrated. We tried not to let the conversation with ourselves go off the rails, because we knew that that can turn every climb into a hell.

We stayed together until we turned left into the Forest. The road immediately went sharply uphill. 'I'm already done for, Bart,' said David, after about fifty metres. 'I've already exhausted all the optimism I'd saved up over the last few months.'

'Don't talk, David. It costs energy. Concentrate.' I moved in front of him. Joost and André were riding a little way ahead. I could hear David's panting above the engine noise of Laura's car.

'You go on,' he said. 'I'll do it at my own speed.' When I looked around, David was already twenty metres behind me. I caught up with André and Joost, and was surprised by the ease with which I managed to. In my head, Tom Waits launched into the first bars of 'Tom Traubert's Blues'. Usually, tunes I couldn't get out of my head annoyed me, but now I almost felt like singing along: 'Wasted and wounded, it ain't what the moon did, I've got what I paid for now.' I took the lead. André seemed to easily stay on my wheel, but I saw that Joost was struggling. 'Say if I'm pushing too hard,' I yelled—the greatest sentence in the cycling repertoire.

Halfway through the Forest, after about five kilometres of climbing, the world around me went quiet and the commentator's voice I dreaded piped up. I knew it was a sign of fatigue, of autonomous brain activity caused by loss of control.

Peter dead, bike red. Must be heavy, an old Raleigh like that. There was nothing wrong with that bike. Never understood how it could happen. Peter dead, bike red. Peter dead, bike red. That helmet of his, will it help in a fall? It's a killer bike. Soon it'll kill André. I must warn him!

I tried to silence the voice, since I knew it could cause me more problems than the uphill road.

I'm reeling time back in. If I pedal very hard, I'll reel time back in. Each turn of the cranks brings me closer to the past. The tyres are time rolling back. A shame they roll counter to the hands of the clock.

André pulled alongside me. He gave me an energy bar. 'Eat,' he said, 'and stop thinking all those weird thoughts.'

I laughed. Obviously he was having weird thoughts, too.

Laura, Laura. Why did you lure us here? Why do you make old men cycle up far too steep a mountain? Why did you stop my hand? I was so close. I was so close! I caressed you all the way back to 1982. Bart's glorious time machine, come and feel Bart's glorious time machine, he'll fuck you back to the past ...

'Fucking hell!' I cried. Suddenly it went quiet.

We were nearing Chalet Reynard. André and I took the lead in turn. We were not trying to shake each other off; we rode up the mountain in great unanimity. Joost was far behind us, but because of the bends, we didn't know how far.

When we were on the flat stretch before Chalet Reynard, my mobile rang. I got it out. It was Laura. 'The rest of you don't have to wait for David, if you were planning to, because he's in the car with me.' A moment later, I heard David himself. 'I thought I was going to die. I didn't feel like that yet. See you on top.'

'How did you get hold of that yellow jersey?'

'Bought it at a charity auction in Oudenaarde.'

'David's called it a day,' I said to André.

'I was afraid he would. Sensible.'

We started on the stretch among the rocks. I changed to a lower gear, the lowest but one. I noticed that I needed to exert more power to get uphill; my strength was running out. It became harder and harder to stay on André's wheel when he took the lead.

She said: it was a cruel game. A game. A board game, with you as their pawn. Why didn't they just propose it to you? A ménage à trois, why not? That Nietzsche did it quite openly, didn't he? Perhaps you would have gone along with Peter's fantasy. The three of you could have lived on the boat. Cosy.

André had a dogged look in his eyes; he was fighting with himself, but also with old Gerrit. Besides, he didn't have a triple chainwheel like me. He was pushing the Raleigh uphill with 42 teeth at the front. But he was fit and driven, and not ready to give up—his legs must be really hurting.

We passed the spot. I had imagined what it would be like, what I would think. I wasn't sure I would recognize the exact spot, but I had underestimated my memory. I could have pointed out to the metre exactly where he was lying, and when I passed the place, it was as if my wheels were made of lead, as if the asphalt turned to quicksand. I had to haul myself past the place; my eyes were burning; I didn't dare look at André for fear of falling.

Your friend Peter, the poet. This is where he lay. Take a good look! Take a good look, man, and you'll see the asphalt is still red. What was he thinking? What last brilliant line of poetry bubbled up from his brain? We shall never know. You deprived the world of the most beautiful line in the history of humanity. Here is where it happened, here he was riding ahead and looking at the world for the last time. Here he looked at you, and knew he had betrayed your friendship. And that you had fucked his girlfriend. Okay, according to his own plan, but even so. Explosive mix, we call it today.

Come off it, man, I said. Thought I said. Come off it, the road's been resurfaced at least ten times since then. Are you still going to be able to see bloodstains?

I looked to see if I could spot any emotions on André's face, but I saw nothing. Perhaps he was too focused to realize what spot we were passing. He had never cycled here before—perhaps that was the reason. He had jumped out of the car and bent over the dying Peter. In that case, you don't pay attention to where it's happening—it doesn't matter.

There were few people on the mountain, far fewer than I had expected. The long stretches of road you see along the sides of the mountain gave me a feeling of despair. I had the feeling I wasn't making any more progress, although the kilometre counter said differently. André was completely wrapped up in himself. I took the lead again without looking at him.

Are there any answers to be found up here? Haha! What did you get into your head? Here on this bare mountain there are no answers. You're pathetic. Men of 50 should sit quietly in a chair and think about life, and not play tough guy on the Ventoux. It's fear of death, pure fear of death.

Then I saw him. He was riding in front of me. A figure bent over a bike. He was wearing a T-shirt and trainers, which amazed me. I blinked a few times. He disappeared around the bend. Once we were through the bend, I could no longer see him. A little later he was there again, toiling uphill, and I tried to catch up with him but couldn't. It was as if he automatically adjusted his speed to mine.

Can't you see who it is, man? Are you blind? Catch up with him and ask him who he is! Look at those shorts, at those trainers, doesn't that ring a bell? Otherwise, ask André. Can you hear his breathing? He knows who it is! He's going up and down on his red bike, his blood-red bike, and he's hurting. Only you can save him; keep going man, keep going, until you reach the top.

I was in the twilight zone, where you know you're hallucinating but still can't let go of the hallucination. Like a parasite, it sinks its jaws into your reality and you just can't shake it off.

I looked back. 'André,' I yelled. 'André!'

André gave me a quizzical look and had no desire to open his mouth. Perhaps he hadn't even heard me. I turned my head back again and saw that we were at Tom Simpson's monument. I considered giving a salute, but dismissed the idea as ridiculous.

We were passed by a taxi.

One kilometre left. My legs didn't want to go on, and my mind had given up long before. I wanted to stop, but it was as if André was forcing me to keep going with his eyes. I saw that the observatory was leaning towards me. The rider in the trainers ahead of me had gone. I had the impression that my speed was measured in centimetres. I was terribly thirsty, but my two water bottles were empty. In my head, the voice tried its utmost one last time to drive me raving mad before the finish.

Joost, where is Joost? Poor Joost! Joost has made a total mess of things. That's something, at least. But what about you? You just plod on, with that insignificant little life of yours. You're too small even to take the world for a ride. Keep pedalling, prick. Peter had at least finished a poem when he got to the top. And you?

I've finished a book, I swear.

The final bend is a swine. It sucked the last remaining energy out of my legs. The deliverance of being horizontal.

I unclipped. I crossed my hands on the handlebar stem and rested my head on my hands. I was breathing heavily. I realized there was a strong wind blowing. Someone put an arm around my shoulders. That must be André. What was I supposed to feel? Happiness? Euphoria? I was back again after thirty years. I had tricked time; perhaps that should free something in me. It hadn't even taken me that much longer than the last time. But I felt nothing. I sat up and turned to André; I hugged him. I felt that at least: deep affection.

André pointed to the sky. 'There you go, old man,' he said. 'This one was for you. I hope I can look you straight in the eye, now.' I was so moved that tears welled up in my eyes. 'You can be sure of that, André. That will do old Gerrit a power of good. He'll be crying his eyes out, up there.'

'Bloody hell. My legs exploded four times.' He threw the helmet in the air. 'Catch, Gerrit!'

It was some time before Joost reached the top. Laura and David followed him in the car. He was pedalling heavily, but smiling.

Laura and David got out and came toward us. Laura kissed us each in turn. She said nothing. David looked sheepish. 'I really couldn't do it,' he said. 'At a certain moment, my heart monitor hit a hundred and ninety. I started sweating like a pig and saw all kinds of blue rockets heading for me. I thought it was time to stop. I panicked. Today I decided I don't want to die yet. Not a bad result, is it?'

'Great plan, David,' said Joost. 'Perhaps we can do something together. I had some wonderful visions on the way. We'll talk about it later.'

We walked to the pole with the 'Sommet Mont Ventoux 1912 m' sign on it. We stood close together, with our arms around one another's shoulders. David asked an English lady if she would photograph us. She took three photos. Before she took the last one, she told Laura to smile, too, 'just like your friends.'

When the lady had returned David's camera, Laura pointed to a building one loop below. 'That's Brasserie Le Vendran. You need to eat. And drink something other than water.'

'Great,' said Joost.

Laura and David got in the car. We recovered our bikes, but stood still for a moment longer, not wanting to allow the feeling of triumph to dilute by descending again at once.

'Did you see the spot?' I asked André.

'What spot?'

'Where Peter lay in the road. I wondered. Whether you realized we cycled past it.'

'I thought I was being pulled off my bike. I swear I did. It was as if a ghost was hanging on to my bike with full force, trying to drag it to the ground. That bike, man, Gerrit's old Raleigh, just felt that it had lain there before. It was like a traumatized horse. I had to do my utmost to stop it running away with me.' He winked at Joost.

'I had hallucinations of blood on the asphalt,' I said.

André took hold of my head and gave me a kiss on the helmet. 'Calm down, Bart. Of course I knew where the spot was.'

'I said: Good old Peter,' said Joost. 'And: Fuck it.'

'Fuck what?'

'Didn't say anything back, that guy. Arrogant fucking poet.'

Joost was the most elated of the three of us. He seemed to have undergone a transformation. There was no sign of the man who, only twelve hours before, seemed to be disintegrating with despair and rage. Even the plaster on his forehead had disappeared, dissolved in sweat. There was a different look in his eyes; a new optimism had blossomed in him. Even though he had suffered a painful defeat.

We looked out over the plain deep below us—nowhere do you have such a strong feeling that the world is at your feet as on the summit of the Ventoux, and certainly if you've risen above that world under your own steam.

Joost put his arms around both of us. 'Thanks, guys. And sorry, again. It must have been the misery I've been through in the past few months.'

'Sorry again about last night, Joost.'

'Just a shame about the photo.'

'Doesn't matter, André,' said Joost, 'I've got the negative.'

XXXIII

We freewheeled downhill and put our bikes against the side of the restaurant. Laura's car was in the car park, but she and David must have already gone to the terrace. I wanted to tell Joost and André that I had seen Peter cycling ahead of me, but decided to keep it to myself for now. They were too euphoric to talk about figments of the imagination. They had dealt with ghosts of their own, and certainly had no wish to conjure up any new ones.

'In a bit, I'm going to tell you all what I thought of on the way up,' said Joost. 'Christ, guys. Suddenly I knew. Halfway up the mountain. A sort of divine insight that only comes to you above fifteen hundred metres. That's the purifying effect of exhaustion and oxygen debt. It makes everything crystal clear, and it's suddenly completely obvious what you have to do. Now I understand why Moses had to go up the mountain for the Ten Commandments.' We turned the corner and checked whether we could see Laura and David sitting anywhere, but obviously they had gone inside.

André pushed back a chair and sat down. 'Laura and David will be here in a minute. They must have gone for a pee. Haven't sweated anything out.'

Joost clicked his fingers at a waitress. She gave him a slightly irritated look, but with his eyes, Joost transmitted the tempting promise of a hefty tip.

'What shall we do?' he asked. 'Champagne, right off the bat?'

'Large beers,' said André.

Joost ordered. The waitress went off.

André wanted to know what Joost's divine insight was.

'Wait a bit. It also concerns David. Don't you have that, too, thinking of all kinds of things when you're on the road? The weirdest things?'

'I try to switch off my thoughts as much as I can,' replied André. 'I try to turn myself into one big climbing muscle.'

I said that I had seen Peter cycling ahead of me. 'About three kilometres from the summit, I think. Very clearly. He was wearing that tasteless pair of shorts, and was on a red Raleigh. I tried to overtake him, but I couldn't. When I accelerated with all my might, he went faster, too. In those trainers of his. I tried to call to him, but I couldn't get any sound out.'

André looked at me seriously. 'And then?'

'Then he dissolved. I lost him around the Simpson monument.'

'Just as well.'

The waitress put three large glasses of beer on the table.

Joost said he was just going to see where David and Laura had got to. 'Perhaps they're waiting for us inside.' At that precise moment, David, in his yellow jersey, came out of the brasserie onto the terrace. When he saw us sitting there, he gestured wildly. 'Come inside!' he cried. 'Come see!' His Surinamese accent had suddenly returned completely, a sign of big emotional turmoil.

'What's all this, then?' asked André. Joost had already

stood up. He had taken off his cycling shoes and went hurriedly over to David. Joost put his arms round him. 'Jesus Christ,' shouted André. 'Come on, Bart, this is serious.'

When we got to David, I saw that his lips were trembling. He looked at us in bewilderment and couldn't get a word out.

Then Laura came out with a man of about 30 on her arm. The man was wearing a pair of dark sunglasses, and edged toward us. He was blind. We looked. He felt that we were standing opposite him and took off his sunglasses. We saw eyes that looked into nothingness. They were the sweet eyes of Madame Olga. In front of us stood Peter, blind Peter.

Laura laughed apologetically.

'Hold me, Bart,' said André. 'I think I'm going to fall over backwards.' But I had to concentrate with all my might, myself, not to lose control completely. 'God Almighty,' said Joost, 'good God Almighty.'

'That's what I mean.' David's voice had come back.

Laura gave us a moment, and then said: 'May I introduce you to my son? His name is Willem, but that won't surprise you.'

Willem smiled his grandfather's lopsided smile. 'Scusi,' he said, 'my Dutch is poor.' André made straight for him. 'Willem!' he said, as if he were seeing an old friend again for the first time in years. 'I'm André, I, I …' He did not know what to say. I looked on, rooted to the spot. A little way away, an elderly couple looked on in curiosity.

Joost also went up to Willem. 'Holy fuck, you're scaring the life out of me, Willem.'

'This is Joost,' Laura said softly to her son.

Joost whispered something in my ear that I couldn't understand very well. I put my hand clumsily on Willem's shoulder and looked into his eyes. 'I'm Bart,' I said. He put his hand on mine. Laura looked at me. Then I couldn't keep it in any longer. Something heavy surged up from my belly and tried to find a way out through my mouth and eyes. I began crying helplessly, turned to Laura, and could scarcely see her. I put my head on her shoulder and she stroked my back.

'Bart. That's why I had to go. Now do you understand?'

I couldn't answer. I wasn't sure I understood.

We put a couple of extra chairs around a table and sat down. David went to the bar, and a little later returned with six glasses and a bottle of champagne.

'Finally, six glasses again,' said André.

'A climb like that is a real killer,' said Joost. 'Look at Bart. He's completely knocked out.' David filled the glasses. We stood up again and drank a toast.

'To Madame Olga and Captain Willem,' I said.

'To Peter,' said Joost. 'Good old Peter. Good old crazy Peter. Sorry, Willem. This is his last poem.'

'Well put together,' said André to Laura, and gave her a kiss. 'Complimenti.'

XXXIV

We rode down at a controlled pace. The champagne had made us cautious. We stayed together and braked like old men at each bend. Laura and Willem stayed behind us. When we had almost reached the spot, André motioned for us to stop.

We laid our bikes on the verge at the left-hand side of the road and crossed to the other side; there was a pole. Laura had parked the car. André took off his father's jersey and draped it around the pole. We put our arms around one another's shoulders and formed a semicircle around the temporary monument. We were silent. The Ventoux wind drowned out the sound of our breathing, and the gentle weeping that rose from my throat. David beckoned Laura and Willem. Laura gave Willem her arm, and they came and joined us. When they arrived, we closed the circle. We bent our heads together. There were no other cyclists and no cars—the Ventoux was completely ours. I looked into the valley and searched for something, an indication of his presence. I can't remember how long we stood there: a minute, five minutes, or ten.

We stood there until André broke the silence. 'Have we

finished with this fucking mountain now?' Willem began laughing, and it was Peter's laugh. We let go of one another.

'It's a magic mountain,' I said. I hugged Willem.

'Good idea of Laura's, to bring us here,' said Joost.

A strong gust of wind pulled the jersey from the pole. It fluttered down like a leaf in autumn, until it caught on a bush about a hundred metres below us.

'Good,' said André. 'May he rest in peace.'

EPILOGUE

Caffè De Vriendschap (the Friendship Café) in the Lange Hofstraat looked as if it had been there for years, but it had opened in May, and so was only two months old. The premises where the travel agency Eastwest Adventures had been based for almost thirty-five years had merged with Cor Meerdink's fishing-tackle shop to form an establishment that took you back a hundred years in time.

On the frosted glass of the door through which you entered the café, its name was calligraphed in elegant letters. Underneath, in a smaller font, were the names of the owners: Castelen, Walvoort & Tankink.

Anyone who knew the original could see immediately that De Vriendschap was a perfect copy of the celebrated Caffè San Marco in Trieste. The dark, richly decorated mahogany of the bar and the walls, the splendid coffee machine, the grand piano, and the sumptuous panelling, the copper coat hooks on the wall, the brass lamps with white globes, the small tables with black chairs, and the station clock suspended from two steel wires: the designers of Caffè De Vriendschap had searched long and lovingly, and had not compromised. Money had been no object in fitting the place out.

There were portraits hanging on the walls in circular frames, and those who took the trouble to study the people immortalized in them could see that they were cycling legends. You needed to be a real insider, though, to notice that they all had something in common: Mont Ventoux. They had shone, been defeated, or, like the man in the photo above the entrance, died there.

On the wall opposite the bar, next to a framed yellow jersey, was a large black-and-white photo of six young people, arms around one another, at the summit of Mont Ventoux. You might think that it was an arbitrary group portrait—a postcard perhaps—and that no one knew any longer who the young people in the photograph were. That it was a photo that had been hung there because of its aura of friendship and, of course, because the owners of De Vriendschap obviously had a thing about the mountain.

It was busy. A small stage had been built in a corner, with a microphone on it. Almost all the tables were occupied, and at the bar there was such a crowd that you had to be patient if you wanted to order. Behind the bar, a pretty girl of about 20 and a young guy at least two metres tall were working up a sweat.

Waiters in uniforms, also meticulously copied from Caffè San Marco, were going around with silver-coloured trays. One of them, an imposing Surinamer, was the manager, and directed his men to places where he suspected a possible shortage of beer or croquettes.

At the table under the group photo on the Ventoux sat a blind man of about 30 and a beautiful woman who spoke to him in Italian. Next to her sat her spitting image, perhaps twenty years younger—her daughter, you'd think, if you didn't know better.

By the stage, two men were testing the sound. One, dressed in a sharp suit, was bald. The other, tall and with grey curls, was giving the orders. He seemed to be commenting on every action, of his own and of the other man. The bald man appeared to be paying very little attention. He took a couple of posters from a cardboard tube and started sticking them on the wall behind the stage with adhesive tape. On the posters was the cover of a book titled *Spinoza Breaks Away*. When he had finished, he exchanged a few words with the tall man.

The bald man went over to the table where the two women and the blind man were sitting, and joined them. The tall man stood at the microphone, tapped it a few times with routine familiarity, and gestured to the young guy behind the bar. The music, Joe Jackson's 'Real Men,' was phased out. Those present automatically turned their attention to the man at the microphone. The Surinamese manager called everyone to order.

'Thank you,' said the speaker. 'Thank you very much for coming to De Vriendschap this afternoon in such large numbers. My name is Joost Walvoort. Some of you may know me as the son of Doctor Walvoort, and I am one of the proud owners of this café. You may also know me from quite recent press and television coverage. All I want to say about it is that that coverage and the reason for it have changed my life for the better.' The speaker shot a challenging glance at the audience. Perhaps he expected comments on what he had said, but there were none. He went on.

'I want to extend a special welcome to a few people today. In the first place, to Laura van Bemmel and her son Willem, who have travelled specially from Italy to Zutphen for this occasion.' The man pointed to the table where the two were sitting. 'Then,' he continued, 'to my own dear mother, who initially refused to come because this is a non-smoking café, but who is here, after all, after I promised her that she can light up one cigar later.' A distinguished lady at one of the tables gave a friendly nod. Next to her sat a pair of female twins of about 50, and two younger women whose father, from the look of them, had to be Joost Walvoort.

'And now, I'd like to ask Bart Hoffman to step up onto the stage. You know him as the redoubtable crime correspondent of one of our leading dailies. I can reassure all the criminals in Holland: he's quit. *Spinoza Breaks Away* is his first book, but many more will follow, I am convinced.'

The writer made his way forward through the audience. He was visibly ill at ease. The bald man shouted: 'Bart!'

Bart Hoffman stepped onto the stage. Joost Walvoort shook his hand and pointed to the posters. 'I can tell you one more thing: the original title was *Spinoza on a Bike*, but after taking the advice of several friends, including myself, Bart realized that *Spinoza Breaks Away* was better. Breaking away is what it's all about. I give you Bart Hoffman.'

'Thanks for the kind words, Joost,' said Bart Hoffman. 'And it's true that you thought of the title. Thank you all for coming; thank you for letting me make use of this special place to launch my book. If I could turn the clock back over thirty years, you would see me sitting here, together with Laura, David, Joost, Peter, and André. David's father ran his travel agency here, and he always had a well-filled fridge. We sat in this spot in June 1982, on the evening before Joost and I were due to drive south to climb the Galibier, and afterward, the Ventoux. It was here, I assume, that a few days later, Laura, André, David, and Peter decided to follow us to Provence. A lot issued from those two seemingly banal events.'

He paused for a moment. 'And now, I'd like to move on and present the first copy. I'd like to ask Laura to come to the stage.' The woman with whom he had previously shared a table got up and came forward. A silence fell in the café. She was wearing a simple white dress that had probably cost a fortune, and that accentuated the tanned skin of her arms and legs.

'Laura,' said Bart Hoffman, after taking a piece of paper with notes on it from his pocket. 'I am very happy to be able to present the first copy of my book to you. It's one of the things that, until not so long ago, I would have dismissed as totally absurd. If I have learned anything in the past year, it is that life can completely surprise you. The space where we are now, by the way, is also a nice proof of that.' Joost Walvoort, who sat down in front of the stage, applauded. 'Hear, hear,' he cried.

'Joost,' said Bart Hoffman. 'Another model of openness to change. Should you, by the way, have children who need tutoring in physics, then he's your man.' Joost made a dismissive gesture.

'Laura,' he said, 'a lot has happened in the past twelve months. You brought us—David, Joost, André, and me—together in Provence after thirty years. And you've given us a little of our friend Peter back, though it was a painful rebirth, I'm bound to say—' An embarrassed smile slid across his face. Bart Hoffman pointed to the table at which the blind man was sitting. 'Willem, the grandson of our beloved Captain Willem Seegers and his wife Olga.' Bart Hoffman had to stop for a moment. Laura put her hand on his arm. 'I'm turning into an old sentimentalist, friends,' he said. 'We must start on the beer quickly, before things get out of hand.' He gave Laura two kisses and presented her with the book. '*Spinoza Breaks Away* is not only about cycle racing. Actually, it's not about it at all.' He scanned the audience, looking for the black man in the Italian waiter's costume. 'David! Am I right?'

'Quite right. It's about life. Anyway, Spinoza never broke away.'

Laura said a brief word of thanks. When she had finished, she looked questioningly at the master of ceremonies. He gave a sign for her to stay on the stage. The bald man now came forward, leading the blind man. The Surinamese waiter joined them, followed by the master of ceremonies. A moment later, six people were standing on the small stage, just managing to fit on it. They had put their arms around one another.

When everyone had been served, the Surinamer, with his other arm still around the shoulders of the woman, raised his glass. The music was turned down.

'In case you didn't know, my name is David Castelen. I want to propose a toast.' He waited for a moment to build up the tension. Then he shouted: 'To life!' He raised his glass again to loud applause. 'And a toast to love!' he continued. The woman stood on tiptoe and kissed David Castelen. She laughed.

The young guy behind the bar turned up the music again. The waiters ran through the café, topping up glasses of champagne everywhere. The blind man made neighing noises and regularly had to wipe the tears of laughter from his eyes. Then he raised his glass and shouted: 'T-t-to my mother!'

Joost Walvoort made a beseeching gesture. After silence was restored to some extent, and the music was turned down again, he pointed to Bart Hoffman. 'The last toast will be proposed by our best-selling author.' The writer pointed toward the girl behind the bar, and then said, calmly and without raising his voice: 'To Anna Jildau, my wonderful daughter. To Willem. To Laura, Joost, André, and David. To friendship.'

A plaintive guitar rang out, and was joined by drums and a keyboard. 'Train roll on,' sang Lynyrd Skynyrd, 'on down the line, won't you please take me far away, now I feel the wind blow, outside my door ...'

Someone took a photo of the six people on the stage.

Acknowledgements

In January 2010, I received an email from film producer Hans de Wolf of KeyFilm. He wanted to make a film and asked if I would write the script. It was to be about four men and Mont Ventoux. He had already approached a director, Nicole van Kilsdonk.

This book emerged from the work on the script of the film *Ventoux*. Far more than the writing of a book, script-writing is teamwork. Hans de Wolf, Nicole van Kilsdonk, Paul Jan Nelissen, Hanneke Niens, Marina Blok, Wilfried de Jong, Gijs Scholten van Aschat, Leopold Witte, and Win Opbrouck will find in the book the elements they contributed to the film script. I hope they can live with that.

My special thanks to Hans and Nicole for our immensely enjoyable and inspirational collaboration on the script of *Ventoux*.

Sybolt Bouwer, who has more than fifty ascents of Mount Ventoux under his belt, told me everything about the Bédoin of the 1970s and 1980s. A story by Ot Louw was the inspiration for the manifestations of altitude sickness that afflict Bart on the Galibier, and the visions on the

Ventoux. I checked with Weert Schenk on the likelihood of André's criminal activities. Schenk, an ex-amateur racing cyclist, also told me about the old tubular tyres, and the risks riders ran with them. Maarten Keulemans read the sections on string theory, the Spinoza Prize, and Joost's scientific fraud. Wilfried de Jong, a proud owner of a Pegoretti, put me on the track of the Italian framebuilder and jazz-lover. With Wilfried I also rode the 'River Rotte run' described in the book—he mostly took the lead.

Many thanks, guys. Let's go for a ride together again, soon.

In reality, the work of art in André's room hangs on the wall of my own apartment. It is by the Nijmegen graphic artist and sportsman Tom Küsters, who died in 2008, and was someone who knew how to get the most out of life. I still think often of his enormous courage in the face of death.

The lines of poetry quoted: 'Go and sleep, on the desolate plain, / On your side, on her side, / Till the morning flushes you open' are from the beautiful poem 'When the night comes' from the collection *Uitloopgroef* (Exit Groove) by John Schoorl: 'The night brings too much, / Immeasurable Kazakhstan Humours. // Of course you long for / The logic of Pythagoras, / Without linear interruption. // And certainly no Bee Gees, / Or voices from the past, / who know the score / Go and sleep, on the desolate plain, / On your side, on her side, / Till the morning flushes you open.'

Thanks for letting me use the extract, John.

Quotes from Tim Krabbé's magnificent *The Rider* that are read aloud by Joost are in the English translation by Sam Garrett (2002). Jan Kal's poem 'Mont Ventoux' from the collection *Cycling on Mont Ventoux* (1974), which inspires Peter to attempt the climb as well, was translated by Paul Vincent. I also gained information from *De kale berg, op en over de Mont Ventoux* (The Bare Mountain, on and about Mont Ventoux) by Lex Reurings and Willem Janssen Steenberg, the bible of every conqueror of the Ventoux.

I am greatly indebted to my friend Aart Hoekman, who carefully checked the manuscript. I am also very grateful to the grand old man of the Dutch publishing world, Emile Brugman, for his willingness to let me benefit from his huge reading experience and red pen. He was severe but just. With her great knowledge of books and publishing, Marieke Verhoeven kept me out of the wind—she knows what I mean by that. Tom Harmsen, (then still) of L.J. Veen Publishers, was the first to point out that there were the makings of a book in the first treatment for the script. My thanks, also, to Sander Blom, Ronald Kerstma, and the editorial staff of Atlas Contact Publishers.

Finally: without Wilma de Rek, my partner, this book would never have appeared. She read and reread; she corrected; she made suggestions. At the right moment, she said the things I needed to hear to keep my spirits up. By being who she is, she gave me an insight into the mind of an intelligent, beautiful woman.

She even made the ultimate sacrifice: she cycled up Mont Ventoux with me. That is love.

Bert Wagendorp, Alkmaar, 21 April 2013

On the Design

As book design is an integral part of the reading experience, we would like to acknowledge the work of those who shaped the form in which the story is housed.

Tessa van der Waals (Netherlands) is responsible for the cover design, cover typography and art direction of all World Editions books. She works in the internationally renowned tradition of Dutch Design. Her bright and powerful visual aesthetic maintains a harmony between image and typography and captures the unique atmosphere of each book. She works closely with internationally celebrated photographers, artists, and letter designers. Her work has frequently been awarded prizes for Best Dutch Book Design.

The font used for the author's name on the cover is called Akrobat. The font in which the red title is set is called Action. Action is a fairly new typeface, designed by Erik van Blokland (Netherlands) with the screen and moving images in mind. Its casual personality and quirky shapes give a friendliness that is unusual in a straight-sided condensed sans. Rik van Schagen used biomechanical footage to determine the shape of his essentialized cycler pictograms.

The cover has been edited by lithographer Bert van der Horst of BFC Graphics (Netherlands).

Suzan Beijer (Netherlands) is responsible for the typography and careful interior book design of all World Editions titles.

The text on the inside covers and the press quotes are set in Circular, designed by Laurenz Brunner (Switzerland) and published by Swiss type foundry Lineto.

All World Editions books are set in the typeface Dolly, specifically designed for book typography. Dolly creates a warm page image perfect for an enjoyable reading experience. This typeface is designed by Underware, a European collective formed by Bas Jacobs (Netherlands), Akiem Helmling (Germany), and Sami Kortemäki (Finland). Underware are also the creators of the World Editions logo, which meets the design requirement that 'a strong shape can always be drawn with a toe in the sand.'